PLACE

a novel

Hannah Huber

Amsterdam Academy Press

Amsterdam Academy Press
www.amsterdamacademy.com

This edition published 2021 by Amsterdam Academy Press
ISBN 978-9-09035-203-9 (paperback)
ISBN 978-9-09035-355-5 (ebook)
Typeset in Fairfield

Book cover illustration: Eveline Wijdeveld
Book cover design: Cigdem Guven
Author photo: Ami Elsius
Developmental Editor: Andie Huber
Proofreader: Rebecca Blunden
Layout: Lisa Hall
Printed and bound in The Netherlands by Tipoprint BV

FSC
www.fsc.org

MIX
Paper from
responsible sources
FSC® C117418

For Noor, Mary, and Tom

"So, here you are.
Too foreign for home. Too foreign for here.
Never enough for both."

- Ijeoma Umebinyuo, *Diaspora Blues*

Chapter 1

I never really liked the water. Which may sound a little bit crazy but what I mean is, I never liked the dark, open water of rivers, lakes and oceans. The kind where you can't see what's underneath always scared me. I'm the kind of person who wants to know what's ahead, after careful planning, no surprises. Now, like a magnetic pull, the river beckoned me to dive in and swim its length every morning. I'm going to miss the Vecht River. In two weeks' time we'll be out of here, flights are booked. We've lived in the Netherlands for twenty years. The idea hasn't quite sunk in yet.

The realtor is showing our house to a couple from Amsterdam later this morning. Our house has only been on the market for two days, but there are already five viewings scheduled, leading me to believe that our house will sell before we leave for America. The write-up of our house on Funda, the Dutch online real estate site, listed the Vecht River as a main feature, and it's true. I've learned over the years that not only is your house your home, your surroundings are too.

The Dutch like to name their houses. In most cases it's a status symbol. In other cases, it's just for fun or to show a sense of ownership. Names like *Vechtlust*—Estate at the River Vecht, *Slotzicht*—Castle View, and *Vrederust*—Peace of Mind grace the front facades of old stately merchant houses here in Loenen, deemed one of the most picturesque villages in the Netherlands. Back in the 17th century, the water in the Amsterdam canals became so contaminated that boats were sent to the Vecht to pick up fresh water and bring it back to Amsterdam, either to sell in bottles or to use for brewing beer. Wealthy merchants built their weekend and vacation homes along the Vecht, many of which still stand today. Our house was by no means one of those huge wealthy merchant houses, but it was a charming brick house, built in 1900 and called *Vechtzicht*—Vecht view, because we literally looked out onto the Vecht River.

Sometimes I had to pinch myself - this perfect Dutch life that we created was one that most expats only dreamed of, full of *borrels*—drinks with local friends, boat rides, and tennis tournaments. I've heard countless times from expat friends that they felt alienated from local Dutch culture because they didn't speak the language, or didn't have a Dutch partner that served as their link. My international girlfriends in Amsterdam said they would never survive in a small Dutch village. Part of me was proud that I could.

After fifteen years in Amsterdam center city, we moved out here, five years ago, to this idyllic span of water, just 50 feet wide and one of some 200 rivers in the world that flow upstream instead of down. The man-made Amsterdam-Rijnkanaal, which was built in the fifties and runs parallel to the Vecht, took away all the commercial boats. It was mostly pleasure boats and tourists that cruised along the

Vecht. So much prettier, more genteel than the Susquehanna River where I grew up — a great wide muddy river that cuts through central Pennsylvania. Boating season started on April 1st and went through to the end of September. As early as 9 a.m., these pleasure boats paraded by our home — the river is just 30 feet outside our door, with half-naked people enjoying a leisurely day on the water, glass of rosé in hand. That's why it was good to swim before the boats, less dangerous and more peaceful.

I started swimming in the Vecht last year. Now that I was in my forties, I needed to switch up my workouts. I couldn't run every day like I used to. In my mind I was still twenty, but it seemed as if the body started wearing down at thirty-five onwards. Swimming was better for the joints. Plus, I liked having alone time. Alone with my own thoughts.

Beginning in early spring, I'd go for a morning swim at 7 a.m., and continue swimming until the Vecht reached an intolerable 12 degrees Celsius — even a wetsuit couldn't keep out the chill. The metric system became second nature, only for American friends and my mom did I have to convert the temperature to Fahrenheit — in this case 54 degrees. The first time I swam I went without a suit. It was freezing! So I invested in what the guy working at the Triathlon shop in Hilversum said was the best one, a good pair of goggles, and a bright orange floating device to tie around my waist so that the boats could see me.

It took me a good ten minutes of sweating and cursing to get that wetsuit on — it's a task in and of itself. The hard part was getting the suit over my butt, which is by no means a Kim Kardashian butt, but it's round. I wished I could take some of the fat from my butt and put it on my small boobs. Finally, after a few careful adjustments, similar to pulling up a pair of pantyhose, the suit was ready to have the back zipper pulled up by the long string.

My suit on, I waddled across the road, then slowly eased down into the 62 degree water, which is normal for June. Those first 30 seconds were the worst, and then it was fine — I just had to breathe into it. Glancing over at our boat roped up to our dock, the *Blauwe Cactus*—Blue Cactus, a sadness washed over me when I saw the *for sale* sign hanging from the boat cover. So many memories on that boat. Like when Paul surprised me by having two home ports painted on the back — Gettysburg, PA, and Loenen aan de Vecht. I didn't know having two home ports was even an option. Pressing the goggles on tight one last time, making sure there was enough suction, I placed my face down into the water. The sun's rays penetrate underwater, reflecting a cloudy light off my hands out in front of me. A sense of panic took over after about 20 feet — the thought of touching a slimy fish or a ring snake with my foot, or accidentally hitting a buoy headfirst, or drowning of carbon monoxide poisoning, which my mom was always warning me about, but then I tried to block such thoughts and simply glide through the water. One, two, three, strokes then a gulp of air on the side. My thoughts drifted off to how, like fish, the Dutch have completely different words for swim strokes; they call freestyle *borstkrawl*—breast crawl, and breaststroke they call *schoolslag*—school stroke. I could never get used to that.

A blue sign denoting the village of Loenen aan de Vecht's border was my landmark to turn around and I swam freestyle back to our dock. The swim was approximately a half hour, total, just under one mile. I wanted to be back before my husband Paul and daughter Lucy were awake, allowing plenty of time to get ready for a busy day of passport renewal, visa application, and work. My mind was racing with the list of everything that had to happen before our big move: sell the house, sell the boat, Paul's visa, goodbye party, forward the mail, box things up for the movers, Lucy's college forms, office goodbye lunch. The list was endless! Even though this swim was meant to clear my mind, I couldn't help but think of all the to-do's.

Climbing up the ladder Paul had placed by the dock, for easy river access when we first moved in, I inserted my finger under the wetsuit's leg seam, letting the water drip out — enough to fill a small bucket. The man at the shop said this was normal, that's how a wetsuit works; it lets a little bit of water in, your body temperature warms it up, and that's what keeps you warm.

After wringing out my hair, I slipped on my gold flip-flops. *No need to ever go on vacation when you can take a swim in a river right out your front door! God I'm going to miss this. Why are we moving again? Granted, the land we bought in Pennsylvania has amazing views over the apple orchards. Luxe problemen*—luxury problems as they say in Dutch. Hopefully the squishing sound of my flip-flops wouldn't get our three-year-old black Labrador Abby too excited, waking up everyone in the house. Having a dog is great, but it is also a royal pain in the ass at times. Abby is a neurotic attention-seeking furball in my face 24/7.

Thursday morning, 7:30 a.m. I had just enough time to myself to enjoy a cup of coffee, before the whole house woke up. Waiting for the coffee to brew, I looked out the front windows towards the ripples glistening on the Vecht in the rising sun like a sequin dress and was caught in a mesmerizing hypnotic state for a moment. Ever since we moved to the Netherlands, we've always used the same gold standard Dutch-designed Techniform Moccamaster coffee brewing machine, a gift from my Dutch mother-in-law. It worked like a charm yielding a nice full pot of smooth hot coffee each morning. I tried to time the milk frothing just right alongside the brewing process. Grabbing a clean mug out of the drawer, I poured two-thirds full with coffee, the rest with frothed milk, then walked out to the front porch with my towel dangled over me. Taking a deep breath as my own form of meditation and listening to the blackbirds chirping in chorus, I watched them hop from one willow tree to the next, like acrobats. Just as I sat down I heard the shuffle of Paul's feet coming out from our ground floor bedroom. I could recognize his step and morning sounds anywhere.

"You sound more and more like your dad every day, making all those caveman noises when you get out of bed. All that cleansing of phlegm in your throat. It sounds like you're about ready to spit out a bunch of honkeys." I smiled up at Paul shaking my head.

"Good morning to you too." Paul leaned down towards the bench where I was sitting and gave me a puckered kiss on the lips. He's always had a sweet smell to him, like honey. His lips were large and plump, his mouth wide, similar to Mick Jagger. His blond hair looked like a bird's nest. People used to ask him whether he got his hair frosted, as his roots are dark but the tips are blond. It's always been that way. His stubble scratched me, it hurt, but not enough to nag him about it.

"Is Lucy awake yet?"

"No, she's still sleeping. But let her sleep a bit longer. She has her final exam in biology today. Come sit down with me and enjoy a cup of coffee here together for five minutes." I patted the seat on the bench next to me.

"Did you pour a cup of coffee for me already?" Paul closed his old worn light blue Ralph Lauren robe over his boxer shorts. He's been wearing the same robe for 22 years. I bought it for him when we first started dating in Washington.

"No, but it's in the thermos and I put a mug out for you by the frother."

Paul went back into the house for his coffee and I looked back at the river. I'd been watching the river react to the environment ever since we moved in, how it ebbed and flowed, how it flooded during the winter, and how the water level lowered in the summer. A canal, on the other hand, was intentional and measured. It could be controlled. Manipulated.

"What do you have planned for today?" Paul asked as he came back out onto the porch with his coffee.

"You mean, what do *we* have planned for today? We have to drive to the American Embassy in Den Haag to get your visa, and I need to renew my passport."

"Oh right. I totally forgot. What time is our appointment?"

"Ten — I figured that way we can skip the morning traffic and still get a good day of work in at the office."

"Do we have to go together, or can you just go on my behalf?" Paul raised his wide eyebrows while taking a sip of his coffee.

"Of course we have to go together. We're applying for an immigrant visa for you as a spouse of a US citizen. Basically I'm your ticket into the US of A." I put my hand on his knee and gave it a squeeze.

"All right, I better get showered then."

"I have all our documents ready to go. I'll be damned if they turn us away for not having a specific piece of paper! Time is of the essence at this point."

"Thanks for taking care of that Jill. At least one of us is organized." Paul kissed the top of my head while standing up.

"Hey, what time will you be home tonight? Can you cook, please? I'm just too tired and I stopped our Hello Fresh subscription. Maybe chicken quesadillas with your homemade salsa? I miss Mexican food so much — *lekker hè?*"

"Why do you always end your sentences with *hè*? You're becoming too Dutch. I have a couple calls scheduled at the end of the day, so don't count on me being home until at least six. But sure, I can cook." Paul runs his hand through his fluffy hair.

"It seems like they're keeping you later and later each week. Can't they cut you a break?" Paul was in the process of training his replacement, which he seemed reluctant to do after working several years at the ag-tech start-up. What was supposed to be three days working from the office, two days from home quickly turned into five days at the office, and subsequently longer days. But he said that this job at least allowed him to make the right connections for the new job he had lined up in the US, as COO of Leaf Fruit Company in Aspers, Pennsylvania — responsible for fruit distribution across the entire Atlantic Coast. He was excited to start, as he said it was finally the right match to his background and he was looking forward to the amount of responsibility he would have in the organization. So I tried not to get on his case about it. At least one of us would have a steady income until I could line up something.

We'd always planned on giving the Netherlands a good twenty years and then moving to the US, giving both sets of aging parents enough face time. So far, everything was working out according to our master plan. Paul secured that job, and our house was on the market, hopefully soon under contract. Paul found a rental property for us, until construction was finished on the 3-acre plot of land we had bought just outside Gettysburg. We bought the land relatively cheap, because it didn't perk. I didn't know what this meant at first, but basically the soil needed to be just right in order for us to install a septic tank and mound. We had to let the control fill settle for four years, before doing another perk test. Those four years are up and the perk test is scheduled for October. Plus, Lucy received a scholarship for field hockey to my alma mater, Gettysburg College, this fall, significantly softening the blow of the 54,000 dollar tuition fee. Even Abby had all her shots and was ready to go.

My parents couldn't wait to have us closer. That's all my mom talked about, "It's my turn now, finally", and "I can't wait to take Lucy shopping at the outlets", and "Your father can make you your favorite cornbread when you come." It would be nice to be so close to my parents again — they could be there for Lucy, should I have to commute an hour-and-a-half down to Washington, if I'm able to line up a job with NPR, where I had my first internship way back in the day. That's what I really wanted. Hopefully twelve years' experience at Radio 1 helped. We're playing our cards carefully at this point, planning and plotting like we always have. "We also need to finalize our guest list for the goodbye party tomorrow." I glanced over at Paul.

"Oh my gosh — I can't believe that's tomorrow already!"

Paul almost spit out his coffee.

"I know. I'm going to try to take off tomorrow afternoon so I can prepare. Let's just keep it simple. Burgers and dogs on the grill, gin and tonic bar, cooler filled with beer."

"Sounds good to me. I have a Spotify playlist ready to go."

"Good, that's the most important part. I just want everyone to get loose and dance in the yard, like last year's summer solstice party." I looked through the window at the clock hanging inside — 7:45 a.m. "Shoot! If we don't wake Lucy up now, she won't have enough time for breakfast!" Lucy needs almost a full hour to get ready for school. What used to be one minute prep time to brush teeth has turned into a half hour of primping. I had forgotten about all the primping I used to do before school, and smiled just thinking about it, BaByliss Hot Sticks, a spritz of perfume, lip gloss.

"I'll go up. I'm the master at waking up my child and ensuring she's in a good mood." Paul stood up with a smile and stretched his arms. It's true, Paul and Lucy have a special bond. Paul was always strict but loving. He could bring Lucy to tears when helping her with her math homework, but made her laugh even more afterwards with his tickle frenzy and jokes. When Paul and I first met, we watched endless episodes of *I Love Lucy* and had no trouble agreeing on her name when she was born. Easy to pronounce in both Dutch and English, and the name brought humor to our lives.

As I finished up my last sip of coffee on the porch, I received a text from my colleague and friend Marlies: Hoe laat ben je op kantoor vandaag?—What time are you coming into the office today? We have to do our last radio segment together :(.

Marlies and I both worked for the Dutch national public radio station, NPO Radio 1, the Dutch version of NPR. Sometimes I felt like the producers and my editing team weighed in too much. Which is exactly why I started my own podcast last year - *Dutch and Such* - more narrative journalism, it allows me to run the stories *I* want to run and interview the people *I* want to interview. Like the former sex worker who opened up the Prostitution Information Center in the Red Light District. And Linda de Mol, known as the Dutch queen of media, who started her own successful magazine. She gave me a free subscription after the interview.

I texted her back: Hopefully I'll be in just after lunchtime. Have to take care of visa stuff at the American Embassy this morning. We're still scheduled to interview Eva Jinek and her thoughts on Trump's re-election announcement, right?

Two seconds later, ping! OK, I'll see you after lunch and yes, the Eva Jinek piece on Trump and America. I'll bet you're thrilled about that one ;). I can't believe this will be my last recording with Marlies, after twelve years of working together. The team is taking me out for lunch on my last day, next week.

While Paul went upstairs to wake Lucy up, I got in gear for the day. I couldn't help but multitask, even in the shower. As I waited for the water to get hot enough, I did twenty squats and brushed my teeth. I've always been quite the drugstore beauty buyer and indulge myself with products, especially my favorite lavender soap - voilà! I was careful not to reach up for my magnifying mirror - which revealed every pore, every hair. I could spend a good half hour plucking hairs and popping pores, so I placed it on the top shelf of my medicine cabinet, well out of reach, so I wasn't tempted. The smile lines by my mouth and crow's feet by my eyes are badges I wear for raising a child who is almost an adult.

Paul and I had to leave by 8:30 a.m., if we were going to be on time for our appointment at the embassy. I know it's crazy, but even though Lucy was seventeen, I still took great pleasure in making her lunch. I got a kick out of arranging the perfect lunchbox, similar to a bento box with various compartments - one for her sandwich, one for raw vegetables, and a little compartment for the sweet Dutch sultana snack crackers. Paul and I had wanted more kids, but it just wasn't in the cards for us. Lord knows we tried. Lucy was conceived with IVF and born in hospital. I felt ashamed telling people, but felt I had to explain myself — the Dutch pride themselves on natural and home childbirths. There was always that awkward silence when people asked me whether Lucy had any brothers or sisters and I said "no".

Epidurals are not common practice here, and people give you pitiful looks if you tell them you had a cesarean. Not only was it a challenge getting pregnant in the first place, but the birth was not the peaceful home birth I had envisioned and heard about from my Dutch peers. I was in labor for 24 hours before they wheeled me in for a C-section. Luckily, I was able to breastfeed — seeing everything else felt like I was missing out. At least I could talk endlessly about breastfeeding with my Dutch friends, "how many feedings is your baby getting now?", and "which pump are you using?". For the full ten months that I breastfed Lucy, I loved every feeding, how her chubby little hand held my pinky as she stared up at me. I'd sing for her all the lullabies I could remember, as well as patriotic songs like *America the Beautiful* and Willy Nelson's *On the Road Again*, since those seemed to be the only lyrics I could remember from Mrs. Delong's elementary school music class. I was grateful to the *kraamzorg*—a home nurse every Dutch family is entitled to after giving birth, 24 hours of at-home care by a trained professional, spread across seven to eight days. Our kraamzorg, Erna, carved Lucy's name out of an apple, presenting it alongside the most delicious fruit salad I had ever had in my life. Erna changed my bed sheets each day, checked my stitches, disinfected my bathroom, made lunch, and helped me get on a schedule with Lucy. My American friends who were new parents were jealous when I told them. I wished they could have had the same.

After multiple miscarriages when trying for a second, we decided to count our blessings and come to terms with the fact that we were going to be a three-person family. The side effects were just too painful — the cramps, nausea, fatigue. Not to mention the anxiety and stress that comes along with the process. I didn't want to go through IVF again. Both Paul and I came from families with four kids, so this was a tough pill to swallow. I always envisioned having a house full of people at Christmas, four kids, all bringing their boyfriends and girlfriends home with them — loads of stockings hanging from the fireplace mantel. Now life is pretty quiet and, dare I say it, a bit boring, *aangeharkt*—all raked up.

Lucy walked into the kitchen, wearing cropped wide-leg jeans and her favorite grey Dutch brand Scotch & Soda sweatshirt. She had small, gold, dangling seashell earrings, and I could see some concealer caked onto her forehead and nose.

"Good morning mama." Lucy took a seat on one of the bar stools at the kitchen island and poured herself a bowl of chocolate Cruesli cereal. Usually, I try to pick out all the chocolate chunks when she's not looking, in order to control her sugar intake.

"Good morning sweetie. Did you sleep well?"

"Yeah. I actually dreamed about Oma Amerika's house, that I was there in her backyard, throwing a ball for Sadie." Ever since Lucy was a baby we had deemed my parents *Oma and Opa Amerika*. They prefer that over grandma and grandpa, which they say make them feel old.

"I love dreams like that. I've actually had a couple dreams lately that I'm at Oma and Opa Amerika's house — I couldn't seem to get her back door open with my key — as if they changed all the locks I had growing up. Then I woke up. Don't you love how we can travel anywhere in our dreams?!"

"Yeah. Although it made me miss them even more. I can't wait to move closer to them!" She took a big bite of cereal. A drop of milk fell onto her shirt, and I quickly grabbed a dish towel and dampened it for her.

"I know, me too. Glad our tickets are booked. Which reminds me, I want to discuss our first couple of weeks there before your semester starts, maybe tonight over dinner? Maybe we can go directly to the beach for a week when we get there." I regretted saying these words as soon as they came out of my mouth, knowing that of course Lucy wouldn't want to wait until dinner for our discussion.

"What mama?! No, let's talk about it now! Can we fit a week in at Rehoboth Beach first? Pleeeease." She dabbed the dish towel against her small boobs, two little mounds.

I took out the cheese knife and started slicing cheese for Lucy's lunch sandwich. The local cheese delivery man wouldn't come until Monday, and we'd already eaten through a good chunk, so now it was difficult to cut off enough of the plastic rind to be able to slice it properly. Paul has shown me so many times how to do it, but Dutch cheese slicing is a skill I just can't seem to master. Usually I have Paul cut off the rind, so it's easier.

"No Lucy. We don't have enough time for a discussion now. I have to leave the house in fifteen minutes, as do you."

Just then, Paul walked into the kitchen. He'd snuck in a shower while Lucy was having breakfast and was now getting his bag together for work.

"Argh! Where are my bike keys? I want to throw my bike in the back of the car so that you can drop me off at the office after the embassy. I'll bike back to the house tonight."

"If I had a euro for every time you ask me that…"

"That is so not helpful." Paul slammed the kitchen drawer shut and continued to look for his keys. Paul bikes to work in one direction, towards Utrecht, and Lucy in the other direction, towards Hilversum — both have an eight to ten mile commute of about 45 minutes.

"Calm down Paul, we'll find them." I gently placed my hand on his back and rubbed his shoulders.

"Sorry, I'm just a bit stressed, that's all." He looked at me, his eyes softened, and he gave me a kiss on my forehead.

"Can't you give me a lift today?" Lucy's dark brown eyes peered out over her bowl as she slurped the last sip of milk. After one of my Dutch neighbors gave me unsolicited advice that my cappuccinos would be better with *lang houdbare melk*—UHT shelf-stable milk, I switched.

"No, papa and I have to go to the embassy this morning." Just as I looked up to say this to Lucy, I sliced my left index finger with the cheese knife, and noticed the shaved bit of skin on the knife as blood started seeping out of the cut.

"Damn it! I hate these Dutch cheese knives! You'd think after all these years I'd be able to cut a piece of cheese!" Paul rushed towards me with a paper towel.

"Here, hold this on there, tight, apply some pressure."

"This is exactly what I *don't* need right now."

"It'll be OK. We're all a little stressed. Here, let me finish making Lucy's lunch. You put a thick Band-Aid on that, and get ready to go." Paul took the cheese slicer from me and rinsed it off in the sink.

"Thank you." I ran to our bathroom and found the tube of Neosporin that I'd brought back from the US during our last trip. Neosporin was one of the handful of products I always brought back, that and Band-Aids, Ziploc bags, Cream of Wheat, and a stack of Vanity Fairs and People magazines. The Dutch alternatives were just not the same. I applied a large Band-Aid and wrapped it tight around my finger. I grabbed a couple extra Band-Aids and placed them in my briefcase.

"OK, Lucy, we're out of here my love. Can one of you please let Abby out one last time, for a pee, before you leave? And don't forget to lock up!" I gave Lucy a kiss on the head and rushed out the door. Paul followed behind me, scrolling through his phone. He almost tripped over his bike helmet on the way to the car. It must have rolled off of the bench on the front porch. He, like most Dutch people, refused to wear it on his way to and from work. We've had so many arguments about it. His commute to Utrecht along the Vecht is windy, full of twists and turns. I wasn't worried so much about his biking skills — he grew up biking everywhere. It was more the cars that worried me. Especially when people checked their phones while driving. Nothing pissed me off more than when I saw people doing that. It was no use getting on his case about it. He wouldn't wear it. I picked it up and placed it on the front porch, out of harm's way. We loaded his bike into the back of the car and were off.

Chapter 2

We hopped into my chariot, a Jeep Cherokee — another symbol of my Americanness among the Dutch. Supposedly only eight Cherokees were sold in 2019 in the Netherlands, compared to 190,000 in the US. While I know it's not a popular family car, I did like to be unique in this homogenous country, a country the size of Maryland. Unlike in my hometown, in Loenen you can't recognize people by their car, because *everyone* has the same - a dark blue or black Audi, BMW, or Range Rover. I waved to everyone I saw driving by, figuring it was probably someone I knew through those darkened windows.

My neighbor, Friso's head bobbed over the hedges as he walked to his mailbox for the morning paper, and he waved. I remember the first week we moved to Loenen and I talked to Friso about how I was expecting more diversity in a town just twenty minutes by car outside of Amsterdam, to which he responded, "Oh no, it's very diverse here in Loenen — we have yellow Labradors, black Labradors, and brown Labradors." That's one thing I missed about Amsterdam. In

Loenen it was one big, white protective bubble, except for a handful of Syrian refugees.

After adjusting the seat settings (Paul is 6'4 to my 5'5 frame), I turned off the air conditioner. Not really needed today. It was 72 degrees outside. I rolled down the window a crack instead, and the smell of dank polders, canals and cow manure crept their way into the car. The smell reminded me of when Paul and I first moved to the Netherlands. I caught a whiff of the exact same smell when I looked out over the flat green fields between Schiphol airport and Amsterdam from the taxi. Growing up in Pennsylvania, I didn't even know where the Netherlands was. But moving here in my early twenties opened up a whole new world for me. We didn't just come for my cheaper master's program and the opportunity to drive to Southern France in the summer. The truth is, I saw it as a chance to reinvent myself, and to create my own habitat.

*****

I had surprisingly little conflict in my childhood, notable for the fact that I grew up in a town known for its conflict: Gettysburg, where the famous three-day battle, the bloodiest of the American Civil War, resulted in a cumulative 50,000 dead and wounded soldiers. I was the oldest of four, with three younger brothers. John was two years younger than me, and the twins, Ben and Tom, were two years younger than John. Me, the only girl in the family. A place of honor, the trailblazer, the responsible, clear-headed one.

My dad started his own carpentry business, allowing him to go golfing with his friends whenever he wanted. My mom was the secretary at the funeral home just down the street from where we lived. I had a happy childhood. My dad read to me each night. My mom took me shopping at TJ Maxx. Both sets of grandparents lived just a couple of blocks away. My grandfather took me to the Christmas tree farm each year to chop down our tree. My grandmother would hand me pieces of hard candy during the long sermons at the Lutheran Church I grew up going to, just one block away from my house. My parents were never overbearing, they let me figure things out on my own and, because of that trust, I never got in trouble. I simply followed the rules, because I had no incentive to break them. I played kick the can with friends on the streets. I rode my bike around town and played for hours in the tiber — the underground cement tunnel system, where all the town's over-flowing water would go in the case of a flood.

High school years full of Friday night football games, and dances ending with Led Zeppelin's *Stairway to Heaven*, floated by like a dream. But each night, as I stared up at my poster of The Cure's *Wish* album cover that was pasted on the ceiling, the one with childlike drawings of eyeballs and a navigational compass, I asked myself "What's next? Where is this all leading to?" Looking back, for a teenager, I was perhaps too preoccupied with the next step, worried about what I was going to become, where I was going to live, who I was going to end up with.

Towards the end of senior year in high school, I felt a deep calling, like an old wise woman whispering in my ear — "Jill, you're going to do great things in life", at least, that's what I wanted to believe. I had always been intrigued by the news anchors on the NBC News morning show, *Today*. I had myself convinced that I was the next Katie Couric. That idea was solidified when the high school aptitude test that my guidance counselor administered said my inquisitive mind and attention to detail would make for a good journalist. I ended up going to Gettysburg College in my hometown, one of the benefits being I could do my laundry at my parents' (I wasn't entirely ready to leave the warm nest I came from), but also because they had an excellent broadcast journalism program. After graduation, I knew that if I was going to make it in the world of broadcasting, it would have to be either New York City or DC. I believed fate was knocking at my door, especially when, fresh out of college, I got an entry-level job at NPR as production assistant at their headquarters in DC. I felt the gods were telling me, "Jill, you were made for radio, not TV".

So the career aspect — "what I was going to become?", was working out. The "where am I going to live?" part was working out — DC. Next came the "who will I end up with?". After all, I was in my early twenties. Time to really start looking for a life partner, so I thought. When Paul came along, I knew that was my ticket. He could be the one to build a life with. He was an opportunity I couldn't pass up. But what I didn't know, nor could ever imagine, was that it was possible to feel at home in a place other than Gettysburg. But Paul's family welcomed me with open arms from day one, and offered a different perspective.

I'll never forget the first day I walked into the house where Paul grew up, in Groningen. Groningen is a two-hour drive north-east from Amsterdam, and is a small city whose claim to fame is the University of Groningen — founded in 1614, it's the second oldest university in the Netherlands and is ranked as one of the top universities worldwide. That's where I first met Margreet. It was the summer of 1998, the summer prior to Paul and I moving to Amsterdam. We borrowed his sister's burgundy antique Volvo Amazon and parked on the Hereweg, the main artery into the city center, the busy street where Paul grew up. Paul and I walked up to the large brick 1920s *herenhuis*, with its beautiful stained glass windows by the entrance and massive carved wooden door (they don't make houses like this anymore!) to find a man watering red geraniums in a flower box, who looked like a red-headed Santa Claus.

"Jill," Paul said, "this is Bert, my mother's partner." Bert reached out and shook my hand, squeezing it so hard it felt like he almost broke it.

"*Hallo Bert, aangenaam kennis te maken*—Hello Bert, a pleasure to meet you," I said as I massaged my hand as discreetly as possible.

Paul whispered in my ear in English, so Bert wouldn't hear as easily, "Bert has no feeling in his right hand, so he tends to squeeze too hard." I smiled and nodded.

We walked through the oversized front door made of heavy wood, stained a dark espresso brown, and entered a small hallway, covered in white marble from floor to ceiling. Paul led me into the living room — a grand room with 15 foot ceilings where Margreet, who was wearing a gauzy white tunic over black leggings and an armful of clanging gold charm bracelets, ran towards me with wide open arms, "*Jill, jij bent er, welkom! Ik voel alsof ik jou al heel lang ken—*"Jill, you're here, welcome! I feel like I've already known you forever." Her dark friendly eyes narrowed in joy, as her smile widened. I smiled back and allowed her to envelop my body, pulling me in for a big warm hug. And she was right. It did feel like that. I felt so welcome - a blanket of delight and warmth enveloped me. Her hair was salt and pepper gray and just hit her shoulders in length. Her eyebrows were neat and well balanced—like Paul's—expanding all the way across the tops of her eyes. She had a sturdy build, but in a jolly way, as someone who enjoyed a good hearty snack and a full glass of wine.

Margreet took me by my hand and led me out to the backyard, through enormous French doors surrounded by sweet fragrant purple wisteria, smelling similar to freesia and gardenias but not as strong. There, on a long wooden table, draped with a red and white gingham checkered tablecloth was a smorgasbord of food. There were deviled eggs, along with a seafood platter, salmon mousse, *paling*— smoked eel, herring, *garnaaltjes*—North Sea shrimp, and smoked salmon. There were all sorts of dips and spreads, her (as I would come to know) famous meatballs, and fresh *stokbrood*—baguette. Everyone was there, gathered around the table. Margreet's ex-husband, Hans, his new girlfriend, Paul's older sisters, their husbands, and Jeroen, Paul's brother. I took a seat next to Bert, who had since made his way from the geraniums to the backyard. Margreet handed me a glass of cold Cava and a cracker piled precariously high with salmon mousse. No one can fit as much dip on one cracker as Margreet.

"Proost op onze nieuwst aanwinst, Jill!"—"Cheers to our newest addition, Jill!" Margreet raised her glass, and everyone shouted *proost!* as they looked each other in the eye and clinked glasses. I felt at home and at ease here, basking in the love of my new Dutch family. I immediately felt welcome as they passed me snacks and teased Paul, trying to embarrass him with stories of the past, like his first kiss in elementary school, or how cute he was when he cried because his cheeks got so red.

Paul and I got married the following summer, in

Gettysburg. Thirty Dutch people flew over for the wedding, a mix of Paul's family members and his closest friends from high school and college. I remember making welcome packets for our Dutch guests, full of bagels, Hershey's kisses, and brochures of things to do. It was one of the hottest days on record that summer and there was no air conditioning in the church. When I walked down the aisle with my dad, all I saw was a sea of our wedding programs being used as fans. The day prior to the wedding, our Dutch friends went on a Battlefield tour. They came back confused, saying that their guide kept referring to "generally this, and generally that", after which I told them about General Lee, the Commander of the Confederate Army — then everything fell into place. Margreet always said it was the happiest week of her life — having the entire family together and both cultures merging.

Paul and his family discussed things openly; like most Dutch people, they were direct. If something was bothering them, like how Paul's oldest sister would order for everyone before they even had a chance to look at the menu, they'd just come out and say it. That was the Dutch way, and I liked it.

Paul's sisters became confidants — they were like the sisters I never had growing up, but had always wanted. Paul's sisters were interested in the same books. I trusted their judgment on child rearing. They would shower me with hand-me-down hockey sticks for Lucy, and bikes. Paul was my link to Europe and all its goodness. I found myself lost in a foreign language, and discovered the allure of Chanel perfume.

My parents were supportive, knowing full well they didn't have much choice anyway. When I put my mind to something, that was usually it. At the same time, I knew they were wary about sending me off to the Netherlands with some Dutchman. Either way, looking back, I realize how hard that must have been for them, to let go. But in all honesty, it was just as hard for me to let go. Loads of sacrifices were made on my end. Not only my physical belongings, like my car, my apartment, and my currency, but also my high school and college friends, my grandmother (who I would often visit), and things like hot summer nights and the sound of crickets when falling asleep. Plus communicating in my native language on a daily basis, something I definitely took for granted until I spent the next twenty years operating in a sort of third language, somewhere between English and Dutch, depending on how tired I was.

I learned Dutch by watching a popular Dutch soap opera about a bunch of teenagers working in a bar, called *Goede Tijden, Slechte Tijden*—Good Times, Bad Times. I rode my bike five miles to IKEA each way, against the wind, to pick up things to decorate our apartment. I'd drape the shopping bags on my handlebars, or attach them to my *bagagedrager*—luggage holder on the back of the bike, and off I'd go, pedaling against the wind. We went out to the *discotheeks* on Rembrandtplein, sipping on *Passoa Jus*—passion fruit liqueur with orange juice, with Paul's Dutch friends. Moving to the Netherlands was life changing, in that it showed me there was more out there than just Gettysburg. That move to "somewhere else" was my ticket out of small-town America, to somewhere I could build the life I dreamed of when staring up at my Cure poster.

Chapter 3

As we pulled up to the highly secured gate of the US Embassy in The Hague, I saw two guards standing out front, checking cars as they came in. The building looked a lot like my high school in the US, or a prison — lots of brick. A large American flag waved out front. I was nervous and looked over at Paul, who was anxiously twitching his leg. I get butterflies in my stomach every time we have to renew or apply for an official US document. Especially today, because if Paul didn't get this visa that would put a major dent in our plans. You'd think I would get used to these appointments by now, but the adrenaline always kicks in. I checked my bag on the seat beside me, rustling through the papers for our appointment confirmation. As I rolled down the driver's side window, a tall skinny man in a camo uniform approached, with a large firearm strapped over his shoulder — he bent down slightly, toward my window, clearing his throat.

"Good morning. I'm Jill Stone here, with my husband Paul Davenoord. I need to renew my passport, and we're applying for his visa." I pointed to Paul with one hand, while holding up my printout of the appointment confirmation in the other.

"OK ma'am. One second please," his thick American accent caught me off guard. I'm not used to hearing the southern twang of ma'ams, and the sound of it made me feel out of place. He took a step back and said something into his walkie talkie. All I heard was a bleep and a fuzzy sound in return. "Can I see your passport?"

"Here you go." My hand shook as I handed it to him. "Yeah, sorry, my US passport expired, but again, that's why I'm here." I brought both my Dutch and American passports just in case. Once it looked like we'd be staying in the Netherlands for more than a year, I applied for my Dutch citizenship back in 2002. I was so fed up with not knowing what Paul and all his friends were talking about, paranoid they were talking about him and his old fling, that I was determined to learn the language and become a full-fledged citizen. To literally have a foot on the ground here, making the culture my own. I didn't like the idea of being so dependent on one person in order to stay. On the other hand, by getting my Dutch citizenship, I felt it showed Paul how committed I was to him and his culture. I would have never gotten my Dutch citizenship if it meant I had to give up my American. Luckily, I was allowed to keep both. Lucy has both as well. Paul is the only one in our household who has only Dutch citizenship. "Why do you even need Dutch citizenship, Jill?" Paul asked me when I was studying one day for the naturalization exam. I'd joke, "Because if God forbid you and I don't work out — at least I can stay here if I want to!" The thought that my integration process, nationality, and ability to adapt to Dutch culture was dependent on him has been something I always struggled with, making every effort I can to pave my own way.

The man, on whose name tag I could now read *Greg*, had a close look, then handed it back to me. "OK thank you. You may proceed to parking. You have to leave your cell phone and any other electronics at reception."

"OK thank you. We will." I rolled up my window and drove to visitor parking. I glanced over at Paul who was sitting quietly.

"I always feel so intimidated at these appointments." Paul clenched his jaw, "It's as if part of the vetting process for US civil servants is to be a douche. It's like the DMV all over again."

"But it's not just America. Really anywhere that produces some sort of official document must have that as a staff requirement, to make people coming in feel nervous by being as strict and unpleasant as possible. I'll never forget when I took a day off work to renew Lucy's US passport at the Consulate in Amsterdam, they sent me away because the credit card I wanted to use to pay had your name on it and not mine. I wanted to cry. A whole day wasted, and they were so unforgiving. At least at the Dutch Embassy in DC they didn't carry around large rifles on their shoulders. I found that so intimidating. All you need is one mentally unstable person and the whole room is dead." I pulled into the first available spot I found.

"Well, that's a bit extreme. Why does your mind tend to play out all these doomsday scenarios?" Paul turned off his phone and placed it in his bag. "I get it, it's an emotional thing for you, passports, visa's, nationality, dual-citizenship. Jill, you're placing too much weight on an official document. It's just a piece of paper."

Hopefully today would change my bad streak with US foreign service officers. As we walked towards the entrance I had a flashback to when I first met Paul in Washington. The same diplomatic vibe hung in the air. I met him in a similar, large stately building, with glistening white hallways, and people walking around with security badges and piles of papers in their arms. As a young twenty-two year old, it was exciting. I felt special, having access to the Dutch Embassy where Paul was interning, just like we had access today.

In fact, that's part of the reason why, even from a young age, I wanted to be a journalist. It was almost the same as being a diplomat in that you have to be objective, while showing empathy. Like diplomats, journalists have access. Instead of keeping the ties between countries, you keep the ties between listeners and news. Having majored in journalism, NPR was the mecca of all careers for me. NPR was (and still is) the big league. NPR's red, black and blue logo against the pristine green lawn will forever be imprinted in my mind. I was happy to at least have a foot in the door with them, and I quickly fell in love with radio, such a timeless communication medium, and a noble profession. It's been around since the turn of last century and is still with us, hardly changed, except that now there are podcasts. As part of the production crew, I would scope out the newspapers and comb the internet for story ideas. Little did I know that a story lead would *actually lead* me to my future Dutch husband.

* * * * *

Paul Cornelis Nicolaas Davenoord (let's just call him Paul) was interning at the Dutch Embassy in the fall of

1997, working on a policy paper for his master's thesis back at Wageningen University, under the supervision of their Department for Agriculture. My job as production assistant at NPR was tough — long days, crunching to meet deadlines. My boss, Catharine, asked me to set up an interview with Paul "about his research on how public and private partners work together when regulating biotech, especially when it comes to approving new crop varieties, and labeling efforts for foods derived from such crops." Say what?! This sounded like an alien language to me. Catharine and Paul met at some hoity toity ag-tech reception the week prior. Catharine figured it would be a fun assignment for me, seeing as there was a lot in the news recently about Monsanto having recently become an agro-biotech subsidiary of Pharmacia. There were lots of lawsuits between the "new" Monsanto and the old one. "Maybe you can brush up on your investigative journalism skills!" she joked.

I met Paul on a windy October day, two months into my new job. I made my way through the Dutch Embassy security check points and reception to conduct an interview with him. While waiting in the reception area, 22-year-old Paul scanned his pass to the revolving doors leading to the waiting area where I was seated. I was struck by his chiseled face, round spectacles, and soft blond feather-like hair. While he wasn't looking, I quickly powdered my nose to remove any shine and did a quick check to make sure none of my morning mascara had sprinkled black flakes under my eyes.

When Paul got to the reception area, I stood up and shook his hand. I felt a current of electricity shoot up through my arm and wondered if he felt it too. I wanted to look away, so overcome by the sheer touch of his hand, but his intense stare prevented me from even dropping my gaze a degree. My eye started twitching — a nervous tick that I never outgrew. He seemed a bit stern, even for a Dutchman, but there was something about him that intrigued me. He was wearing a dark gray suit that was slightly too big for him in the shoulders. He was tall, and very lean. His gold round spectacles made him look smart and European.

"Hi, I'm Paul, nice to meet you."

"*Hallo, ik ben Jill, aangenaam kennis te maken.*"

Paul was shocked and his icy demeanor softened. He continued in English, "Oh, you speak Dutch?! I've never met an American who can speak Dutch."

"No, unfortunately that's all the Dutch I know. I looked up a couple of phrases before our interview, wanting to make a good impression."

"Well done!" Paul puckered his lips together, raised his eyebrows and nodded his head.

Confession: Despite his intriguing European nature and me being physically attracted to him, I didn't really *like* Paul when I first met him. I thought he was too harsh, too surly, *te nors*—too gruff, as they say in Dutch. Here I was, doing my best to make him feel at ease by speaking Dutch to him, and all he gave me was a condescending "well done".

I don't remember much else about the actual interview, other than that I went through the scripted questions, thanked him, and when I left I looked back over my shoulder and caught him still watching me with a smile. I went back to my office downtown, to transcribe and edit. We casually emailed back and forth, for fact checking.

When the interview was broadcast later that week, Paul called me up to say how much he enjoyed it. He then invited me along with a couple of people from the embassy to his house on Upton Street, where he rented a room, to thank me with dinner. He cooked a simple but delicious *farfalle* pasta with a creamy mushroom sauce. I watched him cook, his tall, easy-going stature confidently commanding the pots and pans on the stove, his blond hair even brighter thanks to the overhead light. His blue striped button-up shirt offset his deep brown eyes and his jeans, well, they fit his buttocks perfectly. It was at that moment that I noted, *"Hey, here's a man who can cook well, and I hate cooking. I'm starting to really like this guy..."*

The more we talked, the more we hit it off. After that pasta dinner, Paul and I started hanging out more and more, at first only on the weekends, then daily. My roommate, Michelle, stopped waiting for me to come home at night. Paul and I went on long hikes along the Potomac River in Virginia, where he reached for my hand to pull me up onto the next rock, as we climbed to get the best view of the Great Falls. He gave me his jacket when I got too cold watching the Washington Capitals play the Minnesota Wild at the MCI center in downtown DC. He put his arm around my shoulder on the metro ride back to Adams Morgan, and it felt so natural, so right. We weren't dating, we were still just friends, but we were doing things together that made it *feel* like we were. One night, we got Chinese takeout and my fortune cookie read, "Your spirit of adventure leads you down an exciting new path". I laughed and showed it to Paul. He smiled and grabbed my hand, squeezing it tight. I placed the fortune in my pocket, then later put it in the drawer next to my bed.

About four weeks after we met, it hit me that I was falling for Paul. We had gone to a record shop on 18th street, in Adams Morgan. A little bell dinged by the door as we entered, and that telltale, slightly musty smell of stacked vinyl overwhelmed us when we walked in. The shop owner greeted us, "We're about to close in ten minutes, but have a look around." Bright lights lined the aisles as we flipped through the music bins and Etta James' song *At Last* started crooning over the store's speakers. *I found a dream, that I could speak to, a dream that I can call my own.* The music went straight through my skin to my heart.

I looked down the aisle at Paul, and knew right then and there: he was the one. The "ah ha!" moment had crept up on me. It wasn't the scientific method I had used for dating in the past, of me scoping him out as a possible dating subject, analyzing what I liked and what I didn't like about him. This was the life partner I'd been looking for. This was the BAM! moment. Right there, in a record shop on 18th street, Washington, DC. My hunt was over.

But if we were to be together, there were a couple of issues to contend with. One, Paul was in a two-year relationship with his college girlfriend, Sanne, back at Wageningen. Although, I was getting the feeling she was more into him than he was into her. At least that's the impression he gave me. Two, how long was he going to be staying in Washington and, if he left, what would happen then? Would I go to the Netherlands? His internship was only supposed to be for three months.

In December, when Paul was almost finished with his internship, he went back to the Netherlands for Christmas. I was extremely nervous about it, fearing this was the make or break moment for our non-relationship relationship. And while we had been nothing more than friends on paper, my feelings for him had been getting stronger and stronger, culminating in my epiphany at the vinyl store. I was suddenly terrified that he would not come back to the US at all.

The only thing I could think to do to keep his attention on me and our simmering relationship was to give him a note to read on the plane. I'm much better at writing down my feelings than saying them out loud, which is ironic when I've found a career in broadcast journalism. But broadcast journalism is about facts, not feelings. I expressed my feelings for him as clearly as possible: *I've enjoyed these past two months with you SO much, and can honestly say I'm going to miss you terribly during the holidays and really hope you'll return. Liefs, Jill.* For the entire Christmas break with my family in Gettysburg I was nervous, pacing around my parents' house, biting my nails, going on extra-long jogs on the Battlefield.

I sat on the same bar stools he and I sat on several weeks before, when he met my parents for the first time. I had invited a bunch of friends from Washington up to Gettysburg, to celebrate Thanksgiving. Now it was just me, drinking coffee with my mom. The house wasn't as immaculate as my mom had made it for Paul's visit. The Today show was on the TV in the background, while I leafed mindlessly through a pile of J.Crew and Pottery Barn catalogues.

My Mom asked: "So, Paul is back visiting his family for Christmas. Is he planning on coming back? Didn't he have a Dutch girlfriend?".

"I don't know mom. But I don't want to talk about it." And I didn't. I'd never been so nervous, and I'd never felt so vulnerable as I did for those eight days. The waiting and wondering. The hoping. *Why did I have to fall in love with a foreign man?* But back in Washington at 3:30 p.m. on January 3rd I heard a loud *bleep* sound in my purse. I looked at my Nokia and saw a text message from Paul, *Net geland. Ik ben weer in het land. Dank je wel voor je lieve kaart*—Just landed. I'm back in the country. Thank you for your sweet card. I jumped up and down holding my phone tightly with both hands. I felt a huge wave of excitement and relief as I texted back, *Welkom terug*—Welcome Back! Hope you had a nice holiday. Looking forward to catching up soon.

But I couldn't stop thinking about how, even though I was relieved he was back in the US, he would only be in my life for one more month, because that's when his internship would officially end. Unless I could get him to stay with me in DC..., but we'd have to find a way for him to secure a visa, an apartment, and a job. But in one month? How on earth? If I wanted him in my life, I was going to have to act, and fast. If I didn't, he would return to the Netherlands. I couldn't let that happen!

That same week, I seized the moment. It was a freezing cold January night. The snow melted slightly during the day, creating a sheet of ice that covered the piles of snow at night. The air was clear and crisp. Thousands of stars twinkled overhead, and I could see my breath. Paul invited me over for a movie. I can't remember which one. It didn't matter anyway, because all I could do was think about Paul leaving. When the movie was over, it was close to midnight. We both had to work the next day, so I slowly gathered my purse and jacket, dreading the cold winter air and the twenty-minute drive home. Paul said, "You can spend the night if you want."

My heart raced. I was secretly hoping this suggestion would come up, and I eagerly took him up on it. I felt like it was Paul's turn to show how he was feeling, as I had already acknowledged mine with the note. Paul had not yet verbally acknowledged his feelings for me. What were we allowed to do? What were we allowed to feel? We had never discussed or acknowledged it, until that night.

"The sheets on the bed over there are clean," he said, pointing to one of the two single beds in his attic room. I crawled into my bed. It felt like Paul was a mile away on the other side, but I could hear him breathing softly. My heart was pounding. My head was spinning. I knew if we were ever going to be together I had to act on my feelings. My mouth opened to speak, and I knew as soon as my lips parted there was no turning back. I took matters into my own hands.

"Paul, are you still awake?"

"Yes."

"There's something I have to get off my chest. I've enjoyed my time so much with you these past couple of months. When you left for the holidays I realized how much I missed being with you. I've never met a guy like you before. I'm falling for you."

Paul didn't say a word. Instead, he ran over to my bed and jumped in it with me. His tall body on top of mine, supported by his strong but not too muscular arms, his hot breath, soft tongue reading me like Braille, like he didn't want to skip a word. His stubbly face brushed against mine. I let go of my tense muscles and let myself be enveloped by him. Our bodies fit together like the last two missing pieces of a puzzle. A sound came out of me that I never experienced before. It was as if I was floating. Afterwards, we laid there out of breath, my head on his chest, rising up and down. We laughed as we stared up at the dark ceiling, both of us saying "wow!" at the same time, then laughing even harder. The next day I felt like a schoolgirl as I walked to my car in the same clothes I had on the night before. My colleagues at NPR gave me a double take, and one asked me if I had a brush, after which I smiled and turned red as a beet.

As our romance grew, we emailed messages to each other all day — from the basement of the embassy to the basement at NPR's headquarters in Tenleytown. Supposedly, interns are always stuck in the basement, wherever they are in the world. Messages continued throughout the week.

It wasn't all easy though. There was the sudden, additional stress of helping Paul find a job, so that he could stay in the US on a work visa. He didn't have anyone except for me, my family, and a couple of embassy friends. I'd check in with him before going out for dinner with girlfriends and find him sitting alone in his little attic room, flipping aimlessly through channels, slouched on the couch, empty bags of chips on the floor, curtains drawn.

Within one month, with the help of embassy colleagues, Paul landed a job as an analyst for an agri-food consulting firm downtown. To make his salary work, he ate lunch from the dollar menu at McDonald's, but annoyingly still managed to stay lean. By this time, Michelle had moved out of my apartment and Paul had moved in. But there was one slight problem — I was beginning to hate my job. I was getting the grunt work, because I was the youngest. My plan to have that be my foot in the door and eventually work my way into a permanent position with NPR was not working out as I'd hoped. There simply weren't any positions available.

We'd been in Washington for a solid year. It was time to move on. I needed to find a different path, and thought that getting a master's degree might help me move in that direction. Paul and I were getting more and more serious about our relationship. What was next? We didn't want to get caught up in the mundane reality we saw around us. We didn't want to find ourselves like our colleagues, working in full-time jobs we didn't like, just so we could pay our mortgage and have two SUVs on the driveway behind our white picket fence, with a one-week vacation on the Eastern Shore. Slaves to capitalism. It wasn't enough.

Paul wasn't in a particularly good spot either. He missed his family. His oldest sister was about to have her first child, making Paul an uncle for the first time, something he was really looking forward to. He liked his job and his colleagues, but he didn't have any close friends and he missed his own high school and college friends. We went over to the Netherlands for the first time together that summer and saw them, but that was so short. I could see Paul slipping — the way he walked around hunched over, his lack of energy, the sadness he wore on this face was like the sun caught behind a thick mist.

Europe was becoming more and more enticing. We knew it was possible to live off of one salary in the Netherlands — all Paul's friends and siblings were living examples. If I wanted, I could pursue my master's degree in journalism there, as opposed to in DC, and receive an education that was subsidized so much it was basically free — compared to having to take out another student loan in the US, the first one of which I was still paying off. More and more reasons kept pointing to Amsterdam as a place that made sense for us. In retrospect, the biggest reason of all was that I had this idea that if I found my romantic partner, the rest would snap into place. Growing up in a rambunctious household, I had felt lonely. When I met Paul, I saw him as a clean slate, a chance to make our own home, to build a life together, our own family unit.

After a particularly grueling day for both of us — Paul had got slammed with a 2,000 dollar dental bill for having his wisdom teeth removed, I found a parking ticket on my car, then my car wouldn't start, making me late for work, where I was yelled at for being late while a pile of papers to copy was shoved into my arms — I said, "Let's try it Paul. Why not? The master's program is only a year, and then we'll know whether or not we want to stay."

"I'm all in! I think it's an excellent idea, and a great way to test the waters. Like you said, it's only for a year, then we can decide what to do next."

We handed in our notice both for our jobs and our apartment. I sold my white Ford Focus to a jovial man in Virginia. I got into a master's program at the University of Amsterdam. Paul's sister, Inge, and her fiancé Jaap went scouting for an apartment for us and sent us pictures of a one-bedroom in the Nieuwe Kerkstraat. We put down a deposit, packed up our things, and went on one last vacation to Rehoboth Beach with my family. My parents drove us to Dulles airport on departure day.

"We're going to miss you guys so much. Call us when you get there!" My mom said, as she wiped her tears away with a tissue.

"OK mom and dad, I will. Don't worry, it's only for one year." We stood facing each other as lines of people moved, like cattle, behind us in the security check.

My dad gave me a big hug. My cheek brushed against his rough graying beard. I could feel his body shaking as he cried, trying to hold it in. He and I both knew it wasn't going to be only one year.

Chapter 4

9:55 a.m., right on time for our appointment. Paul and I made our way through the metal detector and entered a large waiting room with white tile floors. There was a large portrait of President Donald Trump in an ornate gold frame hanging on the wall. His face didn't look as orange as it normally did. His eyes stared at me and followed me to my seat. There was a television mounted in the corner, playing CNN with the volume on mute.

As I waited I leafed through our documents, making sure everything had been filled out correctly.

"Did you bring your contract from Leaf Fruit showing your start date, like I asked you?" My heart skipped a beat with sudden panic.

"Yes, Jill. Don't worry. Here, add this to your pile." Paul pulled out his contract and handed it to me, winking. Seconds later we were called up to the window. "Jill Stone and Paul Davenoord?"

"Yes! That's us." When standing up I tripped over the leg of a chair. Paul caught me just on time. I felt like our name had just been called for the Price is Right and we were running down the aisle.

"Jill, calm down. We have all our documents. We'll be fine." Paul whispered in my ear as we approached the window.

"You're right." I smiled and simultaneously greeted the woman whose name tag read: *Cindy*.

"You're applying for an immigrant visa for your spouse and US passport renewal, correct." Cindy peered at us over her gold rimmed glasses perched on her nose.

"Yes, that's correct. Here's our marriage certificate, passports, visa application, passport application, my husband Paul's contract in the US..." I slid my pile of documents under the window. I could feel my eye twitching, but I tried to let my smile suppress the twitch.

After scanning the documents, and stamping others, she told us to go sit down and wait. Ten minutes later we were called back to the window for a mini interview, making sure everything checked out. We answered questions about where we planned on living, what type of work Paul would be doing, whether or not we had dependents, and how long we planned on staying. Ten minutes later we were back in the parking lot.

"I guess it's now official." Paul put his arm around me, turned me towards him and kissed me on the lips. "I'm as American as I'll ever get. We need to celebrate. America — here we come!"

"It is exciting. But it also feels weird. I mean, I haven't really lived in America since that year after college. Maybe it just hasn't hit me yet." I pulled out my keys to the car.

"There is a lot going on right now. Let's just focus on getting through these next two weeks, then we can really relax, enjoy the summer a bit before my new job starts. Did you hear anything back from the realtor on the viewing this morning?"

"Not yet. They're probably there now. I'll let you know if they call me." We both got into the car and I pulled out of the parking lot, past Greg the security guard. We both waved on our way out. "Fingers crossed. Every bit we get over asking price goes towards our new build." Paul placed his hand on my leg and smiled, looking straight ahead.

While driving on the highway towards Utrecht, my thoughts started racing — imagining what it would be like to move back to the US, to make a home there. There's a part of me that's afraid I would feel like a foreigner in my own country. Gettysburg is a college town, so sure, it's eclectic to a certain degree, with its students and professors — most of them from somewhere else, which brings a certain flair. It's also a tourist town, so that brings a different vibe. I have great memories of working the front desk at the Gettysburg Hotel, in a Civil War era dress over my jeans and t-shirt, and making up beds at the Brafferton Inn Bed and Breakfast. Living in Gettysburg, at least Lucy would always have a good summer job. But it might be too much for all of us to move back to my small hometown of 8,000 people. We decided on Gettysburg over the DC area, because it would put us closer to my aging parents, the land was so much cheaper, Lucy had her college scholarship, and Paul had his amazing job offer at Leaf Fruit. All signs pointed that way. But in the past twenty years I had created a certain "healthy" distance between myself and my family, having moved abroad.

Now, when we go back for holidays it's always so intense. I felt like I was being thrown back to my teenage years, where my brothers dominated dinner conversations, re-hashing video game plays or reciting lines from a movie I hadn't seen. My dad always played his music too loud, or had his head stuck in a crossword puzzle. My mom was always running around trying to make everyone as comfortable as possible — so much so that you couldn't even find the bread, because the countertops were covered with food, should anyone want to grab the occasional Entenmann's donut hole! Besides these familial annoyances, I had to ask, "Where is a better place for me, Paul, and Lucy — as a family?"

I just read a headline in the newspaper last week: *The United Nations has researched the happiest children on the planet - Dutch kids are among the happiest, for the 5th year in a row!* — and it's not just because they get to eat chocolate sprinkles on their bread! I learned that it's mostly because they're given more independence, because the Netherlands was safer than other places in the world, basically allowing them more freedom. I was worried that if Lucy went to America, she might lose some of that independence. But then, there was also a part of me that felt guilty, as if I had given up on America and left my family behind. I felt like I owed it to my parents, and to myself, to return. It was time to give America a chance again, me as an individual, and us as a family. We'd only ever been there for short visits, as a family. Moving back was the fair thing to do for my parents, and for Lucy.

To compensate for my choosing a different path, I've spent the past two decades studying the land of the free, from 5,000 miles away. It was like stalking an ex-boyfriend online — despite no longer wanting to be with him, I couldn't help but wonder what he was up to all of the time. By getting both my bachelor's and my master's degrees in journalism, I was looking at American culture from a journalist's perspective, through a different lens, something I started doing when I moved over to the Netherlands with Paul. I was trained at an early age to look at America from a Dutch perspective, and to constantly compare the two countries.

Pro (I think?): The Dutch don't go to the doctor for every little thing.

Con (I think?): In America we wear bike helmets.

My head was spinning with comparisons, trying to extrapolate information that could point to which one fit me better? Where did I *want* to be? Where did I think Paul, Lucy, and I *should* be?

* * * * *

After our embassy appointment, I dropped off Paul and his bike at his office in Utrecht and made my way to the studio in Hilversum. I rolled the tension out of my neck and turned on my Bluetooth. No sooner had I pulled out of Paul's parking lot, when my phone rang. It was my mother-in-law, Margreet.

"*Hallo lieverd, ik bel je in eerst instantie om te vragen hoe het ging bij de ambassade en omdat ik mijn nieuwe hoorapparaat wil testen*—Hi Sweetie, I'm calling you to check in to see how things went at the embassy, but also to test out my new hearing aid."

"It went well. Your son has his visa."

"I'm so happy for you and your family. Your American roots are such a part of you. You love America, it's in your genes, in your entire Jill. *Beloof me één ding Jill, blijf altijd een Amerikaan!*—Promise me one thing Jill, that you'll always remain an American!"

She always says this, "hold onto your American roots! They are so special!" Which, I used to think didn't make sense — how could I be anything but an American? But over time, the once bright, shiny, optimistic edges of being an American (you can always spot one immediately in a crowd over here, by their uber-friendliness), started to slowly disappear. I didn't smile at everyone quite so eagerly anymore. I didn't greet every passer-by during my jogs. I learned to not broadcast my thoughts to the entire restaurant. Over the past twenty years I've realized how America is slipping further away from me, and that's why Margreet is always warning me to keep a grip on my Americanness, while at the same time letting go of all that I cannot control — like Trump's announcement that he'll be running again for president. Looking back, I think during my fight to not be treated as an American, my efforts to shed my Americanness, I lost part of myself. It was almost too much to bear, so I pushed it under the rug. Something I'm very good at doing.

"Sorry Margreet. I'm getting another call, I'll have to call you back some other time." I lied. But if I didn't, I'd be on the phone with her for another hour. Margreet loves to talk over the phone, which can be fun — but not today. I needed to think about that last radio interview I had to record, once back at the studio in Hilversum.

"OK *lieverd. We spreken elkaar*—OK sweetheart, we'll speak soon." Kissing sounds are interrupted by the bleep, bleep, bleep of hanging up.

Chapter 5

On the highway between Utrecht and Hilversum I thought back to our appointment at the American Embassy. The more people ask, "Are you American?", the more I think about its meaning and my response. As the years passed and I changed, as America changed, the percentage seemed to flip to forty percent American, sixty percent Dutch. And this made me sad — as if I've misplaced something important, like my wedding ring or a cherished letter from my grandmother. There was so much of America that I didn't recognize anymore. When I turned on the news I saw what a soap opera America had become, with all of the hate speech and fear mongering, like Trump building his wall to keep out the Mexicans. The Mexicans are the only ones willing to pick the apples in our orchards in Pennsylvania, where I'm about to live (again). It scared me. My ideal, of moving back to share with Lucy what it's like to grow up "American", had eroded a little bit more with each year that passed.

One year turned into three, which turned into ten, then twenty. After many late night talks, we agreed it was time to give America a try. Now that Lucy was graduating Dutch high school, the timing seemed right. Paul and I had had endless discussions about the Dutch education system versus the American one, and when would be a good time to go back to the States. The college years seemed to make the most sense. A logical time to break ties. The way the Dutch started their standardized testing so early, with CITO's starting in the first grade, always bothered me. It seemed as if Dutch children were placed in a box already, at age twelve — pre-university track—VWO; general secondary education—HAVO; or pre-vocational track—VMBO. Lucy was so nervous about what her high school *advies*—advice would be. Too much stress at the time for a sixth-grader, if you ask me. She ended up going to a bi-lingual VWO high school in Hilversum, but part of me wished she could have experienced an American high school, where we were all thrown together. If you needed more of a challenge, you simply took AP classes, and the only standardized testing I could remember were the SATs, which some colleges (including my own) didn't even require. Not that my scores were bad, I just didn't believe in placing so much weight on these standardized tests. A liberal arts college would be good for Lucy — helping her learn to formulate effective arguments, to communicate well, and to problem-solve. She says she wants to be a lawyer someday.

That's the compromise we made, ensuring a Dutch-American balance, living in both our homelands for a solid chunk of time, and being close to both sets of our aging parents. Because, for every bit of America that I don't recognize, there's something I truly miss about it.

When I felt the America I knew slipping away, I tried to tighten my grip on my Americanness by doing extra-American things. I made sure I had sparklers in the house for

July 4th. I made sure that I had a can of Libby's Pumpkin in the cupboard for Thanksgiving. I made Cream of Wheat for Lucy for breakfast. I shot hoops in the backyard, or danced to Talking Heads at high volume — "Come on Paul and Lucy, it's time for the after-dinner American dance party in the living room!. "

But what beat in my heart as an American was not the holidays or the food — it was the spontaneity, openness, and diversity of the people. But a white person's version of "diversity" is not necessarily an accurate portrayal. With 328 million people, there were a lot of voices, a lot of styles, a lot of room for improvisation and openness — at least that's how I remembered America. That was the opinion of my twenty-year-old self, barely an adult. These ideals were attainable for a white girl growing up in south-central Pennsylvania, but the 2000 census showed that the racial make-up of the borough of Gettysburg was eighty-five percent White and six percent Black, and looking back now, with the knowledge that that life and aspiration was only possible for someone who looked like me, it breaks my heart.

What I missed most about America was my hometown. My hometown reflected the beats of my heart as an American — community, helping, openness, kindness, familiarity. The rec park, where the fireman's carnival took place each year. Selling Girl Scout cookies — "Do you want Thin Mints or Samoa's ma'am?" Summer camp, where you'd spend two weeks mostly with strangers, learning how to *make new friends, but keep the old; one is silver and the other is gold.* All of these events were rooted in the idea of community. Sunday school, Girl Scouts, childhood camps, Adopt a Grandparent — all the activities I did as a child seemed to be scarce here. But, while I grew up thinking this was all there, the combination of living abroad for half my life and becoming older has shown me the underbelly of distrust, and the fear of immigrants and people of color which was there all along. I'm not so sure that a sense of community still exists on the same level it did back then. Kids don't go out and play in the tiber anymore, so I'm told.

The once familiar beats of my American heart have slowly developed into a new, Dutch rhythm. Rather than "you don't know until you try" and "go get 'em tiger", my gut-check has become *"Doe normaal, dan doe je gek genoeg"*—"Just act normal, then you're being crazy enough", and *"afspraak is afspraak"*—"a deal is a deal". Where life includes a dose of sarcasm, and skepticism, where everyone is busy making sure their hedge comes all the way to their property line. It feels like there's less room for spontaneity. But on the other hand, I like how I always know where I stand with the Dutch. Their communication is precise. The polder model — consensus decision making, which solves a problem via dialogue, every party having an equal say. All that consensus, and all those meetings, do result in a government and society that takes care of the people as a whole. What's better? A two-party government like in the US, or a sixteen-party government like in the Netherlands? There has to be a balance! Thoughts like these ricocheted in my head for years.

* * * * *

"There she is! How did it go? Did they strip search you?" Marlies looked up from her computer and took a sip from the straw of what appeared to be a post-lunch milkshake.

"Things went as well as expected. Paul has his visa. Our

move is becoming more and more real with each minute that passes." I threw my bag down next to my desk. Marlies came over and gave me a big hug. Just what I needed.

Marlies was my age, married, no kids. She and her husband, Stijn, had never wanted any. Like me, she's very focused on her career. She says that her career is her baby. But, unlike me, she has bright blue eyes, angel-like blond hair with a choppy long bob cut, fair skin and freckles, big boobs, and long legs. A complete contrast to my olive skin, dark brown hair and eyes, small boobs and athletic frame. Marlies always wears heels and refuses to wear jeans, whereas I always sport a pair of Nike Air Max pretty much daily, Levi's 321 shaping slim jeans and, if I want to dress things up, I'll throw on a blazer over a simple silk blouse. Marlies is calm, grounded, and she has a witty sense of humor which I love. But the funny thing is, she's also messy, and all over the place. Her desk is like a sea of papers, and her lunch containers from the day before usually still lurk there. A complete contrast to my orderly desk, with neatly stacked files and compartments for pens, rubber bands, and paperclips. I'm the restless control freak, always looking ahead to the next step. Making sure the security deposit on the vacation rental is paid way before the deadline. Buying thirty kilos of dog food to make sure we never run out, and that toilet paper is always well stocked. Thank God Marlies is there to remind me to slow down, take a chill pill.

She is the ying to my yang, and we knew it as soon as we met at a broadcast journalism conference years ago. I accidentally knocked a glass of red wine over her white blouse, and she burst out laughing as I was crying and trying to wipe it down with a napkin. We were part of the same cohort of people interviewing for a bunch of reporter vacancies at the time, both having just finished our master's in journalism. This was after I had lived in Washington with Paul for a year, then had moved over to the Netherlands for my master's program. I went to the University of Amsterdam, Marlies went to Utrecht University. The conference was part of a recruitment event for all the alumni of the top three Dutch journalism schools in the Netherlands. The most sought-after radio networks were present, to hold interviews.

Outside of my childhood friends and Loenen social circle, Marlies was my go-to. Because she was so far removed from my regular "Loenen life", I felt like I could tell her anything — almost like a shrink. We'd only known each other for twelve years, but not only did she help perfect many of the radio interviewing and editing skills I needed, she'd always been a good listener if I just wanted to unload after a bad day. We'd grabbed countless glasses of white wine after work, on MOUT's terrace in Hilversum.

"You wanna run through the script one more time before Eva gets here?" Marlies sat back down across from me.

"Nah, I'm going to wing it. After all, it's my last episode. I think it'll be fun to keep it more casual. Plus, Eva speaks perfect English, since she lived in the US until she was eleven years old." I applied ChapStick to my lips — something I always did before an interview, to keep them from sticking.

"That's right. I forgot. I love how we get to interview celebrities. Her television show, Jinek has top ratings, you know. I'm sure that will give our listener rating a huge boost." Marlies took a final slurp of her milkshake, before tossing it in the trash.

"I just hope I don't lose it during the interview, seeing as the subject is so political. Trump supports *everything* that I feel is wrong with America right now — he's consistently opposed to gun control, gay marriage, and abortion. But maybe you heard the same in journalism school: a good journalist does not let his or her political sentiment get in the way of reporting (of course, in private or afterwards it's a totally different story)."

"Yes, I do remember that take away. Well, at least Eva will most likely be on the same page as you. But then, the trick is to not make it a Trump-bashing piece." Marlies gets her mic situated next to her computer. I checked to make sure all the recording software was switched on and ready to go before Eva arrived for our interview, scheduled for 2:00 p.m.

Don't get me wrong - I love my job with Radio 1. It's been an incredible twelve years. I got to do lighter reporting, on topics like how the Dutch set up their enviable bike infrastructure (one of my favorite things about living here!), how drug user rooms have led to less drug addicts (something I feel America could learn from), and how Dutch parliament is run (not as efficiently as they would lead you to believe). It saddened me to see these effective social measures and drug policies, and realize that we couldn't seem to implement them in America. My mom reminded me, "yeah, but America has 328 million people and the Netherlands only 17 million — it's easier to get things done in a country the size of Maryland." I suppose she's right. I'm most proud of the piece I produced on my podcast about TBS—*terbeschikkingstelling* — a temporary posting for criminals with mental health disorders, where they go to a clinic and receive psychological treatment instead of being locked away for life. Depending on how that goes, they could be released under supervision. This is the piece that caught the eye of my former boss Catharine, at NPR, now the executive producer in DC. She reached out via LinkedIn to schedule a phone call with me later that day, to discuss the piece and "other opportunities", although I wasn't sure what that meant.

This job allowed me to stretch my creative mind — to be a diplomat in the broadest sense of the word, bridging different groups of people — and it gave me purpose, helping to expand the minds of my listeners. And isn't that what work is all about — having a purpose? But, there are downsides to every job. The 24/7 on-call aspect of the job wore on me, as did the responsibility of being *eindverantwoordelijk*—ultimately responsible, for my reporting. I had to stay current and come up with stories that would grab peoples' attention, ultimately leading to more listeners. Unlike Marlies, I wasn't one of those people who can compartmentalize, unfortunately.

When Marlies and I got hired to work for Radio 1, just out of journalism school, I saw this job as a way for me to build upon my experience at NPR in the US, while still learning more about Dutch culture — a culture I'd come to love, having spent almost half my life over here. I tried to instill this on Lucy, "If there's something you want, just go after it. Give it all you've got! Life is short and (almost) anything is possible if you put your mind to it." Usually this is met with "Maaamaaa — I know. You say this to me all the time."

Just then, I saw a slender blond woman in a black leather pencil skirt and cream-colored blouse walk into the studio. It was our guest, Eva Jinek. Her steel-blue eyes met mine through the glass window. I took a deep breath, stood up, and walked over to the door to greet her.

"Good morning. You must be Jill Stone? I'm Eva." She

reached out to shake my hand. Her hand was soft, and her fingernails were perfectly manicured and painted bright red.

"Yes, good morning. So nice to meet you and thanks for agreeing to this interview at such short notice. There aren't many Dutch celebrities with an American background. We thought you'd make for the perfect guest for today's topic."

"Dum, dum, dum — Trump's announcement that he'll be running again as Commander in Chief!" Marlies chimed in with a low commercial voice from her desk, as she stood up and walked towards Eva. "I'm Marlies, Jill's colleague. We'll both be interviewing you."

"Great! So where do you want me?"

"Why don't you sit down here, between us, behind this mic. Can I get you anything to drink? Coffee? Water?" I pulled out her chair for her.

"Water would be great, thanks."

"Sure, while I get that, Marlies, can you do a quick run through of how this is going to play out, so Eva knows how long the interview is and what to expect?"

"Of course!"

As I walked past Eva, I caught a whiff of her perfume, sandalwood with a hint of jasmine. Jasmine reminded me of a trip I took with my mom when I was ten to LA, to visit my uncle. I love the scent. I haven't been back since, but the smell has always stayed with me. Coming back with Eva's water, we got situated for the interview and ready to press the 'on air' button, so that colleagues wouldn't disturb our recording.

"OK Eva, ready? In 5,4,3,2,1 — we're recording."

"Eva Jinek, welcome to Radio 1! Big news today, Trump officially announced that he'll be running again in the 2020 elections. I did my homework prior to this interview, and learned that you were born in Oklahoma, grew up in Washington, and moved to the Netherlands when you were eleven years old. Do you still feel American? And how does this news affect you?"

"Yes, good job on the homework, that's right, my entire childhood was spent in the US, so yes, I feel like that's really where my roots are — that's where I was formed as a person."

"Well I must say, you've done an excellent job holding onto your American accent. My seventeen-year-old daughter, a Dutch-American dual citizen, still has the strongest Dutch accent I've heard, even though I spent her entire childhood speaking English to her."

"Well, thanks for the compliment. If she went to a Dutch elementary school, then that explains everything. I really think the accent depends on where you went to school in the early years."

"Do you make it back to the States often?"

"Yes, but not as often as I'd like. I don't have any family left there anymore. My parents, who are Czech, decided that they'd prefer my brother and I to grow up in Europe, before we went off to high school. I remember it took six weeks before I spoke my first word of Dutch."

"And now you host the most popular talk show on Dutch television."

"I know, crazy how things work out." Eva took a sip of her water. "To answer your second question on how this affects me. I have to say I'm saddened by the news. I'm not thrilled about the direction America has taken under the leadership of this past administration. I guess part of me is scared too. But I'm also not thrilled with the direction the Netherlands is taking either. Who's that famous history professor who has been predicting US election results?"

"You mean Allan Lichtman? Yes, predicting them correctly since 1984! Crazy, isn't it?"

"Yes, scary. All these astrologists and academics who say every hundred years or so there will be a pandemic or a world war. It's just too much to digest, and I feel like whoever is President of the US reflects the direction of the entire world, in a sense."

"Heavy stuff." Marlies mouthed to me that we have a couple of calls coming in. "Let's see what some of our listeners have to say, shall we?" I pressed the call receiver button, "Hello, tell us where you're calling from today."

"Hi, yes, my name is Tineke, calling from Oss in Brabant. We all know Eva, but how about you? Jill Stone — we've been listening to you for years at Radio 1, with your charming American accent speaking Dutch. Do you miss America? I'm not just talking about the corn dogs. I know about those, because I was an exchange student way back when, and they served those in the high school cafeteria."

"Thank you Tineke. I completely forgot about corn dogs until you just mentioned them! They were so good! You know, Dutch people used to ask me during my first couple of years living in the Netherlands, "Do you feel more Dutch, or more American?" I'd usually break the answer up into percentages to help explain and make sense of (mostly for myself) which nationality I identified with most, although it does fluctuate with the time of year, like on July 4th or if I'd just returned from spending three weeks in America. I feel sixty percent American, forty percent Dutch, with that additional percentage on the US side because that's where my roots are." I paused and sat up straight. "Oh my gosh...what a long answer to a simple question! And I'm the interviewer here. I apologize. I'm getting off track." My eye started twitching again, and a chill ran down my spine from the air conditioning.

"That's all right. I understand. When you end up living somewhere other than the country you were born in, things get complicated." Eva chimed in, and I felt comforted by her reassurance.

The rest of our segment was easy and straightforward. I didn't veer too far off course from getting her response to Trump's campaign announcement. One thing was crystal clear during the interview: Eva felt another four years of Trump could be detrimental. Marlies filled the remaining five minutes with some back and forth conversation, and I hit "stop recording" right on the twenty-minute mark. This should be an easy piece to edit. Eva excused herself, saying she had another appearance before she needed to go to her own studio, also in Hilversum, to prepare for her live show. We stood up and thanked her.

"When will this segment air?" Eva made her way through the door that I held open for her.

"Tomorrow morning, 9 a.m. I'll be sure to send you the link."

"Great, thank you. I really enjoyed this. Also the part where you said about breaking up your nationality into percentages. That really resonated with me."

"Thank you, that means a lot. I do miss America. We're actually moving there in two weeks, after twenty years!"

"Oh my gosh. You must be freaking out! Maybe we can grab a corn dog there together someday, ha-ha." She gave me one last smile, and walked out of the room.

I sat back down for a moment and sent Paul a quick message, Ahhhh! Eva Jinek was just in the studio. You know how starstruck I am? I'm going to miss this job :-(

"Well, that went well, didn't it?" Marlies gave me a high five. "Jill, I actually have a bunch of back-to-back meetings outside the office this afternoon. Do you think you can finish editing this last episode? We have a pretty clean cut, so it shouldn't take long. I left all the equipment on."

"Sure, no problem. I'll send you the link too when it's done. Hey! Don't forget my goodbye party tomorrow. Are you and Stijn coming?"

"Wouldn't miss it for the world! Your parties are legendary. As are your Gin and tonics! I'll be sad though. What am I going to do without you Jill?"

"You're so sweet. You'll just have to fly over the Atlantic and come visit me! We'll have to enjoy a good glass of wine in Pennsylvania, or cider. Cider's a big thing there now; you'd love it."

"Cider...meh! I'll stick to wine."

"Oh, and because of the goodbye party, I'm going to try to work from home tomorrow morning and take the afternoon off, so I can prepare."

"OK, good to know. I'll see you then at your place. Starts at eight, right?"

"Yes, eight. And don't forget — the dress code is white summer chic."

"You Americans always like to have a dress code or theme don't you?"

"You know it! OK, catch you later. *Doeg*."

Pro for America: Corn dogs.
Con for America: Trump could possibly win a second term as Commander in Chief.

Pro for The Netherlands: tap water tastes delicious, and is always accessible.

Con for The Netherlands: Very few summer sounds and fireflies.

Chapter 6

As much as I loved Marlies' company, it was nice to have the studio all to myself and decompress. I was able to dive in with full concentration. My alarm rang and I looked up at the clock, 4 p.m. I remembered to set my phone alarm, since Catharine was going to call to talk to me about my *Dutch and Such* podcast episode on the TBS clinic that I sent her. Catharine is the only person from NPR I really kept in touch with. She was promoted to senior producer of *All Things Considered* a few years ago, at NPR's headquarters in Washington. *All Things Considered* has bred world famous hosts, like Guy Raz, and the show is less rigid than *The Morning Edition*. Catharine was the best boss a woman could wish for — highly intelligent, warm, and motivational. She remembered things like my birthday, and never said "no" to additional media training budget requests. I saw the area code number 202 flash up on my phone's screen.

"Hi Catharine! I was just thinking about all of you over there in Washington, probably enjoying your second cup of coffee at the office now."

"Hi Jill. Yes, that's right, halfway through my second cup now. How have you been?"

"Good, thanks. Busy."

"Thanks so much for sharing that podcast episode with me!" She was cutting straight to the chase, no beating around the bush for Catharine.

"Glad you enjoyed it. Yeah, as much as I love broadcast journalism, narrative journalism has always had my heart. I love sharing other peoples' stories, not so much the hardcore news, which nine out of ten times is so negative."

"I'm with you, Jill. That's exactly why I love working for *All Things Considered*! But I've always had full faith in you, and in your news and narrative journalism skills. I was blown away by your podcast — so concise, so informative, respectful towards the interviewee, yet curious enough to draw out the right answers for listeners. That's actually why I wanted to speak with you." I shifted in my seat and felt the deep wrinkle lines doing their work on my forehead. "Jill, there's a position that just opened up at NPR, as their European Correspondent. I think you would be perfect for it. Can I entice you to consider?"

My jaw dropped, my heart rate shot up and I felt like it might explode. This was a HUGE opportunity — to cover all of Western Europe for NPR! To cover news, commentary, interviews — informing millions of American listeners during their commutes. I swallowed the lump of sheer surprise in my throat.

"Catharine, wow! I must say, I totally didn't see this coming. I'm speechless. What an honor to even be considered for this position!"

"I know, but it's not public information yet. In fact, I only found out yesterday at a staff meeting, but I immediately thought of you for this — your solid voice, the work you've done over the years for Radio 1, and when I listened to your podcast it all clicked! And you know, with NPR, once you're in and doing a decent job, you're golden. You'd be the perfect European correspondent, this would be a great step in your career." Bless her, Catharine was always looking to advance the careers of NPR's women.

"What would a typical day look like on the foreign desk?"

"Well, you'd have to write a daily memo, after scoping out the European news. Your assistant can write a raw rundown of links to news items from around Europe. You can use that in your own research and daily conversations with people, and your daily memo would then go to everyone in the DC network. It'd be a mix of fact and opinion, your analysis, and your take on the EU that day. Some may be longer than others, depending on what's happening. We want to know if it's worth paying attention to the riots in France, or the elections in Germany. Besides the daily memo we'll want news spots, once a day, minute-long news items with any breaking news, and feature stories." I scribbled down notes, trying to keep up with all the information she spurted out at me. "Why don't you take some time to think about it? Do you think you can let me know by the 30th? That way I can keep the job announcement from being published, if we already have a match I can vouch for. The position will be well sought after. There are only seventeen foreign correspondents for NPR. You'll get your own assistant in the Netherlands, and you'll have a whole editorial team here at headquarters."

"Wow, yes! Thank you. Letting you know by the 30th should work. I just want to discuss it with Paul. When would the position start?" I didn't want to ruin my chances, by telling her that everything was already lined up for us to move to America in two weeks.

"In September. Jill, I totally get it. It's not a decision that should be taken lightly. But Jill, do keep in mind that this would be an opportunity of a lifetime and a total career jump. Not to mention that the salary is probably a lot better than what you're making now. I'll send you more details via email, OK?"

"OK, thank you Catharine."

"Thanks Jill. Take care, and we'll be in touch."

"Bye Catharine." I hit the red phone button to hang up, and once I was sure the line was cut off I screamed, jumping up and down. But then I plopped down in my desk chair and stared at the screen in front of me, rubbing the wrinkles on my forehead. My ecstasy was blocked by some invisible force. I felt like two wizards were at war in my head, pointing their wands against each other. How would Paul take the news? He had a job lined up. We had our land in Gettysburg, and the builders were lined up! Our house was on the market. Lucy had her scholarship. My parents were expecting us to move, they'd be devastated. Paul had already put down the deposit on our rental, for until we started building work. This was insane. The timing was totally off! Why couldn't this opportunity have been here ten years ago? Why now?! Lucy was going to freak out. She was so looking forward to going to an American college, where she could make new friends and play on their hockey team. But I couldn't help but wonder how she would be, in the thick of it. Sure, she's been to the US in summertime, but to actually live there? Same goes for Paul. He's only lived in Washington with me for one year. Wouldn't he feel lonely? Won't he miss his family and his friends? Catharine's curveball made me doubt our entire plan. I didn't know whether I was even ready to be back in my hometown. I was right back at square one. So many questions flashed through my head: *Focus Jill, focus. First finish this piece, submit, then go home and let it simmer.*

****

As I drove across route N201, the longest arterial road in the Netherlands, which runs East to West towards Loenen, I looked out to the left — across the Wijde Blik lake, which connects to the Vecht. I saw a couple of windsurfers, and people picnicking along the strip of recreational beach by the water. To the right, people rowed boats down the canal. Traffic was light and I couldn't wait to get home, to enjoy a glass of wine in the backyard. First I'd have to get things ready for the quesadillas, as promised. I wanted everything to be ready by the time Paul and Lucy were home, so we could have a good discussion about this NPR job opportunity.

I made a left at the BP gas station and drove along the one-mile long dike that wound along the Vecht towards our house. Lucy's bike was gone, which meant she was at field hockey practice. I opened the door and threw my keys on the counter, where I found a note: *Abby's been out for a poo and pee at 4:00! Liefs, Lucy.* She's so responsible. Sometimes I worry that, because she is an only child, we've made her too responsible, too grown up, too uptight. It would be good for her to loosen up a bit. Maybe America would be a good influence on her.

I turned on the sound system with built-in speakers — one of the features I loved about this house — and browsed my "recently played artists" in Spotify: Khruangbin, a band from Houston, Texas whose name I could never pronounce, but whose music was perfect for cocktail hour — a mix of classic soul and psychedelia that felt like a warm bath. I poured myself a big glass of Verdejo wine, and added an ice cube. The Dutch aren't big on ice. When my dad came over to visit, that was one of the first things he commented on, "Why can't these damn Dutch figure out how to add ice machines to their fridges?" to which I responded, "Because it normally doesn't get that hot over here, dad. They think we Americans put too much ice in our drinks." I missed him.

It was 6 p.m. I took some chicken out of the freezer so it could defrost for our quesadillas. I lined up other ingredients on the counter, so it would be easier for Paul to throw them together once he got home — jalapenos, tomatoes, lime, cilantro, tortillas, sour cream. Abby came and laid in the corner of the kitchen, watching me as I swayed my hips to the music. I took a big sip of Verdejo and felt the day's events slide off my shoulders. Looking out the front window towards the Vecht, the ripples shimmering in the evening sun, I was reminded how good life was in Loenen, the life Paul and I had built for ourselves.

Just then, I saw Paul roll onto our driveway with his bike, all sweaty. Abby got up to greet him as he walked into the kitchen.

"Hey! Oh nice, thanks for getting everything ready." Paul gave me a quick kiss on the lips, then worked his way over to the fridge and grabbed a can of Heineken.

"Welcome home." I tried so hard not to blurt out the NPR job offer right then and there. "How was your day?"

"Good. Busy. We had the marketing team come in and make another promotional video."

"Glad to hear." And I was. Ever since Paul had left his government consulting gigs to work at this crop intelligence start-up, he'd been much happier. More tired, but happier. Especially now that he'd carved out a role for himself in America. Just then, Lucy walked into the kitchen.

"Hi papa, hi mama." She walked straight to the fridge and started perusing the shelves.

"Excuse me, no. We're going to have dinner in twenty minutes! No snacking now."

"Oh, but I'm so hungry." She stomped her foot lightly and pushed the fridge door shut.

"You'll just have to wait. How was practice?"

"Good. We have a tournament Saturday, against Laren. Can I spend the night at Julie's house Friday and ride with her to the game?"

"Sure. You know, that's actually handy because we have our goodbye party, so I was going to try to arrange for a sleepover for you anyway, as it'll be a bunch of forty-some-year-olds here partying, with loud music."

"Yeah, I definitely don't want to be around for that." Lucy rolled her eyes.

"Why don't you two set the table for me? Let's eat outside on the patio, it's so nice out." I opened the cutlery drawer, creating easy access for Paul and Lucy, while I grabbed a cutting board to chop the cilantro.

Our house faces east, so the sun rises at the front, which is also where our access to the Vecht river is, and the sun sets behind our house, giving us long western sun for dinners on our back patio. The patio is just off the kitchen — perfect for outdoor meals and barbeques. Paul and I both grew up in homes that faced east in the morning and had the setting sun behind the house. It was one of the things on our wish list, when searching for homes outside of Amsterdam. We searched for a good two years, within a ten mile radius around Amsterdam, before falling in love with this house beside the Vecht.

To my surprise, the lilac tree was in bloom. It had taken quite a beating from rogue basketballs, since the hoop was set up next to it. My parents always had a lilac tree in their backyard when I was growing up, so for me, it was like having a piece of home in Loenen. Its sweet smell carried over to the patio, where we sat down to dinner.

"*Eet smakelijk*—Bon appetit." I raised my glass to Lucy and Paul.

"*Eet smakelijk.*" They replied back in unison.

"Well...I have some news." *How am I going to start this conversation? How I start it could make it or break it.* I put my fork and knife down beside my plate. Paul and Lucy looked at me with half interest — I always have some sort of news, usually involving a new travel destination or an idea for a themed birthday party.

"Well, to tell you the truth, I was originally just planning on discussing our summer holiday plans with you tonight — that we could possibly fit in a week at the beach, before papa's new job starts. But, I got an unexpected phone call this afternoon." Now I had their full attention.

"Is one of your parents sick?!" Paul's tone became one of concern, his eyebrows raised.

"No, thank God." I took a deep breath and just blurted it out, "NPR headquarters called me and offered me a job as their European Correspondent! Not only would this be a substantial pay raise; it's a great career step." I held my breath waiting for their response.

"Wow honey, that's great. Congratulations. When do you

start? I guess that means you'll be commuting down to DC? My commute will only be twenty minutes to Aspers, so at least one of us will be close to home. DC is only just over an hour away."

"Actually, it doesn't start until September, but it's not there. It's here. I'd be working remotely, out of the Netherlands, covering Europe. Lucy, you could still start college in the US. I can come over during the breaks to visit, or you could fly back here. I'm sure we can work something out. You are the youngest in your class, which means you could also consider a gap year — get an internship, travel a bit. You don't necessarily have to start college this fall. You could defer your scholarship. Gettysburg College isn't going anywhere. And Paul, you just said the other day how much you love working for this start-up, I'm sure Leaf Fruit would be fine with you working remotely for the first half-year, or year? They're not going anywhere either. And the build, we'd just put that on hold, and take this house off the market asap." I gave away that I had already given this some thought.

There was dead silence. Not even the all-too-noisy grey herons were making a sound.

"Jill, are you insane? Do you even realize what you're saying right now? I want to support you, you know that, but it's just that we have everything already lined up. Our goodbye party is tomorrow! It's been twenty years, and we always said...Leaf Fruit Company already gave me an email address and business cards. I've paid the first three months of rent for our rental property."

"What?! I thought you just paid the deposit?"

"Well, yeah, I was going to tell you tonight. It's not like that's a big deal, seeing as we're supposed to move in there in two weeks."

"I know, it sounds crazy. But I'm never going to have an opportunity like this again. It's NPR! There has to be some way we can make this work." I felt my face turning red, my stomach turning. "I mean, we do have the perfect house here on a river, in a beautiful village, with nice people, good healthcare, no guns, and now I have this amazing job offer with NPR *in* the Netherlands. Why pick up and leave this all behind?"

"I'm confused Jill — why wouldn't we?! This move to America is what we always planned. We always said after twenty years we'd give the US a try. I thought that's what you wanted?"

"Because Paul, this is the opportunity I've — correction, *we've* — been waiting for. Maybe you can work remotely for Leaf, at least at first, giving me at least a year to try this NPR job, or take some time off and pursue photography. I'll be making enough that we could live on one salary. You know, it's easier to live off of one salary here than in the US."

"No way. Period. Why are we even still talking about this?"

I let the silent pause take over, so I had more time to think of what I was going to say next. But I shouldn't have waited, because Paul butted in.

"Lucy, you're half American, half Dutch. I think it's important that we spend more time there, to be more in touch with the American half of you."

"Papa's right, mom! You guys finally had me convinced. I am actually looking forward to America. I'm fine with making new friends. I'll be fine. I could do with a change of scenery. Plus, I have this hockey scholarship! I *want* to go to college in America!"

Lucy stood up and took her plate to the sink.

"Lucy — it's not up to you. Of course, we have your best interests in mind, but ultimately this is our decision. We're the parents. We're the ones paying the bills." I took a sip of water to soothe my dry throat from all the talking.

"I'm not staying!" Lucy stormed into the house and headed towards her room upstairs.

"Lucy, get back here! Your mother is not finished talking." Paul tried to be helpful.

He looked at me, "Wouldn't it have made more sense to discuss this just between the two of us first?"

"I know, I'm sorry. I wasn't expecting to get a job offer and was so excited — this is a dream opportunity for me."

"But like Lucy said, we are ready for America. Not everything can fit in the perfect little plan, Jill. You have to be flexible. Not everything can be like perfect little dominos, all lined up."

"Yeah, but when we made this plan, America wasn't what it is now. There's a narcissist president and metal detectors in schools."

"I know, I'm worried about that too. But there are plenty of nice, level-headed, people in America. Not everyone carries a gun."

By now, my wine glass was empty. I could already feel a slight buzz. As tempting as it was to grab another glass, I stuck to my water.

"How long is the contract for?" Paul was used to Dutch contracts that typically start with a one-year trial, after which the contract could become permanent.

"It's indefinite. Timing wise, I could do this job through Lucy's college years. There's nothing wrong with Dutch universities. You went to one and turned out great. American colleges charge a shit load of tuition, so they can fund their state of the art gyms with climbing walls. I'd rather have a great class and professor, than a climbing wall or 5-star cafeteria food. Maybe we should go inside and continue this conversation." I was afraid our neighbors would hear us.

"There's no conversation to continue, Jill. Bad time to bring this all up. You should have discussed it with me first, before bringing Lucy into it." Paul slammed down his fork onto his plate, crushed his beer can and shoved his chair under the table. "I need some air."

"Where are you going?!" I couldn't believe how far south this conversation had gone, so quickly.

"I don't know. I'm just going to take the boat out for a while. I need to clear my head." Paul walked out the side gate, crossing the road towards our dock by the Vecht.

I was left alone at the table, Abby looked up at me, begging for scraps. "Shoo, Abby!" The Khruangbin album came to an end. All I could hear was a lawn mower in the distance. I walked to the fridge and poured another glass of Verdejo. At this point feeling numb was the only option, as I sat back down and stared towards the setting sun. Direction west.

Chapter 7

Loading the dishwasher — a mundane task I despised. The sun's late afternoon rays poured into the kitchen, showing all the dust particles floating through the air. It was still bright outside — typical for June, when usually the sun doesn't set until 11 p.m. The Netherlands is the same latitude as Quebec, which means long days in the summer and long nights in the winter.

I hadn't seen Lucy since she had stormed upstairs a half hour ago, so I decided it was time to pay her a visit. Unfortunately, like me, she stayed stuck in an argument for quite some time. It was a delicate game to reset her mood. I grabbed the pile of laundry lying on the steps. There was always a pile of something that needed to go upstairs. Her door was closed. I knocked softly.

"Hey Lucy. Can I come in?" No answer. I slowly opened the door. Lucy was sitting up on her bed with her wireless headphones on, my old MacBook on her lap. I sat down next to her and carefully laid my hand on her leg. Her eyes were firmly fixated on the screen, pretending I wasn't there.

"What are you watching sweetie?" She yanked off her headphones and closed the laptop.

"*Modern Family*."

We've been binge watching *Modern Family* for the past year. It's such an easy feel-good show and it covers so much — race, homophobia, migration, sex education — basically, all the difficult conversations are handled through the lives of the characters, making my role as a parent covering these topics easier. I let her watch it when she wants. I figure the show is good for Lucy's English — she watches without Dutch subtitles. If I could learn a language by watching a television show, so could she. Just me speaking English to her and the occasional visit to the US wasn't enough, I felt. Those three-week visits were like a quick fix of Botox. Not that I ever had Botox, but I can imagine — you still had wrinkles in spite of it, like you're still homesick—*dat blijft*.

"Look. I know I kinda sprung all that on you out of the blue. But the truth is, this job offer was also presented to me out of the blue. I just want us to give it some thought, it's a very rare opportunity for me — a once in a lifetime kind of thing, career-wise. But I also know our move, your scholarship, is not something to be taken lightly. I know everything now points to America. I don't want to disappoint my parents, just as much as you don't want to disappoint Oma and Opa Amerika by not moving there." I put my arm around her.

"But mom, you don't get it! Did you ever consider that maybe I want a change of scenery? And you know how much I love field hockey — this is the opportunity of a lifetime for *me*, to play for Gettysburg College." Lucy looked down and fumbled with her bedspread.

"I get it, but I've experienced both US and Dutch

universities. Both offer great programs, depending on where you go. We can always work something out. We could defer your admission, you could do a gap year, or you could still go, and papa and I would come visit you during your breaks. I mean, after all, you're almost officially an adult." Tears started to fill in Lucy's eyes. I ran my hand through her thick hair, pulling it back into a ponytail with my fingers, like I did when she was ten.

"Look, let's take the weekend to think about it. Maybe it would help to make a pros and cons list. Pros for America — you'd be closer to Oma and Opa Amerika, you have the field hockey scholarship, the weather is slightly better... Pros for the Netherlands — you can ride your bike everywhere, there's ice skating in the winter, you can take the boat out with friends in the summer.

"But I don't like riding my bike everywhere." Lucy interrupted.

"Just do me a favor, make a list this weekend and we can discuss it on Sunday night. How about that?" I nuzzled my nose against the side of her face and kissed her cheek.

"OK. I guess I can do that. I just want us to all be together, that's all." Lucy leaned her head against my shoulder. Guilt stabbed me in the heart. When we first moved to the Netherlands, I worked odd jobs while studying for my master's. I then took a couple of years off while we went through the IVF process and had Lucy. I was so relieved to finally have a baby, I wanted to be able to dedicate all my time and attention to her. It wasn't until Lucy went to school, at age four, that I took on the job at Radio 1 and, it's true, it is a busy job. I'm on the road a lot and spend long hours at the studio. But I love my job at Radio 1! It fulfilled me, especially since I knew having more kids wasn't in the picture.

This job was everything to me outside of Lucy and Paul. But Lucy was right. Family was more important than a job.

"I know Lucy. I think we all have to get used to the next stage. You, graduating high school and going off to college. Papa and I with new jobs. The move. Everything's shifting. I know I've been on the road a lot, it's just that I love my job. I hope you can find a job you love someday too. I consider myself lucky. It took me years to get where I am today."

"Do you think if you would have had more kids you would be home more? All the moms I know with more kids seem to be home more." Lucy broached this question carefully, choosing not to look me directly in the eyes, perhaps afraid of hurting me. I was taken aback. I told myself that I'd made peace with the fact that no more kids were coming, but Lucy's question brought back old fears that I hadn't done enough to have more kids. Should I have pushed myself and Paul harder to keep trying? Maybe one more embryo transfer, and that would have been the one? Ever since that first miscarriage, after Lucy, I'd had tinnitus in my right ear — a constant whooshing hum. Sometimes it's louder than others, like when I lay in bed at night. And sometimes that constant whooshing sounds like 'what if, what if, what if?'.

"I don't know Lucy. All I know is that I thank my lucky stars I had you. You and your dad are everything to me. Being the NPR European correspondent means I would have to show up at the studio most days, and I'd still have to be on the road a lot, that's true. But the flip side to it is, what better timing, because you're essentially going off into the real world? You're going to college. For the first time, you'll be living on your own. *I'll* be the one who feels like I never get to see *you*." I squeezed her tight. "Come, let's walk to Hans en Frietje and get an ice cream for dessert."

"Really?! Yes!" Lucy shot up. "Let's ask papa to come too."

"Oh, he went off on the boat to clear his head. I'll leave him a note and tell him to meet us there when he gets back."

We walked together to the local snack bar — it's a small place on the corner of our main street that offers sweets, along with the usual Dutch fare like *kaastengels, bitterballen* and *patatje oorlog*. Lucy showed me a bunch of TikTok clips on her phone, and updated me on who's dating who in her class. Lucy had a boyfriend, Faas, up until two months ago. He was nice, but it was nothing serious. She broke up with him because of her upcoming move to America. She didn't want to be tied down. When we returned home, Paul still wasn't back. I was slightly worried. It wasn't like him to be gone so long. I called his cell phone, only to discover he'd left it behind — I saw it ringing in the kitchen. It was 10 p.m. and still light out, but it was time for Lucy to go to bed.

"Can't I stay up and wait for papa?"

"No sweetie, it's exam week. I'm sure he'll be back soon. I'll ask him to give you a kiss when he gets back."

"OK, goodnight mama. Thanks for the ice cream." Lucy kissed me and I caught a whiff of my Ariel detergent on her shirt as she headed up the stairs. Just before going up she said, "I was just really looking forward to Gettysburg College — the whole campus life, dorms, making some new friends. I get where you're coming from though, mama. You always wanted to work for NPR. You listen to it every day and talk about it all the time. I wish we could have both, you know?"

"I know sweetie. It's hard. I feel so lucky to have so many more opportunities and choices, with two countries. But it seems like there's always an ocean to cross with every decision

I make." I blew her a kiss. "Don't forget to brush your teeth!"

Watching Lucy go upstairs reminded me how the ocean between had always made things more difficult. Like the time I had to say goodbye to my 98-year-old grandmother on her deathbed over the phone, because Lucy was just a few days old, and I was in no state to fly across the ocean to say goodbye in person. To this day I often think, *Was there no way I could have flown over with Lucy? If only my grandmother could have lived one more week, maybe I could have made it on time to say goodbye, and hug her one last time.*

* * * * *

I made myself a cup of chamomile tea, plopped down on the couch, and turned on the news. Headlines: the Russians deny they had anything to do with the MH17 flight crash; former French president, Sarkozy, to appear in court for corruption accusations; protests in Hong Kong; and, for the first time in a hundred years, a wolf is born in the Netherlands. I turned off the television and started making a grocery list on my phone for tomorrow's goodbye party:

*sausages
*burgers
*buns
*olives
*gin
*tonic
*ketchup
*mayo
*chips
*watermelon
*beer

*eye make-up remover pads (might as well, if I'm at the store anyway)

I noticed I had a missed call. Must have been when Lucy and I went for ice cream. I checked the voicemail and there was a message from our realtor, asking me to call her back tomorrow during office hours. Just as I finished listening, Paul came into the house. He looked tired and sweaty.

"Hey." Paul joined me, plopping down on the couch. He smelled strange — cigarette smoke mixed with something else. It was that something else I couldn't quite put my finger on.

"Hey. You were out there for a long time. Why do you smell like cigarettes?" Paul didn't smoke. He hadn't since his freshman year of college, when he and his housemates made a bet that whoever lit up their next cigarette had to dish out 500 euros. He hadn't touched them since.

"Oh yeah — I saw Ruud out on the Vecht with his boat. We anchored our boats next to each other for a while. He gave me a beer, and I must have been standing in his fumes."

"Oh? How's Ruud doing? Did you remind him about the party tomorrow night?" Ruud is the father of Lucy's best friend, Julie. We've known him since our first month in Loenen. We immediately clicked with him and his wife Roos, and would go out on "couple dates" before they got divorced last year. Ruud had had an affair with his golf trainer — it was short lived, but was just enough to push their marriage over the edge. Ruud and Roos were always very different to begin with, one of those couples which make you wonder why they're together in the first place. I worried sometimes that Ruud wasn't the best influence on Paul. Paul definitely drank more when he was around Ruud. I felt like Paul felt sorry for him somehow, and therefore never said "no" to meeting up.

"Yeah, he's looking forward to it. He also mentioned Lucy spending the night at Roos', since he's coming to the party and she's not. You know how they don't like to show up to parties together." Paul started yawning. "I'm going to take a quick shower and then go to bed. I have to get up early tomorrow. We have a big client meeting tomorrow."

"OK, I'll let Abby out one more time and lock up. By the way — we got a bid on our house! Asking price."

"You're kidding? That was quick."

"I know, now it all feels so real, the move."

"Let's sleep on it."

I started making my rounds through the house, turning off lights, shutting down my laptop, getting coffee set up for the next day, so all I had to do was press the "on" button. Paul dried off, put on a pair of clean boxer shorts, and crawled into bed next to me. He kept his reading lamp on, as he scrolled through the messages on his phone. I turned towards him and looked at his face in the blue light of his phone. His glasses were perched on his head.

"You OK?" I rolled more towards him, lying on my side.

"Yeah. Why?"

"Well, you haven't talked much since you got home really, except to say you were going to take a shower."

"Yeah, well you did kind of drop a bomb on us tonight. It's a lot to take in."

"I know, I'm sorry. I had a good talk with Lucy about it though. I told her it might be good for her to make a pros and cons list. Maybe we should do the same. Lists have always helped me make tough decisions."

"Have you really given my situation any thought? I mean,

come on, working at Leaf Fruit means I'd finally have a job I like — no more analyst or consultancy bullshit, but the real operational stuff. I'd have a real stake in their company."

"I know, I realize that."

"Do you? Do you really? Because sometimes I wonder. You're gone pretty much ninety percent of the time for your work, and when you are in town, instead of spending time with me, you're off swimming, or drinking coffee with the neighbors, or out playing tennis with one of your 'mom' friends."

"I thought you liked that I've managed to create a social life for myself. May I remind you that we're in *your* homeland, not mine?! It's not like Dutch circles are the easiest to break into. If you weren't part of some sorority or fraternity in college here it's next to impossible to make friends!" I could feel my blood pressure rising and my face turning red. "At least in America small talk and openness is normal. I'd rather have that any day over closed social circles!"

"Oh don't give me that shit. You know, technically speaking you are Dutch. You have a Dutch passport. Besides, what do you think America would look like for me? I wouldn't know anyone there except for *your* family and *your* friends. And you know what, I'll be just fine."

"Oh yeah, I forgot, you're one of them — those Dutch people who can't seem to break away from their comfort zones. *Lekker saai*—boring!" By now, I was sitting up in bed and hunched on my knees.

"You know… just forget it. I'm done talking." Paul turned off his reading light and phone and laid it on his nightstand. I turned away from him and pulled the comforter up over my head. I'd rather go to bed angry than continue yelling and have things escalate even more. Hopefully, we could wake up and forget about it. Margreet always said it's best to talk things over in the morning, over a good cup of coffee. I hope she's right.

Chapter 8

I woke up to the sound of fake birds chirping, and a soft dim light mimicking the rising sun. I'd blocked the real sun with my blinds. My Philips Wake-up lamp is a gentler way to wake up than the typical loud *reh-reh-reh* sound of other alarm clocks. Paul snored softly beside me. Usually I let him sleep a couple minutes extra, while I fed Abby breakfast and turned on the coffee machine.

I still felt a bit broken from last night — an argument hangover. Not sure which is worse, hangovers from drinking or from arguments. I hoped the coffee would fix things, and we could move on with our day. My mood lightened when I looked over at the calendar hanging on the fridge, reminding me of today's goodbye party! I live for summer, and this party was the ultimate way to celebrate the warm weather while saying goodbye to our friends. I made a carefully curated guest list, combining various circles on purpose, instead of the same-old-same-old circles. Unlike the Dutch, who prefer to sit and socialize with the same people they've known their whole lives, I like to mix up crowds like a salad and see what comes of it.

Paul joined me in the kitchen, as I poured our coffees with frothed milk.

"Good morning." I handed him coffee in his favorite mug.

"Good morning." He took it, and we both walked towards the porch. We both sat down in silence and watched the ripples on the water and the sun slowly rising ahead of us. There wasn't a cloud in the sky, and the sound of wood pigeons—*roekoeën* carried on a soft breeze towards us. I perched my feet on a little wooden stool in front of me and decided to break the awkward silence.

"Are we good?" I squinted my eyes and hunched up my shoulders.

"Yeah, sure Jill. I'm just waking up."

"OK, sorry." We sat in silence for a couple more minutes. I decided to just let it go. No need to rehash last night. Best to focus on today.

"I'm taking off work this afternoon. I have an appointment with the dentist at 1 p.m., and plan on doing grocery shopping for the party afterwards. Is there anything you need from the store?"

"Um…, I could use some more hair gel."

"By the way, how long has it been since you were at the dentist?"

"Well, you'll be pleased to know I was actually there just two months ago, in April." Paul was now waking up and softening a bit.

"Ah, good you're taking care of those pearly whites! The older we get, the more maintenance needed, so I'm told. Do you think you can be home by 5 p.m. to help with the barbeque?"

"Yeah, that should work. I have my last call at four, then I'll head home."

"Great."

Lucy came out onto the porch yawning, dressed for the day but her hair tied up in a towel.

"Good morning papa and mama." She gave us each a peck on the cheek and remained standing.

"Good morning sweetie. Want to grab some cereal and come out here and eat it with us? It's your last official day of high school! Can you believe it?"

"No, I can't. It feels weird. Yeah, I'd like to eat my breakfast here with you. I'll be right back. Anyone need a coffee refill?" Paul held out his mug for Lucy. She was so considerate to ask. Maybe she was being extra sweet, because I'd treated her to ice cream last night. Lucy returned with her bowl of chocolate Cruesli and a full mug of coffee for Paul. I made space between us for her to sit down.

"So you're going to pop by the house between school and hockey, and grab an overnight bag for Julie's?"

"Yep."

7:30 a.m. — time to get in gear. Since I'm working from home today, as soon as I can get everyone out of the house, I can fit in one quick swim before my interview airs, and get some work done. I went through the morning motions that had become second nature — I could do them blindfolded. Pack Lucy's lunch, two slices of brown bread with cheese, just a light spread of margarine, a couple carrots and cherry tomatoes, one slice of white bread with something sweet — chocolate sprinkles—*hagelslag* today, with butter. I choked back a few tears as I closed her lunchbox for the last time.

Paul and Lucy were all set to go, backpacks on, their bikes ready to take off in opposite directions by 8 a.m. I waved goodbye, blew air kisses, and returned to my bedroom where I spent ten grueling minutes putting on my wetsuit. Floating device? Check. Goggles? Check. Flip-flops? Check. Towel? Check. I waddled across the front yard, crossed the small street, and entered the black iron gate to our *overtu-in*—over-garden, what the Dutch call gardens that back directly onto the river. I threw my towel down by the trunk of our cherry tree, walked out onto the dock, and let the morning sun warm up my black suit. I secured my goggles, and lowered myself into the cold water. I scanned the backs of the houses on the other side of the river facing me, just fifty feet away. We have a private back yard, but people who live on the other side of the Vecht have their backyards *on* the Vecht, so we can often see pretty much everything they're doing. There's one nosy neighbor in particular, Geert, who loves to sit with his arms crossed and feet up, staring in our direction. We call him the *burgermeester*—mayor, keeping watch over the neighborhood. At times this is helpful, like when the cover blew off our boat in a storm, or when my parents came to visit and he offered to take our picture from across the water. It's like having an additional lifeguard on the water.

"*Goedemorgen!*" Geert called out from his deck.

I couldn't ignore him now. I took my goggles off for a second and raised my hand to wave.

"*Goedemorgen* Geert."

"Getting ready to leave? I saw people looking at your house yesterday, has it sold yet?"

"Not yet." I spit out some river water I had accidentally gulped.

"Well, if you can get that much for your house, I might just put mine on the market and downsize." Geert crossed his arms over his beer belly. "Well, you'll be missed. It was always fun watching Lucy swim out there on your dock with her friends."

"Time flies, that's for sure. We really enjoyed living here, in Loenen. If you're ever in the States you should drop by." As soon as the words left my mouth I wished I could take them back, as Geert is the type of person to take me up on the offer.

"Well I just might. I think I have your email address somewhere." Geert turned to walk towards his computer in the house.

"I actually have to get back to the house. Take care Geert."

"Oh sure. OK, take care Jill."

Once back at the house, I showered, threw on some clean clothes, and got out my laptop. I listened to my last Radio 1 segment, including my recording from yesterday's interview with Eva Jinek. Brief, straightforward, yet light-hearted at the same time. I sent the interview link to Jinek's production team, as promised, then started going through my inbox. There was an email from the realtor, with the official offer on our house. There was also an email from Catharine, with more details on the NPR position. The job description did look appealing — regular daytime hours, and working independently, as well as with an editorial team back in Washington. I could hire my own assistant, and my jaw dropped when I saw the salary: 100.000 dollars! Catharine wasn't kidding when she said it's a step up from what I'm making now. I would no longer have to hold out on getting a new pair of Nike Air Max, or a new winter jacket for Lucy. We usually got hand-me-downs from Paul's sisters' kids, so it wasn't often that I treated us to new clothes.

It always surprised me how quickly the hours passed. I made myself a quick grilled cheese sandwich, let Abby out around the block, then grabbed my car keys and shopping bags as I headed out the door. Just then, the realtor called my phone and I clicked it away. Paul and I hadn't really got to discuss it yet.

Seated in the waiting room of the dentist, where it smelled like mouthwash, I flipped through a Dutch magazine, browsing the latest summer fashion. The buzzing sound of dental hygiene equipment hummed through the door. The woman who'd had a dental practice here for years recently retired, and supposedly a new woman had taken over the practice. The door opened, and an older man scurried out, waving goodbye over his shoulder.

"Jill Stone?" A tall woman with a light blue uniform and white sneakers stood at the door. Her clear, fair skin looked radiant and smooth. Her golden blond hair was pulled up in a bun. She wasn't wearing any make-up, from what I could tell, but had naturally long eyelashes and a wide smile with perfectly straight white teeth, which made sense seeing as she's in the business. She had extraordinary pale blue eyes.

"Yes, that's me." As I walked towards her, I reached out to shake her hand.

"Hi, I'm Sofie. *Kom verder*—Come on in." Sofie motioned towards the coat hanger, so I could hang my purse. I noticed she was not wearing a ring, something I automatically look for on people, for some reason.

"Nice to meet you Sofie. Welcome to Loenen! I hear you're fairly new?"

"Thank you. So far, so good — such a nice change from city center Amsterdam."

"Oh, where did you live in Amsterdam?" About ninety

percent of Loenen's population is composed of people who have moved away from Amsterdam after having a couple of kids, seeking more green space. Loenen is part of what's been deemed Amsterdam's Lake District, just a stone's throw away, and much more space.

"In the Plantage neighborhood, which was loads of fun, but tourists are taking over the entire city it seems. It's just not the same. I actually know Annelies, who used to run this place from dental school. When she said she was retiring and looking for someone to take over I jumped at the opportunity!"

"Oh my gosh! We lived close to the Plantage neighborhood, in the Nieuwe Kerkstraat, for fifteen years. Which street did you live on?"

"Plantage Kerklaan!"

"Wow, that's so close. And to think in all those years we never ran into each other doing groceries on the Jodenbreestraat, or in Oosterpark, crazy. I totally get what you're saying about tourists. The street changed entirely! We used to have block parties, eating *pannenkoeken* while watching soccer on a big screen in the street. Now it's all Airbnb and rolling suitcases."

"It's such a shame. How long have you been in Loenen?" She asked while switching the chair to a lying down position.

"Five years now, and I love it. Here, you notice the seasons so much more than in Amsterdam. I'm from a small town in the US, so it feels like I have a slither of it here, with more space and a driveway. I live in a brick house, *Vechtzicht*. And you know, it's funny, have you also noticed how people love to size each other up by talking about real estate, when we tell people where we live? - 'Oh, we looked at that house too', meaning they didn't like the house we bought for some reason, but stop short of saying why."

"Yes. The first question people ask me is which house I bought." She laughed, while putting on her rubber gloves.

"Ah ha, see! And probably the next thing - what do you do for a living?"

"Yes, although they find out soon enough, when they come here for a check-up. Hey, that's so cool that you're from the US. I've only ever been to Florida and New York before - loved both. What brought you here?" Discreetly, I tried swallowing a big gulp of saliva, which grossed me out, but I wanted to keep talking while she cleaned my teeth.

"Long story short: a Dutch husband, and a master's program."

"Ah ha."

"And one year turns into three, which turns into twenty! One child, a dog, and two houses more, and here we are still — to my parents' great dismay. But that's all changing. We're actually moving to the US in two weeks. That's why I wanted to get my teeth cleaned one more time, before having to look for a new dentist over there."

"Oh my gosh! That will be quite the big move then. Nice for your parents." I could taste her rubber gloves as she moved the small mirror around with one hand, and picked away tartar with the other.

"It is a big deal. I'm trying to come to terms with everything. There's so much involved in a move. Anyways, enough about me. Glad Loenen has a new resident! By the way, I hope you don't mind me asking, but you smell so good — what perfume are you wearing? I've been obsessed with perfumes since I was a teenager, and I don't recognize your scent. It's very unique — a bit of sandalwood, musk maybe?"

"Thanks. Yeah, you're not the first one to ask me. I bought it at a special perfume boutique in Amsterdam, called Scent." I didn't want to pry too much for the name, but at least I now knew where she bought it.

"I know it's short notice, but I'm throwing a party tonight, it's actually our goodbye party. You're welcome to come! It'd be a good way for you to meet some new people. It'll be like your welcome party."

"Oh, that's so American of you, so spontaneous. I'll try to stop by!"

"Great, it starts at eight. *Vechtzicht* by the windmill, can't miss it."

"Yes, I live just across the river, a couple houseboats down. Here, go ahead and rinse." She pressed the button to raise my chair to the seated position, and dispensed a cup of water to rinse while she took off my bib.

"Thanks Sofie! Hope to see you tonight. I'm off to do groceries for the party."

"Thanks for the invite. Nice to meet you. And Jill, one more thing, you may want to consider using those dental sticks instead of floss. They're better for your gums, and the older you get, the more maintenance you need." *Argh — easy for a sassy thirty-some-year-old to say. I already regretted inviting her to the party.*

* * * * *

Although the Dutch usually like to spend an entire afternoon going around to individual specialized stores, I opted for the local Jumbo supermarket, as it had everything in one spot. I parked out front, backing in so that my trunk faced the store, for easy loading. I love being able to drive to the grocery store here and load the trunk of my car, as opposed to doing groceries with the *bakfiets*, or walking three blocks with heavy grocery bags.

I grabbed a cart, took out my grocery list, and started my rounds through the shop. It was relatively quiet, which for a Friday afternoon I supposed was normal. The shopping carts are smaller than the ones in America. I hoped I could fit everything for the party in one cart. As I began to gather cases of beer, bottles of soda, chips, dip, it occurred to me: that was how I pictured living as an American in a small Dutch village. Hosting parties, throwing the doors open, inviting in anyone who wanted to come. I'd always pictured sitting outside with friends and neighbors. I held on to every café chair we'd ever owned, keeping them in the basement until they were needed for an event. Paul would hand them up the treacherous steps to me, one by one. I spotted Roos across the produce aisle and made my way over to her.

"Hi Roos! I hear Lucy is spending the night at your place tonight. Thanks in advance, although I wish you could make it to our goodbye party."

"I know, me too, but you know, it's just too hard to attend social events when Ruud is there too."

"I can only imagine. Loenen is such a small town."

"Well, that's just it. People are only ever interested in talking about real estate or divorce. This town thrives on gossip." Roos weighed her plum tomatoes.

"I'll bet this past year has been particularly hard for you."

"Yeah, and you know, everyone's already chosen their side. Some are on his, some are on mine. It's just too awkward and tiring, quite frankly, to be exposed to more than you have to. But we decided to both stick around in Loenen so we could be there for Julie."

When I first found out about the divorce, I asked Roos why. She said, "It was a combination of his fling with his golf trainer and his love for alcohol." But, when I asked Ruud, he said, "irreconcilable differences." There was probably truth to both sides. They did argue a lot, and their lifestyles were on opposite ends of the spectrum - Roos a health freak, and Ruud couldn't care less. I could only imagine how relieved Julie must have been that the yelling had stopped, despite how sad it must be to have her parents living in two separate houses. I guess he had to prove to himself that he still mattered to women, so he had a little fling. Of course, the whole town found out soon enough. One of the moms from Lucy and Julie's school, Anouk, saw Ruud leaving the shed next to the golf carts, the trainer following right behind him as he adjusted his pants, and suddenly the gossip was rampant. The affair was short lived, but it did solidify Roos and Ruud's differences, and their eventual separation and divorce. Paul and I were careful not to take sides in front of Lucy, but the truth was that I was on Roos' side. I would be devastated if that happened to me. Frankly, I'm afraid Ruud's behavior might rub off on Paul if they hang out too much. I don't blame Roos for wanting to avoid social gatherings where he'll be.

"Well, you'll be missed. But let's get together sometime soon and go for a goodbye walk. Maybe next week sometime?"

"I'd like that."

"OK, well, a walk it is. I'll text you next week with an exact time."

I pushed the cart to the meat section, to pick out beef for the burgers. Just then, my phone rang — it was Marlies, checking in. She didn't know yet about the NPR offer, and

I wanted to tell her before tonight's party when I probably wouldn't have much time, so I picked up and put in my ear buds to multitask.

"Hi Marlies! I'm at Jumbo, so I might sound distracted, but I can talk and shop at the same time."

"Ha-ha, you little multitasker. I listened to our last radio segment — well done! I must admit, I shed a tear."

"Thanks babe. Even though I missed you yesterday afternoon, it was good to have those hours to crunch and get it done."

"Are you ready for tonight? Stijn and I are looking forward to a good party. It's been a while." I continued working my way through Jumbo, loading items and striking through them on my list.

"Yes, just about. Just getting all the food now. Hopefully Paul will be home on time to help fire up the barbeque. Hey Marlies, you're never going to believe what happened yesterday at the office." I paused, giving her ample time to guess, which I knew she wouldn't.

"You saw a mouse?! I saw one scurry under our desk, and set up a trap yesterday morning."

"No! Ewwhh, gross. I hate mice. No, Catharine called me and asked if I would be interested in being their European correspondent, based here in the Netherlands!"

"AHHHHH! WAT?! DAT MEEN JE NIET. AHHH!— What? You're kidding!" I had to take out my earbuds. She was screaming so loud. "That is awesome news Jill! I'm so happy for you. I mean, ah-hem, obviously I would miss you like crazy at Radio 1 — but what an amazing opportunity! Please tell me you said 'yes'!"

By now I was almost at the register, but pulled off to the side so I could focus on our conversation.

"No, I haven't said yes, yet. It's complicated. I mean, it's not just me, there's Paul and Lucy. Plus, we're supposed to move to America in two weeks for goodness' sake. The thought is surreal. I have until the 30th to let them know my answer."

"Oh my gosh — you must be dying inside! Well good thing your party is tonight, then you have the week to think about it."

"Yes, in that sense I'm kind of glad the party is tonight, because it's all I'm thinking about really. Stay or go. Take it or leave it."

"Well honey - either way, consider it flattering that they thought of you. *Dat is niet niks*—that's a big deal."

"Thanks Marlies, I know. I am very flattered. OK, I'm going to check out now. I'll see you tonight, and don't forget, the dress code is white summer chic."

"*Ja ja*, OK. I know, you've mentioned it twice now!"

"Sorry, *dag* sweetie."

"*Dag!*"

I loaded my groceries onto the conveyor belt, where a young man with whiteheads stared at me and scanned my groceries, letting them pile up at the end. I had to bag them myself.

Mental note: In America, most places bag your groceries for you = Pro.
In America, shopping carts are larger, so you can fit in more groceries = Pro.
In America, the bread isn't as fresh as here in the Netherlands = Con.
Maybe the pros and cons list was a bad idea. It was going to drive me crazy.

Chapter 9

Back at the house, I laid out my special white Ibiza dress that I bought online, specifically for the goodbye party. Truth be told, I was influenced by an ad on Instagram. I saw a lot of other women in Loenen with a similar dress and thought, why not join them? I looked over at Abby for approval, who was lying in my bedroom in the corner with that look on her face only dogs can make, as if they're saying, *Honey, you think you have problems? I can't even talk!* "How can you not like this dress Abby? It's summer and light, and it twirls when I dance." It didn't deliver exactly what it promised when the model was wearing it — it hung a bit more on me. Less flattering. It did, however, cover my disappearing waistline, and it was already 7 p.m. — it would have to do. I put beers in the cooler, and set up the gin and tonic bar in the back, including stacks of lime, cucumber, and a small dish of cloves. I was annoyed with Paul, who for some reason was late coming home from work. He had to scramble to fire up the barbecue and rake the grass from yesterday's mowing session, so it didn't stain peoples' white shoes.

"Where the hell were you Paul?" I placed the salsa and chips out on the counter.

"I got stuck on an important call! Sorry, but work has slightly more priority than this goodbye party." Paul changed out of his work clothes, and put on a white button-up shirt, white chinos, and his Adidas sneakers.

"Closure is important, Paul. You're always stuck on a call. You'd think just this once you could make it home early. I took off the entire afternoon to get ready, and specifically asked you to be home on time to fire up the grill and help out a bit." I sliced up the buns and placed them on a tray, ready to load up and dispense, too busy and too annoyed to make eye contact.

"Don't worry so much. Everything doesn't have to be perfect." Paul grabbed his grill tongs and mitt, set them by the Weber, then headed over to me and enfolded me in a hug. I felt myself stiffening, at first. I was so focused on setting up for the party that it felt like a diversion we didn't have time for. Then I allowed myself to relax into his hug, to appreciate his familiar warmth. "I get it, saying goodbye is emotional. Everything's going to be OK. Try to enjoy yourself tonight, OK?" I nodded my head, and leaned in more. He kissed me on top of my head. There was a soft warm breeze that carried the dank scent of the Vecht, mixed with the sweet smell of freshly cut grass. Paul mowed the lawn yesterday. He started raking the yard again, to the playlist he'd put together for the party, playing softly over the outdoor speakers. I knew from past experience that, once guests started rolling in, I'd be too distracted to turn on the music. I placed a couple of tiki torches in the corners of our yard and hung up outdoor lights on our patio, which I'd transformed into a dance floor. I blew up white balloons and hung them out front, so it was clear to guests that they were at the right place. Setting up for a party is my favorite bit, almost better than the party itself, and certainly better than tearing a party down and clearing up.

"Hey Paul, want me to pour you a drink? Loosen up a bit before people start rolling in?"

"Yeah, I'll have a beer. Gotta go easy on the G&Ts. They don't always sit so well with me." He was right, if he had more than two he'd be on the couch all the next day, milking a hangover. I got Paul a beer and fixed myself a gin and tonic, adding some cloves. Around 8 p.m. guests, all dressed in white, started arriving — flowing steadily into our backyard. Our neighbors were first to arrive, followed by a couple of Paul's colleagues from work, friends from his fraternity and their wives, his ex-girlfriend Sanne and her husband (*I didn't know she was coming!*), a couple of my international girlfriends from Amsterdam, and parents from Lucy's school. I saw Paul fist bump a couple of his buddies, while flipping burgers. I ran around making sure everyone had their first drink in hand. After that, it was up to them to grab their own drink from the cooler or G&T bar. I made a couple of trips back to the kitchen, to make sure the food was well stocked. From time to time, I looked over at Paul at the barbeque, checking in to make sure he had everything under control. A few men kept him company, while women mostly clustered around the appetizer table. He looked up at me and winked.

At first, conversations were brief, keeping it to "thanks for coming!" and "you look great!" and "aren't we lucky with the weather — the perfect temperature." But as the night went on and more alcoholic beverages were consumed, conversations became longer, slightly more slurred. Paul had turned up the music, the stack of paper plates in the trash can was higher, the floor tiles by the gin and tonic bar stickier. To my great satisfaction, people started dancing on the makeshift dance floor, a hand aimed upwards, or a drink balanced in one hand, the other twirling in the air to the beats, or resting on the hip of their partner. If *Prince* or *James Brown* played, I was out there with them. I felt a light and happy buzz.

While on the dance floor, getting my groove on to *Let's Go Crazy* with Marlies, I looked over at Paul again and saw him talking to a pretty blond woman, her back turned towards me. Her butt was perky in her tight white jeans. Her thighs didn't touch. She was wearing green stilettos, and a white sleeveless top. Someone passed her, forcing her to turn to the side. I saw her sleeveless top was a plunging V-neck, showing a lot of cleavage. I had a better view of her face now. It was Sofie! *Sofie the dentist ended up coming*?! I didn't see her come in, but then again, I had stopped paying attention to everyone who was here. There must have been at least fifty people crowded into our backyard by now. I hadn't seen her out of her dental environment, out of uniform. Her blond hair was down, just below the shoulders, and had that windblown look — as if she'd used that saltwater beach hairspray. These Dutch women seemed to have such effortless beauty. Her hand was wrapped around one of our expensive wine glasses. Strange, I hadn't put any wine glasses out, knowing how easily they can be knocked over and break. Paul was animated, using his hands to explain something. Sofie started laughing hysterically. Paul's not *that* funny. Marlies noticed that I was distracted.

"Hey Jill, what's up? Why aren't you dancing?" She gave me a little shimmy.

"Oh nothing. I just noticed Paul talking to a woman who I just met today." I pointed discreetly in their direction. Marlies looked over her shoulder then back at me.

"She's pretty. Who is that?"

"Her name is Sofie. She moved here last April from Amsterdam. She's the new dentist here in town."

"I can tell, her teeth are gorgeous."

"Well, she sure is smiling a lot over there with Paul. Does something seem weird to you, or is it just me?"

"I'll send Stijn over there to check it out." Marlies knew I tend to overthink things.

"Stijn, why don't you head over there to Paul. Looks like he could use a refill." Marlies gently pushed Stijn in Paul's direction.

"Oh, OK." Stijn, having no clue what Marlies and I were up to, made his way over to Paul and Sofie, while Marlies and I continued to dance.

Sofie smiled at Stijn when he came over, and stepped aside, making more room for the three of them. I saw them conversing casually, smiling and chatting. Five minutes later, Stijn walked back over to us and started dancing while talking.

"*Ik ben er weer*—I'm back."

"What were you guys talking about over there?" I asked casually.

"They were talking about photography."

"Oh? What did they say about photography? Is Sofie into photography too?"

"Yeah, supposedly, but once the conversation got more technical and they started talking about their cameras, that's when I checked out."

"*Zie, niks aan de hand*—See, nothing to worry about."

Marlies leaned over and nudged me in the arm. She then surprised me by tapping her wineglass loudly with a knife, to get everyone's attention: *ding ding ding*. *Oh my gosh, a goodbye speech?!*

"Could someone please turn down the music?" Marlies yelled. The chatter subsided. I felt the attention in our backyard shift towards us, as faces swiveled, people gathering in a half circle. "Paul, come on over here next to Jill." Paul made his way over, with a bashful smile. I rearranged my expression into one of surprised delight. Next thing I knew, a projector switched on behind us and projections appeared against the side of our house — someone had managed to quickly hang up a large white screen. A slideshow of photos submitted by friends and neighbors started playing. People started oohing and ahhing, as photos of de *Avondvierdaagse*—a traditional Dutch walking event that was banned by the occupation forces during World War Two and therefore is celebrated today, boat rides with our neighbors on the Loosdrechtse Lake, and *schoolplein borrels*—schoolyard drinks, flashed across the screen. My mom was always amazed that parents drank wine on the schoolyard during school events. "That would never happen here in America!", she'd always say. Marlies gave a heartfelt speech about how much she loved the stories I told her at work about my life in Loenen, and how sorely we would be missed. As a joke to end her speech, she handcuffed Paul and I to our back porch and pretended to swallow the key, only to release us and present us with a photo album that everyone had contributed to, showing pictures of our boat (with its two home ports) floating down the Vecht River. I remembered Geert snapping that one — he must have placed it in our neighborhood WhatsApp group. "Something to remember us all by. Whenever you're homesick for the Netherlands, just pull out this album. You'll always have Loenen aan de Vecht as a home port."

Marlies' words brought me and Paul to tears. The Dutch are so good at skits and meaningful speeches. It felt like our wedding night all over again. Everyone clapped, then we turned up the music. I drank another G&T to sustain my light buzz, and continued to dance. At one point Paul Simon's *Late in the Evening* started playing. Everyone lined up in a conga line and started circling around the yard. I found Paul in the line, his hands around Sofie's waist, and felt a slight pang in my stomach. I convinced myself it was nothing. It was just a conga line, for Christ's sake. Roos' ex, Ruud, was in front of me and I had trouble even keeping my hands on his hips — he was all over the place, completely off beat, but I was too buzzed to care. We all ended up in one big circle as *Bust a Move* by Young MC started blasting. Ruud, who by this time was wasted, dove into the center of the dancefloor and started breakdancing. Everyone clapped their hands to the beat yelling, g*o Ruud, go Ruud, go Ruud*, as he attempted to spin but landed in the grass, getting grass stains all over his pristine white pants and button-up shirt. Every party needs a guy like Ruud, to liven things up. Someone has to be the one who dives into the center of the circle and dances. One of Paul's college friends pushed Paul into the center of the circle, knocking my expensive wine glass out of Sofie's hand. *Argh! There goes twenty euros of hard-earned cash!* The glass shattered all over the dance floor. Seeing this, I quickly ran to grab a dustpan and small hand broom from the kitchen. When I returned, I saw Paul's ex-girlfriend from college, Sanne, dancing with Paul on the dancefloor as I swept up the broken glass. Sofie bent down to help me pick up the shards with her perfectly manicured hands.

"I'm so sorry Jill."

"Don't worry about it." I clenched my jaw, thinking of the money it was going to cost me to replace.

After tossing the glass shards into the trash can, I returned to the dance floor where Sanne and Paul were the only ones dancing — everyone had gathered in a circle around them. Sanne, the one I thought could jeopardize our newly budding love in Washington. Sanne, who had a two-year relationship with Paul in college. Sanne, who supposedly had more feelings for him, than him for her, during his internship in DC. Well, judging from how they were dancing on the dancefloor I'd beg to differ! Their bodies were intertwined. Sanne grabbed the Hawaiian lei around Paul's neck and pulled him in — they jokingly danced forehead to forehead. I could feel my heart racing, my face turning red. I swallowed a lump in my throat and felt a tingling sensation in my stomach, making me short of breath. I could feel Marlies looking at me out of the corner of her eye. Her left hand reached out towards me, trying to block me from doing something I might regret, but it was too late.

"What the hell is this Paul?!" I went up to his side pushing him away from Sanne, giving her a mean glance as if she was trash. Sanne backed away flabbergasted. Everyone was flabbergasted. The music was still playing but everyone fell silent, watching. Watching to see what I'd do next. Something had snapped inside me, call it jealous rage.

"Aren't you married, Sanne?! Keep your hands off Paul!" Marlies came running up behind me and softly placed her hands on my shoulders, trying to calm me down. I pushed her hands off my shoulders and walked up to Sanne's face.

"He broke up with you about twenty-one years ago, remember?! So maybe it's time you kept your hands to yourself?" Sanne didn't say a word as she stood in shock, her mouth gaping wide open.

"Jill, stop! We were just dancing." Paul came to stand between me and Sanne.

"Just dancing, Paul?! Is that what you call it?" I could see guests slowly leaving, our neighbors, Sofie, Paul's colleagues from work, as discreetly as possible. Others didn't dare, because they were caught in the frontline. "Looks like there's still a little chemistry there, if you ask me."

"Don't be ridiculous Jill! We were just dancing." He let out a laugh, which made me feel even more ridiculous, and walked towards me with open arms. He grabbed me and pulled me in tight for a hug. "Jill, you're overreacting. I know you're under a lot of pressure with the upcoming move, the NPR job offer is weighing on you, but now you're just seeing things, and stressing about things that aren't there."

By now I was regretting the past two minutes and my outburst more than anything, but it felt too late to take it back. I had already made a complete fool of myself. I didn't know where to turn, or what to do. Here I was, ruining my own goodbye party. The party I had been looking forward to for so long. The party that was going to bring people together and give us closure. Tears welled up in my eyes. The only thing I could think to do was to run inside and hide. That's exactly what I did. I ran to our bedroom, closed the door, plopped down on my bed, and sobbed into my pillow until I fell asleep. My final cognizant thought was of Roos, at home on her couch with the girls, watching *The Voice*—a quiet oasis compared to here. I wished I was with them.

Chapter 10

My head was still spinning from last night, even though I had taken two aspirins before bed. The air was stale in our bedroom and I could smell the alcohol evaporating from Paul's pores next to me. His mouth was hanging open, his lower lip smooshed and curved, as he produced a steady snoring sound. I heard the neighbor's dog, Boris, barking and tried blocking the sound by putting a pillow over my ears.

It was late, 9 a.m., which for me was sleeping in. I sat on the edge of the bed, taking my time to put on my sherpa-lined slippers that I'd conveniently placed next to my bed, and grabbing my gray sweatpants and maroon hoodie that were within arm's reach. I shuffled into the kitchen, gave Abby her dog food, and made a pot of coffee, even though I wasn't convinced yet that I could stomach anything. After last night's drama, I had forgotten to prepare the coffee before bed, like I always did. I heard the last guest leave around 1 a.m. about a half hour after the embarrassing debacle. Paul must have stayed up to clean up the mess from the party, in his own drunken state. One thing we had in common was that we couldn't stand waking up to dirty dishes and a full counter. I looked around me and saw some remnants of last night's party that he had missed — empty gin bottles, the tiki torches, some shriveled balloons, and a white sweater someone had left behind.

As I waited for the coffee to brew, supporting myself by leaning on the counter, I tried to recall everything that had happened last night. My memory was foggy. I remembered Ruud getting way too drunk, like he always does, and breakdancing. I remembered him smelling of weed when I had walked past him. I remembered Stijn and Marlies dancing close, laughing. Small scenes flashed by, like a slide projector. One of Paul's college buddies peed in our bushes, and I remembered being annoyed. Why couldn't he have just gone to use the bathroom? Then I remembered watching Paul make Sofie laugh hysterically. And his hands on her hips during the conga line, his palm just above the little Levi's label on her butt pocket. A flash of jealousy turned the heat in my body up, and caused my neck to turn red. Then I remembered Paul and Sanne, dancing closely together before I went after them like a screaming banshee. I remembered Marlies trying to protect me from myself. I remembered Paul's colleagues trying to shoot the basketball, and the ball hitting my lilac tree. All these bad flashbacks make me want to return to the landscape of American barbeques, which seemed mild in comparison.

Paul walked into the kitchen, moaning and groaning.

"Want me to make you an egg? They say it helps with hangovers."

"God, no!" Paul started gagging and ran for the bathroom. Abby stood outside the bathroom door, concerned, wagging her tail. A solid minute later Paul came out and sat down in the living room, next to the kitchen. "Sorry. I should have seen that coming." He wiped his mouth with his sleeve, popped into our bathroom, and returned with his toothbrush.

"How many drinks did you end up having last night?"

"Oh God, I don't know. I don't even want to think about it, or I'll throw up again." Paul put one hand on his forehead, the other making a stop sign in the air. *This is going to be a fun day.* "Just give me a couple minutes to wake up, then I'll be fine."

I looked at our family weekly calendar on the fridge and saw *Margreet and Bert - dinner.* I'd completely forgotten that Paul's mom and her partner were coming over for dinner tonight, something we planned weeks ago and definitely couldn't cancel. We should be feeling better by the end of the afternoon, I hoped. I grabbed my coffee and went to sit on the front porch. I saw a couple of sloops, out already for a Saturday morning cruise. The sun was strong already in a bright blue sky, no clouds. The hydrangeas were in full bloom, showcasing their pink, white, and purple shades. Lucy's hockey game should be starting soon. I told myself I could send her positive vibes with my thoughts. It would be great if she scored today, for her last game on Dutch ground for a while. Sometimes, she's too sheepish when it comes to asking for the ball on the field, but she's never sheepish when saying what she wants from me.

I was hoping we could fit in a family walk today. Over the years, I'd learned it was always best to approach Paul and Lucy with new ideas when we were out in nature, walking around. The *Zonnestraal* estate was the perfect backdrop for broaching the NPR job again. I hadn't had enough headspace yet to fully weigh the opportunity. My heart seemed to say yes, but my mind was stuck on Paul and Lucy. Now was as good a time as any to make my own pros and cons list. I walked to the dining room table, grabbed a piece of paper from there, as well as Paul's receipt from the new camera he'd bought, and a pen, and walked back out to the front porch. I drew two columns on the back, and at the top I wrote: pros and cons for leaving the Netherlands...

Cons:
*I'd miss out on an amazing job opportunity as NPR European correspondent operating out of the Netherlands.
*Feels less safe in America, with all the guns and mass shootings.
*Lucy saying goodbye to her high school friends (but she'd be doing that anyway).
*We'd see less of Paul's family, who I've really come to love.
*I'd miss the coffee, bread, and less processed foods over here.
*I'd have to set up things like internet and phone providers, and find a doctor, gynecologist, all that stuff.
*It's like a full-time job in and of itself to move - packing, what to do with the car, finding a new home.
*I'd miss Marlies.
*I'd miss the Vecht.

Pros:
*The bagels, coffee ice cream.
*I'd be closer to my high school friends. A couple

have moved back to Gettysburg and I'm looking forward to hanging out.
*US college could be fun for Lucy.
*Fresh starts are good. You don't know until you try!
*Groceries are packed for you.

Nine cons so far, five pros. This was why this is a good exercise. I'd keep this list to myself. Maybe I could come up with other things this weekend. I tucked the piece of paper in my robe, just as Paul came out to join me.

"Come sit here — the fresh air will help." I patted the seat next to me.

"Thanks. Yeah, you're probably right." Paul sat down next to me. I moved my thigh against his, and thought about how different our two legs were, mine small and smooth, his thick and covered with hair, long and strong.

"Look, I'm sorry about last night. I'm so embarrassed. I know I made a complete fool of myself."

"I don't want to talk about it now." Paul readjusted a pillow in his back.

"OK. Hey, I was thinking, once Lucy gets home from hockey, let's all go to *Zonnestraal* for a walk."

"Sounds good."

"You know, my friend Emily posted on Facebook the other day that cicadas are expected to come out from under the ground again in the summer of 2021. Remember that one summer we visited DC and they were everywhere — splattered all over the road, and on my windshield? It was like Armageddon! It's so crazy to think that they've been underground the entire time we've lived over here! It's almost like they're on the same schedule we are."

"Yeah, they were super gross. I'd never seen anything

like it, and it will be too soon if I ever see something like that again!"

"Bugs aside, I liked living in Washington with you. Remember all those runs we did together, training for the Marine Corps Marathon?"

"Yeah. I figured if I wanted to hang out with you, the only way I was going to see you more was to train with you."

"Remember how we'd get in all those little tiffs because our adrenalin was so high? By the end of a 10-mile run, you'd storm off in one direction and me in the other. But we always knew we could find each other at the Java Coffee House on 16th and Q Street."

"Yes I remember, but it was usually you who stormed off. Similar to last night."

"Um, I thought you didn't want to talk about it now."

"No, you're right, I don't."

"I couldn't even remember what or who had set me off, most times. All I remember is that Java Coffee Houses's oatmeal cookies were the best on the planet. All the calories we'd burned running were replaced by that one cookie." This is what I'd always loved about our relationship; as much drama as there was, mostly caused by our different styles of communicating, there was also love. Most of the time we operated on this middle ground together.

Although rough at times, those were fun years, when we were first getting to know each other and exploring DC together. When you're living in the moment, you don't realize how special those years in your early twenties are. With so much energy you dream big, anything seems possible. The older we get, the more cynical we become. I'm not sure I'd want to live, nor could live in our old neighborhood now. There'd be too many things that would annoy me — the rats, the drug deals, the sirens, the parking tickets. But at the time — although these things were still annoyances — we just dealt with it. We were happy to have milk in the fridge, and to be able to pay our rent.

Each year, when we would go back for our summer holiday, we were sure to fit in a day in DC, reminiscing. Paul would meet up with his old boss, we'd grab a coffee in Georgetown, and then tell Lucy all the stories of when we first met, boring her to death. But walking the streets there the last couple of years had made me sad. I was a visitor, not a resident. That felt different. It was like attending an alumni weekend at a school that wasn't your alma mater. That realization made me doubt that going back to my hometown would feel like home. I felt a deep sense of panic and regret.

"What are you thinking so deeply about over there?" Paul brought me back to real time.

"Oh nothing, just our time in DC. The rats, Georgetown."

"That's quite the combi, yeah. It was fun living there. But all cities are fun when you're in your early twenties."

"True. I feel so old now, even going into Amsterdam. Everyone there seems like they're not a day older than thirty. Are we really getting so old? I feel like I'm still in my twenties. But then I look down at my hands, or in the mirror, or at my skin tags, or my disappearing waistline, which all tell the truth."

"I know, it sucks getting old. I'm going to go take a shower." Paul grabbed the small beer gut he'd been developing and jiggled it underneath his robe.

Roos pulled up on our driveway to drop off Lucy. Lucy and Julie were giggling, and I heard them discussing who won *The Voice* the night before. Roos stepped out of the car.

"Hi Jill. How was the party last night?"

"Oh it was fun. I missed you though."

"Did Ruud behave himself?"

"Oh you know, the usual. He broke out some good break-dance moves, that's for sure." I didn't want to say too much, seeing as Julie was within listening distance.

"Well, the girls and I had a fun night, with pizza and The Voice. Lucy — tell your mom the good news!" Roos opened the back car door to let Lucy out.

"We won our game, and I scored!" Lucy smiled ear to ear, as she climbed out of the car with her overnight bag and hockey stick.

"That's great news! Congrats *dames*—ladies!" I peered into the back seat at Julie. I was sad to have missed Lucy's official last goal on Dutch soil.

"They really did play well today, I must say." Roos gave both girls a look of pride, as she crossed her arms and nodded her head in approval.

"Well, I'm sorry I missed it. Thank you for bringing them. Lucy, what do you say?" I helped Lucy with her bags.

"Thank you Roos."

"Oh you're welcome sweetie. Have a good weekend! Jill, shall we do our walk on Monday after work?" Roos gave Lucy a big hug and climbed back into the car.

"Yes! Sounds good." I blew Roos a kiss as she pulled out of the driveway. I put my arm around Lucy, and walked through the gravel towards the house.

"We're going to go on a family walk later, at *Zonnestraal*. Your father's taking a quick shower. Do you want me to make you an egg sandwich or something before we go?"

"Oh man. Do I have to go? Can't I go hang out with Pleun instead? I only have a couple more weeks with my friends here." Lucy pulled off her hockey socks and shin guards as we entered the house and threw them on the floor.

"Um, excuse me. Come back here young lady. Remember what we discussed? I'm not your maid. Dirty clothes in the hamper, pick up your shoes and other stuff off the ground." I said pointing. Even though I said this a thousand times a day, it never registered. *Was that a Lucy thing? Or a teenage thing?*

"OK moooommmm." Lucy rolled her eyes, and headed upstairs for a shower. "Why don't you and dad go together? I just want to chill at Pleun's house today. I'm tired from my game." She yelled down from the top steps.

"All right. That's fine. Just be home by five, because Oma Margreet and Opa Bert are coming for dinner."

"They are?! Yay! OK, no problem. I'll be home by five. Thanks mom!"

When Lucy and Paul had showered and dressed, we all ate a quick egg sandwich in the kitchen. Lucy took off on her bike to Pleun's house, just a few blocks away. I filled up a couple of water bottles, then grabbed Abby's leash and a poop bag. Paul grabbed his new Canon camera — the EOS M50 model he'd just bought as an upgrade, claiming it would give him more flexibility than the entry level model, albeit still expensive, camera he had before — and off we went.

Zonnestraal — a former sanitorium for people with tuberculosis in the 1920s — was a short, twenty-minute drive away. Now it was used as public grounds, where dogs could run off the leash through heather meadows. The parking lot looked busy when we got there, but we found a spot without any trouble. Paul and I strolled towards the soft sandy paths. This is one of my favorite Dutch landscapes — wide, open heather meadows. Abby jumped through the heather like a bunny. She sniffed the butt of every dog that passed, and moved on, always looking back over her shoulder at us, part of her pack. Ten minutes into our walk I couldn't wait any longer, and brought up the NPR job. We didn't have a ton of time to decide — just until the end of the month. Paul was right, we should first decide on this together, then bring Lucy into it.

"So, Paul, have you given my potential NPR correspondent job more thought? Did you try the whole pros and cons approach? I have mine right here as an example. Maybe that's the best way to start this conversation." I pulled out the crumbled piece of paper I'd transferred from my robe to my jeans pocket. I read my list out loud to Paul. He laughed at the coffee ice cream bit. At least he saw the humor. "So, your turn?"

"Look, Jill. I don't think a pros and cons list is the way to go about this. You know I love it here, and my parents. It's just, everything is already lined up for America. We are moving. In two weeks. I can imagine that it feels weird. Scary, even. But it'll be fine. I have a good job lined up at Leaf Fruit Company. Lucy is going to love Gettysburg College. You could easily find work in Gettysburg, or DC. Why go shake everything up, just so you can take a strategic career move? Where does that leave us? Me, and Lucy? We have such a good plan." Paul threw his hands on my shoulders and pulled me towards him, I looked up at his earnest eyes, then looked down at the sandy ground.

"I get what you're saying Paul. I like America too, and I'm happy you're able to line up a job so easily and that Lucy has this scholarship, which by the way, she could hypothetically still go over and start, with or without me. It's just, life is short. Why not give this NPR job, *my* dream job, a try?

And, why wait? This opportunity is here now and may never be available to me, to us, again. We left DC so we wouldn't both get caught up in the American dream of working full-time to pay for the white picket fence, two SUVs in the driveway, and one week of vacation each year. Do you really want to go back to that?"

"But Jill, had Catharine never called you and told you about the job, we wouldn't even be having this conversation right now."

"Yes, but did you consider that with the salary I would make with the NPR job you could become more serious about your photography? I just think it could be fun. Plus, we could be with your parents longer and they're not getting any younger."

"Yeah, but it's not fair of me to deprive you of more time with your parents. Plus I like your parents. I miss them. I'm actually looking forward to hanging out with them more." Paul threw a stick for Abby.

I knew when I married Paul that my life would be more complicated than if I had just settled down in Gettysburg with an old fling. I could have had a life running the local coffee bar with Matt, or planning events at the cider orchards with Steve.

"Well, that's just it. I feel like I'd never forgive myself if I didn't take this opportunity, allowing us to be closer to your parents in their old age. They're a good ten years older than mine. I realize there's so much that plays into this decision. You had a rough time adjusting in DC. You missed your family and friends. You had your ups and downs. I honestly think my being over in the Netherlands for so long contributes to my volatile state and outbursts, like last night. When you're not on your home turf, you're more vulnerable.

But this NPR job would make me feel more connected to America, while living in the Netherlands."

"So you're blaming your jealous rage last night on the fact that you're not living on your home turf?" Paul looks at me, raising his eyebrows.

"Well, yes. I'm more vulnerable over here, which makes me *onzeker*—insecure." An elderly couple sitting just ahead of us along the trail on a bench looked up towards us, so I lowered my voice. "Look, I'm sorry for last night. I don't know what got into me. I'm sure this whole move to America plays into it. "

"Well, it was pretty embarrassing, especially for me and Sanne. But we'd all had too much to drink. Look, let's just forget about it. Hopefully everyone else will too." I felt like we're getting somewhere now. Paul took my hand in his, but his hand felt like stone. It was there, but it might as well not be.

As we made our way back to the car, I took a deep breath, inhaling the smell of the heather mixed with sand. The sun felt warm on my face. The remnants of my hangover had slowly dissipated. It was true, we had a good plan to move to America. But despite our plan, I still couldn't help but want to stay.

Chapter 11

While folding a load of laundry in the living room, I saw a gray Renault Kangoo minivan pull into our driveway. I walked out to greet our dinner guests. Margreet, Paul's mother, stepped out of the passenger side, her arms wide open, gold bangles clanking by the sleeves of her oversized white blouse. Margreet has always had a simple yet sophisticated style, less is more. Her salt and pepper gray hair was pulled back in a hairclip. I caught a whiff of her Chanel No. 5 perfume. She grabbed a basket in the backseat, which was filled with the usual Dutch treats — meatballs, *pannenkoeken*, and a pan she was giving us, plus large Tupperware containers filled with something else. She usually spends a day in her kitchen before coming to visit, so she can shower us with food for our freezer. She also likes to unload some of her dishware each time she comes, "I'm alive now, and don't want you all to have to worry about cleaning out my place when I die. I want to see people enjoy my belongings." While I love the actual gifts, it always feels a bit morbid to take things from her, knowing she is cleaning out her home in anticipation of her own death.

"Oma and Bert, you're here!" Lucy ran out to greet them.

"*Hi lieverds! Ik heb jullie zo gemist*—Hi darlings, I've missed you so much!" Margreet wrapped her arms around Lucy, pulling her in tight. Bert made his way over to me by the front door and gave me a big kiss on the lips. He does this to everyone in the family. Me, being a germaphobe (Paul says this is an American stereotype — "You guys started this, with antibacterial wipes!"), wiped off his kiss when he wasn't looking. I loved Bert though. He was one of the gentlest, kindest men I'd ever met.

"*Wat kan ik voor je inschenken?*—What can I get you to drink?" I asked Margreet and Bert, as they stepped into the house.

"A glass of white wine would be wonderful!" Margreet set her basket down in the kitchen, and started unloading its contents into the freezer and onto the counter.

I remembered the shattered glass from last night's party. How I'd screamed at Paul, in front of everyone.

"I'd love a beer," Bert said, as he took a seat. It was a two-hour drive for them, from Groningen. Margreet doesn't drive, and Bert's getting on — eighty-three years old this year. Paul entered the kitchen and said he had to check some work emails in the other room.

"Hi Bert, hi mom." He gave them both one kiss on the cheek. "Bert, do you want a glass with that beer?"

"Yes please." Bert poured his IPA into the glass.

"It's so clean here." Margreet scanned the kitchen.

"Oh, you think so? Well thank you. Yeah, we had our big goodbye party last night. Paul and I gave everything a good wipe down afterwards."

"Oh yes, Bert and I are the same. I can't sleep if the house is a mess. Jill, I'm making dinner for you guys tonight.

You're busy enough as it is. I have everything right here. It'll only take about twenty minutes for me to throw everything together, so go pour yourself a glass of wine."

"Oh my gosh, Margreet. Thank you. What a treat!"

After pouring myself a glass of wine I sat down next to Bert. As I watched Margreet cook, I had a total feeling of *déjà vu*, remembering the very first day I met her, now well over twenty years ago. If someone told my younger self that, *someday you'll be having deep philosophical conversations with your Dutch mother-in-law*, I would have declared them clinically insane. But it's true — my Dutch language skills are at my best when I'm talking to my Dutch mother-in-law. The words just flow out of me. We get each other on so many levels. She often tells me how she had to become seventy-years-old to have the wisdom women have today, that there's so much more parents have to deal with today than when she was a parent. She doesn't know if she could do it. We talk about everything, from what a Dutch columnist wrote in the weekend's newspaper and what is our new favorite white wine on sale at Gall & Gall, to our new year's resolutions. And, what's most special is that it didn't take us long to get to this comfortable place.

Lucy's piano music made its way into the kitchen from the other room. She was showing off her latest tune for Bert, who also played. Bert walked up behind her as she filled the air with beautiful notes. I watched him from the kitchen, as Lucy played and Margreet cooked. He picked up a framed black and white photo Paul had taken of Lucy when she was young, on a swing outside the farmhouse where Bert and Margreet now live. Paul had picked up photography from his dad. I'd framed some of his work over the years, the photo of Lucy being one of my favorites. I was glad Paul had a hobby, something outside of his work that he enjoyed.

"Dinner's ready!" Margreet called out from the kitchen. We sat on the barstools surrounding the large, black granite island. Margreet laid out her *aardappel gratin*—potato dish, and *draadjesvlees*—beef stew. "A bit of a hearty meal for the summer, but you know me, I only make hearty meals."

"Doesn't this look delicious!" I grabbed a serving spoon from the drawer. Margreet took a big gulp of her wine, then placed a napkin on her lap.

"Mmmm, smells good oma!" Lucy sat between Margreet and Bert.

"*Eet smakelijk!*" Margreet gave everyone a signal to go ahead and eat, by nodding her head.

"*Eet smakelijk!*" Bert, Paul, Lucy and I said in unison.

After the first couple of bites, Margreet took another sip of her wine, "How was the party last night?"

I looked over at Paul hesitantly, "Well, it definitely was eventful. There was broken glass involved, dancing, and yelling." The room fell silent as Margreet looked over at Bert and then to Lucy and then Paul, her eyes ending at me. She was careful not to judge.

"Jill." Paul stared me down, begging me with his eyes not to go into it, but he knew better. I'd always been able to discuss things openly with Margreet. She'd always been open about her divorce — how she had two men in her life, how she got jealous easily. In fact, we'd always bonded over our jealous tendencies. Margreet and Paul's dad, Hans, divorced when he was ten. Margreet fell in love with Bert, who was a family friend. Hans and Margreet slowly drifted apart. Margreet went off with Bert, and Hans found his new partner, Linda. They're all on good terms, and see each other often. Frankly, I've never seen such an amicable divorced couple. Margreet always says, "I have two men in my life — my soulmate Bert, and the father of my children Hans, I love them both." We'd always had deep philosophical conversations about motherhood, letting go, self-reflection, usually based on articles we'd both read in the Dutch weekend newspapers.

"Basically, I made a fool of myself after seeing Paul dancing with Sanne."

"Oh Sanne?! Jill, you know Paul doesn't have feelings for Sanne, that was so long ago. He chose you!"

"I know. I just had too much to drink. We all did. I don't know what got into me."

"Well, don't beat yourself up about it. Last time Bert and I had an argument, I was so angry that I threw red wine all over my white curtains!" Margreet belted out a boisterous laugh.

"Well, strangely enough, that does make me feel better. I've gotten so angry before at Paul that I've thrown *Chocomel* all over him."

We both laughed hysterically. Paul and Bert looked at each other and rolled their eyes. I put my fork and knife down, and wiped my mouth with my napkin. Margreet started coughing, as if a drop of wine had gone down the wrong tube. Margreet continued to cough. Lucy rushed to get her a glass of water. Bert patted her hard on the back, until the coughing passed.

"How are your parents doing, Jill?" Margreet and my parents had always gotten along well. They emailed each other for birthdays, and we always planned in a visit to Groningen whenever they came to visit me in the Netherlands.

"They're doing well, thanks. They're getting very excited to have us over there. My mom keeps sending me articles from the *Gettysburg Times*, so that we're all up to date on what's going on locally."

"I can imagine! I've felt guilty all these years, having you over here with us. Poor Chet and Sally, having their daughter and granddaughter so far away. As much as I'll miss you three, won't it be wonderful for your parents to have you back?" The more Margreet talked, the more emotional she became, as tears filled her eyes.

"I know, but I'm having major separation anxiety from the Netherlands. I've spent the majority of my adulthood here, and I can't help feeling as if this is all a big mistake. I mean, as familiar as America is, it's also so unfamiliar. It's hard to explain." Looking up at the ceiling I tried to contain my tears, holding them in and pressing my lips together.

"What does your heart say, Jill?" Margreet had a knack for boiling things down to what the heart wants.

"That's just it — I wish I knew. My heart isn't speaking to me right now. She's asleep or something. We've always said we'd move back to America after twenty years, but it just snuck up on me so soon! I don't know if I'm ready. And to complicate things even more, I just had the most amazing job offer dangled in front of me. I don't know if or when another offer like this will come along, career-wise."

"Oh?! What job offer?" Margreet's eyes widened.

"NPR — National Public Radio, where I interned when I first met Paul, offered me the job as European Correspondent, in the Netherlands." I shot a look over at Paul, who rolled his eyes and shook his head.

"Jill! My goodness. That sounds like a big deal." Margreet tried to take the temperature of the room before saying anything else. "You've always been very career-driven. Unlike me. I mean, when the kids were small I went back to school for my master's in education, but that was mostly thanks to

Bert. I never really had to go into an office. But times are different now, aren't they?" Margreet has always encouraged me to pursue my career. She's been my cheerleader throughout my years at Radio 1. "I'm sure you'll figure things out and do what's best." She glanced over at Paul again, who had his head down, looking at his food.

"Yes, well we still have a couple days to think about it."

Paul's phone made a ping sound, with a new message.

"Sorry guys, I have to take this in the other room." Paul swiped on his phone, pushing his barstool back and making his way towards the living room.

"No phones during dinner — house rule." Lucy spurted out like a robot.

"I know, but this is important." Paul closed the door behind him.

"I'll say one last thing about it, Jill. Just be sure to follow your heart, and the rest will work itself out. It took me seventy years to figure that out, so I'm saving you a ton of time by sharing that knowledge with you now."

"Thank you Margreet, you're always so wise." I raised my wine glass and clinked it against hers. "I'm so glad you and Bert were able to come this weekend. It's our last time together in this house!"

Paul came back into the kitchen and placed his phone out of reach.

"Everything OK?" I asked.

"Yeah, just a work thing that I needed to take care of. Coffee anyone?" Paul switched on the espresso machine.

"No, thank you. Just make one for yourself. I'm going to finish this glass of wine, then head to bed." Margreet folded her napkin and gently placed it on the granite island in front of her.

"I put clean sheets on the guest bed — everything's ready for you to dive in." Groningen was just too far away for them to come just for dinner, plus Bert didn't like to drive when it was dark.

"Thank you, Jill — you always take such good care of us." Margreet took one last sip of her wine, set her glass down, grabbed me, and gave me a big hug, whispering in my ear, "I know you'll do the right thing. Just follow your heart." She and Bert went into our guest room for the night.

Pro for taking on NPR job: I wouldn't have to leave my mother-in-law. I love that woman.

Chapter 12

A morning dove woke me from a deep sleep. I looked over at the alarm clock – 8 a.m. Not bad for a Sunday. Walking out to the living room I saw Paul and Lucy were already awake. Paul was reading the Dutch NRC weekend newspaper. Lucy was drawing on the iPad.

"Are your mom and Bert still sleeping?" I walked over to Paul and gave him a kiss on the lips. He kept his eyes on the paper. Lucy didn't look up from her iPad either, when I gave her a kiss on the head.

"Yes. Haven't seen them yet."

"OK, I think I might go for a longer swim today. If they wake up before I'm back, could you make them breakfast?"

"Of course."

"Thanks." I started walking back towards the bedroom when Lucy asked, "Can I go with you, mom?" Now her eyes were on me. I thought for a moment, caught off guard. This was not like her to ask to come along. Maybe she wanted to get something off her chest.

"Um, sure honey. You've never swum that far before. Do

you think you can make it?"

"I think so. We can always turn around if I can't, right."

"Of course. You're right. We can always turn around. OK quick, go put on your swimsuit. I want to go before all the boats come out." Lucy jumped up from her chair and ran upstairs. I looked over at Paul, who put his paper down and smiled.

"That's nice you're going together for a swim. I don't think you've ever done that before."

"No, you're right. We haven't. It'll be nice."

The water was warm enough to swim without a wetsuit. I was excited about the prospect of letting my legs move freely underwater. We quickly ate a banana, and I had a cup of coffee so that there was something in my stomach. Lucy and I scurried across the road, towel, goggles and floating devices in hand. The morning light was soft. There was a slight breeze, but not enough to ripple the water. The sky was blue, except for a wisp of clouds off to the west. I climbed down the ladder first, dipping my toe to test the temperature, then eased my legs and torso into the water, followed by my arms and shoulders. I waved to Geert, who was sitting on his back deck facing the Vecht. *Ah, our surveillance camera is awake.* The curtains were all drawn down at Sofie's house, from what I could tell — about 150 feet away, it was difficult to see. I treaded water in front of our dock to get used to the temperature and closed my eyes, letting the morning sun penetrate my skin as Lucy carefully eased into the water.

"How was your party, mom? Was it weird saying goodbye to everyone?" Lucy and I synchronized our breaststroke next to each other.

"It was fun! But yeah, a little strange and sad. Julie's dad

128

did some breakdancing." I glanced over at Lucy.

"What? You're kidding."

"No. He's pretty good."

"I believe it."

We swam in silence, until I decided to break it with chit-chat.

"You know, it's now officially past the summer solstice, and that's"...

"Your favorite day of the year." Lucy chimed in, in unison. "I know mom, you say that every year — how sad you are that we're now going in the 'wrong direction' with daylight." Lucy rolled her eyes, and laughed.

"I guess you didn't get my cosmic astrology genes. That's one thing I won't miss here, the dark Dutch winters — those dark weeks that never seem to end, where the cold goes right through your bones. Thank god for my sunlamp and vitamin D capsules. I don't know if I could survive the winters over here without them."

"But the winters are cold in Pennsylvania too." Lucy said, matter-of-factly.

"Yes, but we don't get those week-long windstorms, or two weeks of rain. But then again, I haven't lived in the US for twenty years, and with climate change, who knows what 'normal' is anymore."

We approached the *Glashut*—a row of houses that used to be a 19th century glass factory, our halfway point, and we stopped to tread water as a break, then continued back in the direction we had come from. We listened to the rhythm of our strokes in the water and our breathing, ducks splashing, swans flying overhead.

"Mom, can I ask you a strange question?"

"Sure, go ahead."

"Where do you want to be buried?"

"You're not rid of me yet young lady!"

"Ha-ha, I know. That's not what I meant. You better live to be at least one-hundred. But I was just wondering the other day when I passed the graveyard, where would you want to be buried?"

"That's a good question. I guess I'd want to be cremated, and have half my ashes spread out in Gettysburg, where my roots are, and the other half here in the Netherlands, maybe in Loenen, in the Vecht?"

"Really?" Lucy's eyes widened, and she stopped swimming for a second, treading water.

"Yeah. People do that, you know. Both have played such an important role in my life. I don't think I could choose one over the other. You might fall in love with a particular place someday — China, Spain, Bolivia, it could be anywhere. Then you'll know what I mean. That place becomes a part of your DNA."

"Yeah, but the Netherlands is my home. I was born here."

"Yeah, but look at Queen Maxima. She was born in Argentina, but is now Queen of the Netherlands. I would imagine she calls both places home."

"I guess you're right. I mean, Gettysburg does feel like home a bit, since we've been going each summer."

"Exactly, and it's that feeling, like a warm blanket, no matter how hard you try to kick it off, it stays enveloped around you — that's home."

As we headed back towards our dock and the windmill, we passed Sofie's house along the way. The curtains were still drawn. We climbed up the ladder, and dried ourselves off.

"Thanks for letting me join you, mom."

"It was fun. Thanks for coming. You did a good job keeping up. I guess it's all that biking to and from Hilversum." I gave her a hug and felt her cold cheek against mine. Paul was in the *overtuin*, trimming our hedge.

"Want me to make you two an omelet?" Paul asked.

"Oh yes please! I'm starving."

"Me too." Lucy added.

"Come on, let's rinse off." Lucy showered upstairs in her bathroom, me in mine. After breakfast, Margreet and Bert headed back to Groningen, her basket now empty and hanging on her arm as she got into the car. I spent the rest of the morning catching up on the laundry and vacuuming.

Usually my mom calls on Sundays — a good day for a catch up, since during the week I'm too busy with work. Growing up, I'd call my mom every day at the funeral home. Seeing as she was their receptionist, I knew I'd always get her on the line first. My mom always sounded happy to hear from me, and was always there to provide a listening ear, whether I had just called to tell her that Jeremy and I broke up, or that I couldn't find my basketball shorts for practice. I hope Lucy and I have that kind of relationship throughout life — where she calls me often, even to update me about the smallest things, no matter where she ends up in the world. Because I only saw my mom once or twice a year, those little phone calls about nothing made it feel like she was closer.

Like clockwork, my mom called at 2 p.m. Netherlands time, 8 a.m. Pennsylvania time.

"Good morning, Jill."

"Hi mom."

"How are you? Did you go for a swim?"

"Yes I did, and Lucy joined me this time."

131

"Oh, how nice. You know, I was getting a bit worried about her. I had her on the phone a couple times. She's so quiet. Are you sure she's doing OK, emotionally?"

"Argh, yes mom. She's fine. She's always been a bit quiet, you know that. She has a lot going on. I mean, her high school graduation is tomorrow."

"I saw your post on Facebook, her backpack hanging out the window with the Dutch flag. I love how you guys do that over there. I deposited some money in her US savings account and sent her a graduation card. Did the card arrive yet?"

"Aw, thanks mom. That's nice of you. No card yet, but it's Sunday, so I'm sure it'll arrive this week."

"Hey — before I forget to tell you, and you find out from one of your brothers, I had one of my episodes the other day. Nothing to worry about, everything's fine. I was checked out at the hospital, and they sent me home."

"What? What kind of episode? Mom?! Are you OK?"

"Yes, yes. That's why I didn't even want to mention it, but it's best you hear it from me. Remember last year when I was driving home from the dentist, and didn't know where I was or who I was for a good ten minutes?"

"Yes. That was scary. They diagnosed you with stress-induced amnesia right?"

"That's right. I was stressed because I had to go to the bathroom really badly and there wasn't one around. Well, that's exactly what happened this time. I went out to eat with your brother at Ernie's Texas Lunch, had some stomach troubles, then blanked out again. John took me to the ER, everything's fine. I just thought you should know, that's all. It's nothing, and they can't do anything about it."

"Well, jeez mom! That worries me."

"Don't worry. You have enough on your plate. I cannot

wait to see you! Did you guys decide whether or not you're going to fit a week in at the beach?"

"Well. Here's the thing. I have other big news I want to share with you." Silence on her end, in anticipation. "I got a job offer from NPR! To be their European Correspondent!" My mom, an avid NPR listener, nearly choked over the phone.

"What?! Jill, that's awesome! Congratulations! You're going to take it right? Washington is only just over an hour commute from Gettysburg!"

"Well, the job is actually over here, in the Netherlands. We're still figuring everything out."

"What about Lucy's scholarship? What about Paul's job at Leaf? What about your rental place? Your land? Your.."

"I know mom. Believe me, I know." There was a long silence, so much so that I thought either the line had broken or that she had hung up. "Mom? Are you there?"

"Aren't we good enough for you over here?" My mom sniffed.

"What?! Of course mom. That's not it. It's complicated. I've been over here for twenty years. I can't just close the door. I know the timing isn't great, but I want to seriously consider the opportunity. I don't think there will ever be another one like it."

"I guess I just feel hurt, that's all. It's just unfair. They've had you for so long. Now it's my turn. I only get to see my granddaughter once a year. It's just not enough." I could feel myself getting annoyed now. I didn't want her words to weigh into my own decision-making process. I regretted telling her. I should have waited. Of course I'd like to be able to drop by for a quick coffee and catch up, like all my Dutch friends do with their mothers. I felt like I had missed out on a lot, seeing as I'd never really had my parents close by to babysit, or come over for a Sunday dinner, like Lucy's friends' parents could. An *Oppas Oma*—Grandmother close by who babysits, was simply not an option for me. Margreet lived too far away to come babysit regularly when Lucy was little.

"I have to let them know my decision by the end of the month. Don't worry, either way we're coming over this summer for a visit. The question is whether or not we'll be staying."

"Well, I'll keep my fingers crossed that's a no. It'd be like a dream come true to have you guys back on this side of the pond for good."

"Don't pressure me mom." My jaw tightened.

"I know, I'm sorry. It's just, you know, we'd love to have you back home over here. OK, keep me posted."

"Will do. Love you mom, bye."

"Love you too sweetie."

As I hung up the phone, I thought about the word *home*. When Paul and I first moved over to the Netherlands, I learned the idea of *home* can mean different things. I used a mini cassette recorder to document my experiences during my first year, and would mail the cassette tapes to my parents or my best friend back home, Anne — must have been the journalist in me. Lucy found my mini cassette recorder the other day and brought it to me. I pressed play, nervous at what I might hear — it had been so long:

> *"Hi Anne! It's Feb 24th, 2000, 3:40 p.m. here in the Netherlands, 9:40 a.m. for you in America. We're off to a birthday party this afternoon for one of Paul's high school friends, Rens. I'm bracing myself for hours of*

sitting around in a circle, first a round of coffee with cake, then a round of savory snacks, like Dutch cheese and ossenworst with mustard. They always start with the sweet and end with the savory.

So chickadee — let's see. It's windy here today, like always. I have a new thing called wind therapy. When you walk outside the wind literally blows you away. Because of the flat landscape, there's nothing to block the wind. When a dog tries to poop outside it can't, because the wind blows the dog and the poop away. The wind is incredible. But that's why I call it wind therapy, because you can curse, yell, and shout anything and no one will hear you, as the wind is so strong — it just takes your words away. Even the person right next to you won't hear them. I hate it, but I love it, you know what I mean?"

I paused the tape and told Lucy I wanted to first listen to it all on my own, as I couldn't remember saying any of this. Crazy how fast we forget. I was afraid she might hear something she shouldn't. Even though she was seventeen, I didn't want to corrupt her young mind with her uncensored twenty-four-year-old mother, so I sent her away, pressing play again once I was alone.

"My parents are coming to visit in March, which I'm looking forward to, but I'm also kind of worried about the two worlds colliding. I'm excited to show them the Kijkshop though — where you browse the items for sale behind a glass cabinet, write down the number of the item you want to buy, and bring that number to the cashier. Kijken means to look — brilliant!"

I hit pause and smiled, remembering how happy I was that they did visit me that first year, so I could show them the land I was falling in love with, so they could see the immense flat landscape and witness how strong the wind was. This tape was not only insightful for its day-to-day details, but my younger self surprised me. Memory is a strange thing, like a movie and a dream wrapped up in one. How was I able to move over here as a twenty-three-year-old and basically start a new life!? How did I manage to solidify relationships with all these people? How did I bike in that wind, to and from my classes at university? Listening to that tape again, I closed my eyes and could picture the bike route I took each day to class. Starting on the Nieuwe Kerkstraat, then hanging a right by the skinny bridge, continuing up along the Amstel River, bumping all the way on my saddle because of the brick streets. Crossing over by Waterlooplein, passing the white round opera house, then over two bridges, up along a canal towards Dam Square. Just behind the royal palace was the P.C. Hoofdhuis, where my professor and twelve other students awaited, in a small classroom overlooking the Singel canal, blue and white trams running by in the distance. I had to pinch myself each day, just looking at the beauty around me, the historical buildings dating from the 16th and 17th centuries, when I was used to American Civil War era buildings being old.

When I first heard Dutch being spoken, it sounded like someone coughing up phlegm, to me. I would get headaches from concentrating so hard on each word, my fingers numb from constantly flipping through the pages of the Dutch-to-English dictionary, looking for words and translations. I developed a callus on my throat, so that I could handle the hard guttural sounds. The Dutch language had become my new obsession, and I was on a mission. Because, the sooner I could learn Dutch, the better I could integrate, and what's the point of living abroad if you're not going to integrate?! Plus, I was sick of not knowing what Paul and his friends were talking about — it seemed like they switched from English to Dutch, whenever there was something they didn't want me to hear. There's a difference between being an expat who's just here for a couple of years, and an international who is in it for the long haul. Once my master's program was over, and we had made our agreement — twenty years in each country — I transformed from an expat into an international.

Even though I didn't know where The Netherlands was before — the country with 16 million people at the time and 2.8 times smaller than Pennsylvania — it was engraved in my heart from that year onwards. For better or worse, I was officially a dual citizen.

As much as I loved America and missed Washington, it was refreshing how the Dutch saw the world in a direct, no nonsense way — Dutch government uses the consensus model to reach agreements. Women wore thick HEMA tights and boots or rain pants on their bikes, so that biking could continue in the winter months. If someone asked, "How does this skirt look on me?" they'd get an honest answer, "Not so great — try this one." Being in a small country, it seemed as if people were more respectful towards their environment. Distances between destinations were shorter, so nine out of ten times riding a bike made more sense than driving a car.

While not all things were unicorns and rainbows, Dutch kids really did grow up eating *hagelslag*—chocolate sprinkles, on their bread. The first time I saw our nieces eating chocolate sprinkles on their bread for breakfast I was AGHAST! It looked like mouse poop, for starters, but after trying it I came to love and appreciate this Dutch treat. *Alles met mate* the Dutch would say. Everything in moderation. That wasn't just with food, but with everything — cars, houses, amount of time for visitors. *Bezoek en vis blijven drie dagen fris*—visitors and fish both stay fresh for three days. But the most important lesson that year about home was that it has to be *gezellig* — there's no translation that does justice to this word, but "cozy" comes closest.

Chapter 13

I heard Lucy knocking on our bedroom door.

"Mom! It's 8 a.m. We're going to be late for my graduation ceremony!" I shot up straight in bed. Paul threw off the duvet, completely disoriented.

"What? No, we're fine. It doesn't start until ten, sweetie."

"OK, but please get up and get ready. I don't want to be late."

"Don't worry. More importantly, what are you wearing? Come here, I can't see." Lucy walked towards my bed and twirled, in what appeared to be a dark-green dress with three-quarter sleeves and Doc Martens. "You look cute."

"Can I pick out your outfit today, mom?"

"Sure, why not. This is your big graduation day." Lucy was good at putting outfits together. She went to my closet and pulled out a pair of wide-leg navy pants and a cream-colored sleeveless blouse.

"How about this?" Lucy laid it out on my bed.

"Nice. I like it. Thanks."

"Are you going to pick out my outfit too?" Paul sat up

in bed, laughing.

"Yours is easy papa. You always wear the same thing anyway, Polo shirt and khakis — voilà!"

"Come over here Lucy." I patted the space between Paul and me in bed. Lucy smiled and walked over in little steps. "You're not too old to come give us a big group hug, are you? I can't believe my baby is graduating high school today! Ahhhh." I pulled her wrist, so she plopped down between us and sank my face into her soft hair that smelled like sweet flowers. "I better bring a pack of tissues with me."

"Mom, you'll be fine. If anything, a shot of caffeine will get you through the ceremony and all those calling of names."

"Oh yeah, I forgot about that part. How long does the ceremony last? I have to be back in the office for my goodbye lunch." Paul kissed Lucy on the cheek and got out of bed.

"I don't know. An hour and a half, something like that?"

"Oh, that's fine. Hey, maybe tonight we can go out for dinner to celebrate, when I'm back from work?"

"Yeah, I'd like that."

"Great, I'll be a bit later tonight. Is that OK?"

"That's fine. I was going to hang out with some friends and go out on the lake this afternoon, anyway. We're taking Pleun's parents' boat. I'll make sure I'm home by eight."

We got in gear. I let Abby out, Paul loaded his and Lucy's bikes in the station wagon (they wouldn't fit in the Jeep). I poured coffee into a travel mug, and grabbed the car keys. Lucy trailed behind me, eating a bagel wrapped in a piece of paper towel. We drove along the dike towards the N201, direction Hilversum.

"Argh! The drawbridge is open. It's always open when you're in a rush." The joys of living by the water.

"Chill, mom. We'll be fine." Lucy pressed the radio tuning button until she found a station she liked.

This put us five minutes behind. I drove ten miles over the speed limit to make up for it, getting us to Lucy's school just on time. As we pulled up I saw loads of teenagers, all dressed similarly to Lucy — cropped wide leg jeans, Nike Air Force sneakers or Adidas Stan Smiths, sweatshirts with names of American cities like Santa Monica or Chicago — the Dutch youth love wearing apparel that states places they've never been to but that sound cool. It's like how when you wear a University of Amsterdam hoodie in America it's cool, but when you wear it in Amsterdam, not so much. A sea of bikes lined the school parking lot. Many of her classmates, including her ex-boyfriend, Faas, were leaning against the side of the school, smoking a cigarette before going inside. Faas looked over at us and gave a sheepish smile. He was nice, but I thought Lucy could do better. Someone with a bit more charisma. Someone more self-motivated. Too many of Paul's friends started smoking when they were in high school, and still smoke to this day. I couldn't help but think of all those years their lungs had been taking a beating. I saw Lucy's English teacher, meneer van de Bilt, heading towards the entrance. He spotted me and waved. He started walking over to our car. He was wearing an old looking woolen sweater, with a moth-eaten hole in the shoulder. His balding head glistened in the sun.

"Hi, Jill! Did Lucy tell you she got a 9 on last week's test?"

"She did tell me. A 9 is great! We're so proud."

"It would have been a 10 if she didn't have that American accent. Good luck in America, Lucy. You'll do well I'm sure. The *6jes cultuur* isn't really a thing over there, from what

I'm told — they appreciate good grades and high achievers." He leaned in the car window, and patted Lucy on the arm.

"Actually, we do have a similar saying in the US, 'Cs get degrees', but we won't go there now." Meneer van der Bilt was the only one who laughed at my joke. I wasn't about to go into how annoyed I was at his comment on the American accent. It was graduation day, so no point. The Dutch teach British English in their school system, and this wasn't the first time Lucy had been reprimanded for her American accent.

The ceremony lasted just as long as Lucy said it would. After a couple of speeches from her teachers and the handing out of diplomas, a group photo was taken. I cried my way through a pack of tissues. Paul occasionally took my hand to comfort me. My heart filled with pride and joy when I saw Lucy cross the stage. Where did the time go? If I couldn't make it through her high school graduation with dry eyes, how was college graduation going to be? Or her wedding day? Of if/when Lucy gave birth? Her whole life flashed before me and, for some reason, that whole life was in the Netherlands.

After the ceremony, and lots of picture taking, Lucy disappeared into a sea of friends. I drove Paul to his office and helped him unload his bike.

"Have you heard anything from the realtor about the viewing?"

"I missed a call from her the other night. She left a voicemail asking me to call her back, and I totally forgot until you mentioned it. I don't have the mental capacity right now to deal with it. Too many decisions, too much going on. I'll try calling her back today. We'll see you at 8 p.m., then? I'm going on a walk with Roos at five, so I'll be back around six." I stood on my toes so I could reach to give Paul a quick peck on the lips. "Have a good day. I gotta run. My goodbye lunch with Radio 1 is today."

"Oh that's right. Have fun."

"See you tonight!"

"Yes, OK. Love you. See you tonight."

Radio 1's studio is several blocks away from Lucy's school — in the Hilversum Mediapark, where most Dutch channels have their headquarters. Marlies was already behind her desk, ticking away at her keyboard, when she stopped typing and looked up at me.

"*Goedemorgen schat. Alles goed?*—Good morning dear. Everything OK? How are you feeling after Friday night's party?"

"Oh Marlies, I'm so embarrassed. I don't know what got into me." I threw my bag down next to my desk and turned on my computer. The new message alert was at 113 — a new high for my inbox.

"Don't be too hard on yourself, Jill. Everyone had too much to drink."

"Yeah, but was it just me, or were Paul and Sanne dancing way too close?"

"They were dancing close, but nothing to worry about. They were just having a little fun."

"Well, if that's your way of trying to make me feel better, it has worked. But I can't seem to shake the weird feeling about Paul. As if his mind is somewhere else lately. And the way he was carrying on with Sofie! How animated he was, as if they were already good friends! They've just met!"

"Jill, I sent Stijn over there to check on them, remember? You have nothing to worry about. Paul loves you. He's with you. You guys are married, you have a daughter."

143

"I know, I know. But something's off. Ever since I told Paul about the NPR job he's been more distant. I'm glad he's back into photography, but sometimes it seems like he's living on a different planet from me — it's hard to explain. I feel like we're growing apart."

"Try not to look into it so much, Jill. Maybe America *would* be good for you guys. A fresh start?" Marlies reached across the desk and squeezed my hand. "I have to head out to a meeting. Are you going to be OK?"

"Yes, I'll be fine. I have a busy day ahead to distract me anyways."

"Don't forget your goodbye lunch today. It's a surprise where we're going, but I know you'll love it."

"Can't you give me a hint?"

"One hint — it's by no means chic."

"I'm OK with that, ha-ha. McDonalds?"

"Close. OK, stop guessing, just wait until 1 p.m."

"Oh Marlies. If I end up in America, what am I going to do without you?"

"You give me too much credit." Marlies blew me a kiss across the desk.

Scanning through the subject lines of the new messages in my inbox, my eye was drawn to one with the subject line: *your land*, from my mom. I had told her not to use my work email address. Although immediately annoyed, I couldn't help but open her message and view the photos she'd sent me. She wrote that she was out for a drive and took a bunch of pictures of the plot of land we'd bought to build on one day, with rolling hills, orchards in the background. I have missed rolling hills. I imagined what it would be like to wake up there in the morning with that view, going to Lucy's field hockey games and stopping by my parents afterwards, grabbing a crab cake sandwich and virgin Bloody Mary for lunch with Lucy. I imagined us sitting in the town square and catching up on life as we watched all the tourists passing by.

My phone rang, bringing me out of my reverie. It was the *makelaar*—realtor, they must be calling about our house.

"*Hallo, met Jill*—Jill speaking."

"Jill — we have an offer on your house."

"Oh my gosh." My heart rate shot up. I wished I could hit pause on life right now. My words were caught in my mouth.

"The couple from Amsterdam that I showed the house to the other day made an offer — asking price. You'd be wise to take this Jill. What do you want me to tell them?" I stared out in front of me.

"Let me discuss it with Paul and get back to you. Is that OK?"

"Do you think you can let me know by the end of today? I don't think we should keep them waiting too long."

"Yes, definitely. By the end of today, I'll call you. Thanks so much. *Dag*—goodbye." As I hung up, I looked down at my hands now inflamed with eczema. That always happens when I'm stressed. Ever since living in the Netherlands, I've developed all these strange ailments, or paid witness to things with Lucy that I don't recall having myself, growing up in America: *krentenbaard*—raisin beard, *luizen plague*—lice plagues, and *waterwratjes*—water warts. You wouldn't think it would be so different, especially in a first world country. But, besides adjusting to a different climate, there's an entirely different ecosphere of bacteria! I was usually embarrassed to tell the receptionist at the doctor's office my date of birth, which they always asked for to look me up in their system. I was afraid that they'd think: *Oh, her again - the hypochondriac American!*

The next hour was spent answering emails, reaching out to partners to let them know I was leaving and that they would do best to contact Marlies from now on. Come 1 p.m. I was starving. I saw a handful of colleagues gather at our door at exactly one, all smiling. Clearly, they were trying to keep our lunch location a secret.

"OK Jill, ready for your send-off lunch?" Marlies, who had since returned from her meetings, got up, took my arm, and pulled me towards the door.

"I don't know, am I?" raising my eyebrows, I hesitated behind her. She took a bandana from her purse. "You're not going to blindfold me are you?"

"Of course! Otherwise it won't be a surprise."

She and our team guided me to the front entrance, where we hopped into a vehicle. We only made a couple of turns, and approximately ten minutes later we all stepped out.

"OK, ready, I'm going to take this off in 1,2,3!" Marlies ripped off the bandana and there, across the street, I spotted the Dutch snack bar chain, FEBO. Food was also a huge part of the integration process for me. I tried the raw herring, the *filet americain*—cured meat. But nothing says Dutch cuisine to me more than FEBO! Marlies handed everyone a few euro coins, "compliments of Radio 1". Scanning the snack options, I inserted a two-euro coin into the slot, then opened the little vending window and took out a delicious, steaming *frikadel*—all the left-over parts of various animals, minced together into hot dog form. To top things off, I ordered a *patatje oorlog*—French fry war. My guess was that they called it "war", because it literally looks like a war zone, with every sauce imaginable piled on top of the french fries. While standing in front of the FEBO, all crowded around a white plastic standing table, I dug around with my little plastic fork, making sure that there was just the right balance between the *pindasaus*—peanut sauce and mayonnaise, to go onto my delicious fry. My mouth watered as I took the first bite of the French fry war. I felt its warmth go down my throat and into my stomach. When I went to throw away my plastic plate, I noticed two guys with JanSport backpacks on (one dark green, one navy), West Virginia University baseball caps, and New Balance sneakers, passing by on the sidewalk, "Holy shit dude, do you feel it taking effect yet?" *I'm assuming they're talking about the pot they've consumed.* "Yeah, startin' to feel it. Hey! Watch out for the bike!" They didn't see the bike path that's parallel to the sidewalk, as they made their way across the street. An angry cyclist rang her bell, "*Pas op, kut toeristen!*—Watch out, fucking tourists!" I had to smile to myself, thinking how glad I was that I'd been able to "pass" as Dutch all these years. I'd taken on their casual clothing style. I'd learned their language. I knew to always look left, right, left. Granted, the whole traffic coming from the right has a right of way thing still gets me sometimes, but other than that…

Later, I thanked my colleagues for the wonderful lunch, which had come with a few speeches and goodbye gifts, including a Dutch cheese knife and bottle of champagne. I shut down my computer for what might be the last time, and carried a large bag filled with my belongings to the car. I felt sad, like I was saying goodbye to my family, because that's what my colleagues had been for the past twelve years. Before driving back to Loenen I tried calling Paul, to tell him about the offer on our house, but there was no answer, so I sent him a text. It wasn't five yet, so I still had time to get back to the realtor.

As I drove back to the house on the N201, with the radio on, there was a news alert about how the government was going to address water safety in an effort to reduce accidents. *Finally! I hope they patrol along the Vecht and lakes more often — someone died out on the lake last year from a speedboat injury!* Every time I was out there I was reminded of how dangerous the water can be. Too many people drowned each year in dark water, either because of rip tides, or people who drank too much while out on their boat.

When I pulled back up to the house, I was greeted at the door by Abby, wagging her tail. The boat was gone. I could have sworn Lucy said she was going out in Pleun's parents' boat. I also noticed Paul's new camera that had been laying on the dining room table this morning was now gone. Maybe he took it to work. Maybe I should ask him more about his photography, show more interest. It wouldn't be that much longer when it would be just the two of us at home — when Lucy moved out. I couldn't think about that now, without feeling a deep emptiness inside.

Roos arrived in her car and parked on our driveway. I grabbed Abby's leash on the way out and walked outside to greet her.

"Ready for our walk?" Roos pulled her hair back into a ponytail.

"Yes — looking forward to it. I've been sitting on my butt most of the day." I locked up the house and we walked out towards the road. "Which way should we walk? Towards Vreeland or Nieuwersluis?"

"Let's do Nieuwersluis, for a change."

Roos pulled out *salmiak* from her back pocket—Dutch candy that tastes like black licorice, and looks like a black worm with beige insides. "Want some of this?"

"No, thanks. My tastebuds are too American for that."
She shrugged, and put the plastic sandwich bag full of candy back in her pocket.

Nieuwersluis is a small village between Loenen and Breukelen, out towards Utrecht, where Paul works. The Vecht river runs through them all. I thought how lucky Paul was to have such a beautiful commute to work along the Vecht on his bike. He took this route every day.

"So how have you been, Roos? I feel like we're always so rushed when we talk — either dropping off the kids or picking them up, or quick exchanges at the grocery store. I'm glad we have a chance to really catch up."

"I'm OK. I just acquired a new client, so that's added to my workload." Roos works at an ad agency in Amsterdam. As long as I've known her she's worked for the same company.

"Well, I can imagine it's nice, in that sense, to have a couple days to yourself, without a child and a husband to take care of."

"Actually, it's terrible. People always say how nice it must be to have time to yourself when you're divorced, but I'd much rather have us all together. I miss Julie when she's not there. It's terribly lonely."

"I never thought of it that way. Sorry, didn't mean to assume. My 8th grade world history teacher always said, 'never assume because it makes an ass out of you and me.' Well, I guess I just made an ass of myself."

"No worries. It's a common divorcee misconception."

We'd made it to the Cronenburger bridge, about three-quarters of the way around our 5K loop, when we heard sirens. We stopped just before crossing, and two police cars and an ambulance came at full speed in front of us, crossing to the other side of the Vecht, heading towards Nieuwersluis.

"What the heck?" I looked at Roos confused.

"Looks pretty serious!" Roos raised her eyebrows.

All of a sudden, I got a terrible feeling in the pit of my stomach. I immediately thought of Paul, who should be headed home on that same road in about twenty minutes. I thought of Lucy, out on the boat with her friends.

"Paul should be heading home soon on that road. I better call him to let him know he should go a different way, because it will be blocked off." I reached into my pocket for my phone, scrolled through my recent call history, and clicked on his name.

"That's a good idea."

"I'm getting his voicemail straight away. He must be on another call, or has his phone switched off."

"I'm sure he's fine. Maybe he already left, saw what was up ahead and took a different route via Breukelen."

"I hope you're right."

"You worry too much Jill."

"I know, you're right."

I shook off my negative thoughts and *what if's* and continued to walk the rest of the route with Roos. About twenty minutes later, as we approached my driveway, I was telling Roos how excited I was to hang out Lucy's backpack with a Dutch flag for graduation, when my phone rang. No caller ID. I picked it up.

"Mevrouw Stone?"

"Yes?"

"Officer Petra Visser here, from the Vechtstreek police force." My heart rate shot up and my face froze. My hands started shaking uncontrollably, I could hardly hold the phone to my ear. Roos grabbed my arm and stared at me in full anticipation.

"Are you the wife of de heer Paul Davenoord?"

"Yes."

"Your husband was in a boat accident just now. He's alive, but in a critical condition. He hit his head on a bridge — he didn't duck on time. We're transporting him by ambulance to the emergency room at Amsterdam University Medical Center."

"What?! Oh my God!!"

"Do you have someone who can accompany you to the hospital? In our experience, it's best to have someone else drive you, when faced with these situations." I looked over at Roos, who was still staring at me with a panicked look on her face. Roos nodded her head, *yes*.

"Yes. I have someone to drive me."

"OK, good. When you get to the Amsterdam UMC, just head straight to the ER. The ICU trauma doctor on duty can bring you up to speed." I didn't register everything she said. All I knew was that I had to get Roos to take me to the Amsterdam UMC, asap. I hung up, my knees gave up, and I fell to the ground. I was in total shock. I didn't know what to do. I couldn't even think straight.

"Jill. I'm so sorry! I could hear everything through your phone. Come, let me take you. We can jump in my car." Roos reached out and picked me up off the ground. "Let's put Abby inside, I'll get my purse and you get your wallet — just in case, you never know." Amsterdam UMC is normally a short fifteen-minute drive away. But of course it was rush hour, so there was traffic, a sea of red brake lights ahead of us. Each minute felt like an hour. In the end it took us double the time. I felt like throwing up from the stress, as we pulled into the designated parking spots for ER and made our way through the sliding doors.

Chapter 14

My paper cup was filled up halfway with black coffee from a vending machine. I swirled it like a glass of wine, staining the upper half of the cup with a black residue. My stomach turned inside out as Roos and I waited for someone to summon me back to where Paul was lying in a critical condition. The woman behind reception peered up through the plexiglass window.

"*Mevrouw*." She looked directly at me. "Do you have any form of I.D. on you?" *Thank God Roos thought to run into the house for my wallet! Funny how, even in crisis situations, we're able to remember some details.*

"Yes. Here's my Dutch driver's license."

"OK, *dank u wel*. I will make a copy of your license. Now all I need is your insurance card, home address, and a contact person for the patient."

"OK. I'm the contact person. My address: Loenenseweg 7, in Loenen aan de Vecht. Here's my insurance card." I slid my card towards her as she typed away on the computer. She looked down at the card out of the corner of her eye and stopped typing.

"Thank you. Go ahead and take a seat. You should be called back shortly." She nodded towards where I was sitting.

Roos rhythmically rubbed my back, which put me in a sort of trance, until the sliding glass doors in front of us opened and a tall man with round glasses and a white jacket came out with a clipboard, looked up and called, "Jill Stone?"

"*Ja! Dat ben ik*—Yes, that's me!" Jumping up, I threw my half full paper cup in the nearest trash receptacle and looked over at Roos.

"I'll wait for you here. *Sterkte Jill*—good luck Jill." Roos gave me a warm smile. I nodded and followed the man through the sliding doors.

"Hello Jill, I'm Dr. Meijer, the Intensive Care Doctor on duty tonight. Our trauma team is back with Paul." He shook my hand firmly. "Before I bring you to Paul, I just want to have you come in here so that I can bring you up to speed." He pointed towards one of their so-called Family Rooms, at least that's what the plaque next to the door said. There was a gray couch, two worn chairs, and a coffee table with ring stains on it. The room was clean enough, but tired. I saw skid marks on the floor, and a corner of the coffee table was chipped.

"Take a seat." He pointed to the couch. I figured the faster Dr. Meijer brought me up to speed, the faster I could go see Paul. "Now Jill, what you're about to see will be difficult. Paul suffered a contusion of the head with some blood in his brain. He's in a medically induced coma, which means he's unconscious, unable to respond to any stimulus around him. Now, that's not to say he won't wake up, but it could take days. We have him on some pretty strong painkillers and sleeping medication. He's lucky he got away with just three broken ribs, the way he fell on the side of the boat. Because his head injury is more serious than his ribs, I'll be working together with neurologist, Dr. Carla Boomsma. I'm Paul's *hoofd behandelaar*—head practitioner, but we'll be consulting on his case the entire time, and you'll be seeing a lot of Dr. Boomsma as well. We're going to keep him here, in a medically induced coma, and monitor his bodily functions. We'll of course keep you informed of his condition. Usually, we keep patients in a medically induced coma for two to three days. Depending on how things go, we'll try to bring him out in about two days, allowing his body and brain time to heal."

At that point, a nurse popped into the room and handed me a clear plastic bag.

"Sorry to interrupt Dr. Meijer, but here are the belongings we found on him." The nurse handed me the bag, with Paul's wallet, camera — at least, what was left of it — smartphone, and a silver bracelet.

"What's this? It's not Paul's." I said, pointing to the bracelet while looking up at the nurse.

"Oh, that was found at the scene. I believe it belongs to the young woman who was with him during the accident. She's back there now."

"What?! There was someone with him?!"

"Yes, and that's a good thing too, because she's the one who called the ambulance. I'm sure she'll have more information for you, since she was there. I assumed you knew her, that she was his colleague or a friend."

I sat up straight in my chair. There was an enormous lump in my throat that kept creeping its way up, until I swallowed it back down. *So that's where our boat was.* There were times he took his camera out with him in the boat to take pictures — his so-called "me time", to unwind. He said he came across so many beautiful things on the water, he wanted to take pictures of birds, like the *zomertortels*—summer doves, and *ijsvogels*—king fishers.

"No. I have no idea who it could be. He usually goes out on the boat with me, or occasionally with his friends." My breath became short, and I got a sour feeling in my stomach.

"We've moved your husband. I'm sorry, is Paul your husband?" Her face turned bright red.

"Yes, he is."

"We've moved your husband to the Intensive Care Unit. He's no longer in the ER." After delivering the news the nurse quickly headed back out the door.

"OK, well, I think we're finished with the briefing." Dr. Meijer grabbed his clipboard and pushed his glasses further up his nose. "Come, I'll take you back to Paul."

I followed Dr. Meijer out into the fluorescent lit hallway leading to the Intensive Care Unit. Nurses in light blue scrubs were rushing around, wearing a determined and focused look on their faces. Dr. Meijer scanned his hospital badge, opening the doors to the ICU. We walked past the nurses' station and made a left towards a room with four hospital beds, all separated by a curtain, ending up at the bed that was farthest to the right. A slit between the curtains revealed Paul's foot. Dr. Meijer slid the curtain further to the side for us to enter, and my heart skipped a beat.

There was Sofie, the woman who had cleaned my teeth just last week, the woman who was at our goodbye party talking to Paul, laughing. Those scenes of her flashed before me. She was sitting off to the side of the bed on a chair, scrolling through her phone, as if she'd been waiting for me the entire time. My knees felt like jelly — I wanted to collapse right there on the floor, because what I saw in front of me was so scary, so surreal. To think it was my husband lying there was too painful to believe. But it was, it was Paul. There must have been ten tubes going into his veins and nose, attached to his chest with monitors. There was a large blue tube hooked up to his mouth, allowing him to breathe. His neck was in a thick brace, and his head was completely covered in bandages. Dr. Meijer placed his hand on my shoulder, "I know this is difficult to see, Jill." Tears welled up in my eyes.

"Jill, I'm so sorry!" Sofie got up and walked towards me. I couldn't process her presence just yet. She was more like a ghost.

"Can he hear us?"

"Yes, we believe so, although he will not respond to stimuli in his coma. But it's still good to talk to him, even if he doesn't respond." I felt nauseous, this was all too much. I looked for the closest receptacle that I could throw up into and saw a beige puke bucket lying next to Paul's bed. Without another word, I rushed over to it and threw up, mostly that day's FEBO lunch. Using a tissue, I wiped my mouth and turned towards Dr. Meijer.

"I'm so sorry. I just couldn't help myself."

"That's OK. It happens — you're not the only one." Dr. Meijer reached out for the bucket and, holding his breath, took it to the closest nurse to dispose of. "Let me give you some time alone with Paul and...I'm sorry, what was your name again, *mevrouw?*" He looked over towards Sofie, who was standing off to the side.

"Sofie."

"Ah yes, Sofie. Good on you to call 112 at the scene of the accident."

"Thank you, doctor." Dr. Meijer exited through the curtain. Sofie turned towards me, her head down slightly.

"Jill, I'm so sorry."

"You already said that. Thank you. The question is, what were you doing with Paul?"

"Oh, he didn't tell you? He's been giving me photography lessons. We were out on a photo safari." Her voice quivered. She started speaking fast. "We were out taking photos, after his work. It was our last session before your move. Paul said the boat was for sale and it was likely the last time he'd be taking it out. We were about to go under the bridge at Nieuwersluis. He turned towards me to take a photo — he said the lighting was just perfect. I was sitting on the back seat of the boat. I screamed "duck!" but it was too late. His head slammed into the cement bridge, knocking him out. He fell down, his middle hitting the side of the boat. The majority of his weight was still in the boat, so I was able to pull him back in. I switched off the boat immediately. There was blood everywhere. It was horrible, Jill. Horrible." Sofie started crying and wiped her nose with her sleeve before continuing. "The whole scene keeps replaying in my head. I called an ambulance straight away. They sent in a trauma helicopter. I wasn't sure he was going to make it, in all honesty." Her face was tight with grief, waiting for my response.

"Thank you Sofie. I'm glad you were there." *Am I glad she was there? If she wouldn't have been with him in the first place, would this accident have happened?* I'm prone to that sort of thinking — it's the journalist in me. What the hell was she doing with him? That would explain their chummy conversation at the goodbye party. But why wouldn't Paul just tell me, if he was giving her photography lessons? "If you don't mind. I would like some alone time with Paul."

"Of course. Jill — if you need anything, you know where to find me." And with that she walked away.

I pulled up a chair and took Paul's hand in mine, carefully moving the tubes so that I could get my hand under his. A symphony of beeps and lights played on the monitor and other equipment next to Paul's bed. Paul's slow and steady heart rate flashed across the screen. There were a bunch of numbers and codes I didn't understand. Softly, I leaned in towards his face, full of bruises and scratches. His face was also swollen. His eyes were closed. He was here, but he wasn't. Inhaling, I smelled his sweet honey smell and kissed his cheek at the only spot of flesh that wasn't covered with something, and whispered in his ear, "You're going to be OK Paul. Stay strong. You have to wake up from this coma. For me, for Lucy." I looked closely at his face, five o'clock shadow, the chiseled cheeks I'd fallen in love with over twenty years ago. "Why didn't you duck?! You moron! I'm so mad at you for that." I gently squeezed his hand. Maybe showing him some emotion while he was in his coma would help bring him out of it. For the next twenty minutes my eyes played ping-pong between the monitor showing Paul's heart rate and his face, all the while holding his hand, gently stroking across the couple of centimeters it was possible to do so.

A tall woman with dark brown hair tied up in a bun and wearing a white jacket gently pulled back the curtain and walked into our section. "You must be Jill, Paul's wife?"

"Yes, that's me." I stood up to shake the hand she was offering me.

"I'm Dr. Boomsma, the neurologist working together with

Dr. Meijer. I can imagine this has been quite a rough day for you. I'm so sorry, but visiting hours are over. I'm going to have to ask you to come back tomorrow. Paul needs his rest. You're welcome to come back tomorrow morning at 8:00 a.m."

"OK. But I hate to leave him here like this."

"I know, but don't worry, he's in good hands. We'll call you if his condition changes. Best thing you can do is go home and try to get some sleep. Do you have children?"

"Yes, we have a seventeen-year-old daughter, Lucy. She still has no idea." Tears welled up again.

"Oh my, yes — that's difficult. I'll leave it up to you, but please feel welcome to bring Lucy in tomorrow. In our experience, when a parent is severely injured, like Paul, it's best to have a good talk with her before bringing her in, preparing her for what she's going to see. Staying honest yet optimistic is tricky."

"I'll do my best, thank you. I would like to bring her in tomorrow. Will you be here?"

"Yes, I'll be here tomorrow. Go get some rest." Dr. Boomsma held back the curtain, gesturing as politely as possible that it was time to go. I reluctantly walked back past the nurses' station towards the waiting room. I almost forgot that Roos had been waiting all this time. She was reading *Privé*, a Dutch gossip magazine, when I found her in the waiting room. Roos shot up from her chair when she saw me walk through the sliding doors.

"Jill! How is he?!" Roos gave me a big hug.

"Oh Roos, horrible. I knew it would be bad, but didn't know it'd be *that* bad." My nose was running like a faucet, my eyes puffy.

"I'm so sorry Jill. Come, let's get you home. Have you told Lucy yet?"

"No! I haven't had a chance. I want to get back to the house before she does, so I can tell her. What time is it?!"

"7:30 p.m". Roos told me, just as I looked at my own watch, as if I needed to have an extra set of eyes to help me because everything was blurry, including my mind.

"She's out with friends on the lake, but she'll be home by eight, so yes, let's get going so I can beat her home."

Roos drove me back. When we turned off onto the Vinkeveen exit towards Loenen I blurted out, "Dr. Meijer said someone else was with Paul during the accident."

"Sofie, the dentist. She said Paul was giving her a couple of photography lessons before we moved to America."

"That's strange."

"I know, right?! Supposedly Paul had his camera wrapped around his neck, as if he was taking pictures when he smashed his head against the bridge. Why would he go out on our boat and give Sofie a photography lesson after work? Why wouldn't he just tell me?"

"Try not to overthink things Jill. Maybe it slipped his mind because he didn't see it as a big deal, just helping out another *Loenenaar* with photography."

"Right after work?!"

"True, that is strange. Do you have his camera?"

"Yes. And his phone."

"Well, maybe there's something there. First thing's first though, get some rest, and bring Lucy up to speed."

"Yes, you're right. Thanks, Roos. I don't know what I would have done had you not been with me tonight."

"No need to thank me. I'm glad I could help."

Roos dropped me off at home. I saw five missed calls from the realtor. I didn't see Lucy's bike. Abby was waiting by the door, wagging her tail. We were all going to go out to

161

eat tonight. Just the thought made me cry. All of a sudden, I felt very alone, and scared. Would Paul ever be able to eat again? The simple things had now become questions. I wasn't hungry anyway, thirsty if anything. As I poured myself a glass of water, I heard the crunch of Lucy's bike tires on the gravel. Poor thing, she had no idea. Now her whole world was going to come crashing down. *Remember what Dr. Boomsma said in the hospital — try to strike that balance between honesty and optimism.*

"Hi mom!" Lucy said cheerfully, as she walked in the door and threw down her hockey bag in the mudroom.

Taking a deep breath, I opened my mouth, but nothing came out. I froze. Tears filled my eyes.

"Mama, what's wrong?!" Lucy came up to me and grabbed my arm.

"Oh Lucy. Come, sit down. I have something I need to tell you." Lucy's face became stricken with fear, her eyes wide. She took a seat at the dining room table. I sat next to her and grabbed her hand.

"Where's papa?" Lucy's eyes darted around the room, searching.

"Lucy, your father's been in an accident…" Before I could get another word out of my mouth, Lucy interrupted hysterically.

"What!!?? Is he dead?! Where is he?!", she screamed.

"No! Lucy, he's not dead. He's in a coma, in hospital. He hit his head on a bridge as our boat went under. He wasn't paying attention. It knocked him out cold."

"Oh my God, no!" Lucy's knees buckled as she fell to the ground, cupping her hands over her face. I crouched down next to her and rubbed her back, just like Roos did to me.

"Lucy, he's going to be OK, we need to stay positive."

"OK?! How do you know?! Papa's in a coma. You don't know whether or not he'll wake up."

"No, you're right, I don't know for sure. But the doctors have him in what's called a medically induced coma. If all goes well, they're going to try to bring him out of it in two or three days. We need to stay positive."

"What are the odds?" Lucy always wants things broken down into statistics and odds.

"I don't know, the doctors didn't give me percentages. All they said was if the tests they run look ok and his vital signs are OK, then they'll bring him out of the coma."

"I want to go to him. Now!"

"We can't. I'm sorry. I was just there — visiting hours are over. I can take you first thing tomorrow morning."

"Why didn't you tell me sooner?!" Lucy looked up, her mouth turned down, face red, snot dripping from her nose.

"Because it all happened so fast. I was walking with Roos when I got the call and he was already being taken to hospital by ambulance. I wanted to go to him first and assess the situation, and figured I it was best to tell you afterwards."

Lucy said nothing back, but rather buried her head deep into my shoulder and sobbed. I sobbed along with her — our bodies shook in unison.

"Come, I'll make you some tea." Grabbing her hand, I lifted her up and walked her to the kitchen.

"Can I sleep with you tonight?" Lucy wiped her snot away with the back of her hand.

"Of course. I'd like that, actually."

After about an hour of Lucy drilling me with more questions that I didn't have answers to, I remembered it was probably wise to inform Margreet of Paul's accident, and my own parents. When I called Margreet she was shocked, of course. After giving her all the details I had, I asked her if she could update the rest of the family, so I didn't have to. She said that she would come tomorrow, leaving Groningen first thing in the morning. Lucy and I put on our pajamas, brushed our teeth, and went to bed. Leaning over, I kissed Lucy on the forehead and squeezed her tight, whispering in her ear, "It's all going to be OK, just get some sleep. We'll go see your dad first thing in the morning. *Welterusten*."

"*Welterusten*, mama." Lucy pulled the duvet further up over her head. I set the alarm for 6:30 a.m., to make sure we'd be up on time, and switched off the light. As I laid on my back, my head started racing at full speed. *What does all this mean for our move to America? Can we even go? What does it mean for the NPR job? What if Paul doesn't wake up for another couple of months?!*

Does his work know? Probably not. I'll have to call them tomorrow, as he definitely won't be showing up.

How will Lucy respond? I told her about all the tubes, the monitors, not to be scared when she sees all that.

I tossed and turned for about an hour before deciding to just get up and get a glass of water. This summer was already a contender for one of the hottest on record, and I could feel the air on my skin pressing against me, making my thick hair heavy. Looking out the kitchen window I saw a full moon outside, its light glinting across the surface of the Vecht. I thought of Paul, just seven miles away, sleeping. Dr. Boomsma said it was wrong to think of it that way — he wasn't *sleeping* — but I let myself anyway: I pictured him with his eyes closed, on his back. I did my best to block out the tubes, the sounds of the ventilator, the beeps. I crawled back into bed. Lucy was fast asleep. Once I laid down, I pictured his soft face, his face beside me in sleep, there on the

164

pillow next to me. I closed my eyes and thought about all the times we'd joked about crazy WhatsApp messages from people in town, other mothers who obsessed about play-dates and sleepovers, or funny things we could do to mess with our neighbors who were so protective of their property line, "we could build one of those huge floating decks and put it right smack dab next to their houseboat, put a couple palm trees on there, a barbeque. That'll teach them!", Paul would say, and I'd laugh so hard my cheeks hurt. I opened my eyes in our dark bedroom, lying there without him beside me, I felt somewhere between sad and numb.

Chapter 15

A startled awakening had me reaching over to Paul's side of the bed, only to find Lucy's arm instead of his. It wasn't all a dream. This was really happening. My husband was lying in a coma at the hospital. One of my greatest fears, was actually playing out. I thought it best to let Lucy sleep a couple minutes longer while I took care of unpleasant logistics, like calling Paul's work to tell them about the accident. Check. Calling the realtor to tell them negotiations are on hold for the moment. Check.

We arrived at the ICU promptly at 8 a.m. The smell of vending machine coffee and the sound of hospital machine beeps filled the air. Nurses were at their station, chatting about their kids, about the day's planning. I held Lucy's hand as we approached the curtain surrounding Paul's bed. Looking over at Lucy, I squeezed her hand and whispered before opening the curtain.

"What you're about to see is going to be difficult Lucy. Are you sure you're ready?"

"Yes mama." Even though Lucy's a good two inches

taller than me, she looked so young, so vulnerable. Her face flushed. It broke my heart. Slowly the curtain revealed her father lying peacefully in a coma state — thick white bandages around his head. "Papa!" Lucy broke down at his bedside, tears fell on his pristine white hospital sheets. It was difficult for her to know where to lay a hand of comfort — too many tubes and bandages. She stroked his cheek with the back of her hand, her yellow and blue friendship bracelet Julie gave her hung loosely around her wrist. Coming up behind her, I pulled her thick hair back into a ponytail in my hands and removed strands that were sticking to the tears on her face. Careful not to say anything and just let her take it all in, I pulled up two chairs beside Paul's bed, and pushed one under her so she could sit. At that moment Dr. Meijer walked in, along with the neurologist Dr. Boomsma who had a friendly smile, with dimples on each side. If I had to guess, she was probably in her late thirties. She wore light make-up and her dark brown hair was pulled back in a tight braid this time.

"You must be Lucy." Dr. Boomsma smiled at her from across the bed.

"Yes." Lucy wiped her tears and looked up at her. "I'm Dr. Boomsma, I'm the neurologist taking care of your dad. This is Dr. Meijer, the intensivist. We're both treating your father. I'm so sorry Lucy, that this happened. Has your mother updated you on his condition?"

"Yes, she has. Is it true that he might not wake up for a while? Will he ever wake up?!" Her last words ended in a high pitched soft shrill as she tried to stay composed.

"We have him in a medically induced coma, which means we can control more or less when he wakes up. He's in what we call a minimally conscious state (MCS). We want to give his body and brain time to heal. Every brain is different, as is every injury, but in your father's case, I suspect we'll bring him out of his coma after two or three days. He has three broken ribs, which isn't bad seeing the severity of the accident. Depending on how his condition is, we'll gradually withdraw the drugs while monitoring his brain activity and other vital signs."

"What does a medically induced coma feel like?" Lucy rubbed her hands together nervously. She's always been curious, wanting to suck up all the information she can.

"That's a good question, Lucy. Well, usually comas are like twilight states — hazy and dreamlike, where you don't have fully formed thoughts, but you still feel pain and form memories that your brain invents to try to make sense of what's happening to you."

"Now you're speaking her language." Trying to make light of the situation, I glanced over at Lucy who had her eyes glued to Dr. Boomsma.

"I'm going to run a test on Paul today. And we'll have the results as soon as tomorrow. Is that OK with you?" Dr. Boomsma looked directly at me for approval.

"Yes, of course, please! *Anything* that will help us know if and when he'll wake up!"

"OK then. Other than that, his condition is serious but stable. He's getting enough fluids, his heart rate is good, his ribs need time to heal. We're doing everything we can to ensure his condition remains stable and hopefully improves."

"Yes, thank you doctor." I turned to face Dr. Meijer, "Did the trauma team present mention Sofie having any additional details that are helpful? Like how fast the boat was going?"

"What?! Papa was with someone?!" Lucy shot me a

169

confused look. Dr. Boomsma looked over to Dr. Meijer, waiting for him to answer.

"Well, I actually have to get on with my rounds. It's common practice for the police to stop by and ..." Before Dr. Meijer could finish his sentence, two police officers stepped into the room wearing a black uniform with a neon yellow stripe across the shirt, a police baton hung from their belts. "That's a coincidence. I was just telling mevrouw Stone that I wouldn't be surprised if the police checked in at some point post-accident, and here you are. I have to get going, so I'll let you speak in private." Dr. Boomsma stared me down, motioning with her eyes towards Lucy, telling me quite clearly that this was probably not a conversation where Lucy should be present. "Lucy, why don't you let me bring you to the coffee corner — we have a machine that makes the best hot chocolate and I think I saw some magazines at the nurses' station."

"Oh, isn't that nice of Dr. Boomsma? You should go Lucy. You haven't had much to eat this morning at breakfast. You could probably use some sugars. Just come back here when you're done."

Dr. Boomsma winked at me. They exited through the curtain and my heart broke for Lucy. I wasn't sure if she really wanted to go, but could tell she was doing her best to go with the flow.

"Hello, mevrouw Stone. We're sorry about your husband. I'm Officer Visser and this here is Officer Kamphuis. We're part of the Stichtse Vecht police and were at the scene of the accident yesterday." Officer Visser extended her hand and shook mine firmly. "Do you have any questions about the the accident yesterday?" Officer Visser came over to my side of the bed and pulled up a chair just a few feet away.

My throat and mouth were dry, making my teeth stick to my lips, "Actually, yes, I'd like to know more about how the accident happened. Paul was supposedly in the boat with another woman?"

"Yes, the woman Paul was with told us she was posing for a photo of her while he was steering the boat. She tried to warn him to duck but he was too late. He collided with the bridge, knocking him unconscious." Officer Visser's voice was calm and steady, showing no judgement, a true trained cop.

"What about Sofie, the woman he was with? Shouldn't she be held accountable for this? Had she not been with him, this would have never happened." I realized as soon as I suggested this I sounded insane.

"No, this was an accident. Not paying attention while steering a boat is the number one cause of boat accidents. Paul was going the speed limit of 6 kilometers per hour. Really no one was at fault."

"Sofie was the one who called 112? Was she the only witness?" I looked towards Officer Visser for confirmation.

"Yes, that's right — we got the call from Sofie. There was one person walking across the bridge when the accident happened, a 56-year-old man who lives in the area. He recalls seeing two people together in the boat, just before they went under the bridge. Then he heard screaming and ran over to the bank of the river to help dock the boat so that the ambulance could get to them. He'd actually like permission to come and visit Paul. He was just as traumatized by the whole thing as Sofie."

"I'll bet. It must have been so scary for him as well." My heart felt warm with the realization that when push came to shove, there were people like that man that ran to the rescue.

"Collisions with bridges and other boats happen unfortunately more often than you'd think. In fact, there have been three accidents on the Vecht River so far this year. I'm sure you've heard the government's plans to make open waterways safer?" Officer Visser laid a hand on my shoulder. "OK, well here's my card, should you have any questions about the police report, or need any follow up. May I tell the man who was on the bridge, meneer Smit, that he can come in and visit?"

I looked over and nodded, "Yes, I think that would be nice. I'd actually like to meet him and thank him in person, so feel free to give him my number so we can coordinate."

"OK thank you, I will. *Sterkte* for both you and Lucy."

"Thank you, officer." She exited through the curtain with her colleague. All these people coming and going was starting to feel like a disappearing act. I sat in silence for a good fifteen minutes, until Lucy came back with renewed energy.

"Hi mama!" She sat down beside me, close to Paul.

"Hi sweetie, did you score a hot chocolate?"

"Yes, and I brought one for you too." Lucy handed me a plastic cup filled halfway with cold hot chocolate and looked over towards Paul. She was still slightly out of breath from walking around. "He almost looks like a baby lying there, so helpless." Lucy cocked her head to the side.

"I know, it's strange isn't it? Paul who's been the tall, strong caregiver now laying there, not able to talk, or lift a finger." A cold shivery ran down my spine. I tried to shake it off. "Oma should be here any minute. She said she would leave Groningen first thing in the morning. It's almost 9:30." No sooner than I said this, the door swung open and Margreet walked in with Bert.

"*Oh nee! Mijn lieve zoon!*—Oh no! My dear son!" Margreet ran to Paul's bedside, hands covering her mouth in disbelief, her gold bangles clanking. Bert stood off to the side, quiet, stoic almost. Margreet reached out behind her to grab both me and Lucy, pulling us in tight to her soft warm Oma body. "Oh Jill, Lucy - this is just terrible—*Vreselijk!* And to think just two days ago we were all sitting enjoying dinner together at our house. And now this?! *Hoe is het mogelijk?*—How is it possible?"

We stood there crying together for a good while. Visiting hours in the ICU are short, so we were asked to sit in the waiting area. Bert offered to go get us all coffee. He took Lucy with him down to the hospital cafe, promising her a *gevulde koek*—Dutch cookie filled with marzipan, giving Margreet and I some time alone.

"Jill, did you find out anything else about the accident? You told me briefly over the phone, but once I heard Paul was in a coma, I checked out. It's like my body went numb. My first thought was — I'm going to lose my son!"

"Oh Margreet, I know, I'm so sorry. I was dreading calling you with the news for that very reason. We need to have hope that everything is going to be OK." Placing my arm around her, I leaned my head on her shoulder and handed her another tissue. "Paul bashed his head against a bridge while taking a picture of someone. He didn't duck on time."

"That damn camera! What the hell was he thinking?!" Margreet threw her hands up in the air.

"He started taking that camera out on the water with him this past spring. He said how beautiful the light was reflecting off the water. I just never imagined photography would lead to trouble, to a coma!"

"Who called 112?"

"Sofie. She's the new dentist in town."

"Well, then that woman is a saint! Thanks to her, my Paul is still alive. He could have died!"

Biting my tongue, I could feel jealousy and anger rumbling in my stomach. And I was annoyed with my mother-in-law calling Sofie a saint. "Supposedly he was taking pictures *with* her. I just don't get how he had to go out after work and take pictures together with some other woman." After saying this Margreet's face became like stone. I can't tell whether she's contemplating the same, whether she's angry at hearing this, or whether she even heard me. "Margreet?"

"Jill, I'm seventy-four years old, I've seen a lot. I know Paul better than anyone. If there's one thing I'm certain of, it's Paul's love for you, your love for each other. You know exactly why you fell for Paul back when you met him in Washington and he knows why he fell for you. You and Paul need each other. You're bound to each other, *veroordeeld* —condemned, or better yet, *schatplichtig*—tributary. That's just how it is — there's nothing and no one that can stop that. It's written in the stars. So if you have an ounce of doubt about Paul and this other woman taking photographs with him, I can assure you there's nothing, and I haven't even met the woman.

"Thanks Margreet, I appreciate that. You know I love Paul too. I honestly don't know what I'd do without him. In fact, one of my biggest fears is losing him. Sure he can be a royal pain in the ass and stubborn as hell, but so can I. I can't imagine being with anyone else. It's just ever since finding out he was with this Sofie woman during the accident, I just can't get rid of this sour feeling in my stomach, it keeps churning and churning. Things just don't add up."

"I'm just saying, no matter what, Paul loves *you*. He

chose *you*. Not that lazy boring Sanne in college. What you have is special. You need to stick together." Bert and Lucy were back from the cafe. Bert held two steaming cups of coffee in his hands, I spotted a cookie crumb hanging in his fluffy beard.

"We're back!" The visit to the giftshop with Bert lifted her spirits.

"We bought papa a *Get Well Soon* balloon. And we brought you a *gevulde koek*." Lucy asked at the nurses station whether she could tie the balloon to the side of Paul's bed.

"Oh that's nice." I grabbed the cookie out of the bag and took a bite. The ground almond center was still warm - it's sweetness brought a moment's comfort.

"We actually should get back to the house. You're welcome to sleep at our place as long as you'd like. Twenty minutes versus two hours for you to visit the hospital each day is quite a difference."

"Thank you, Jill. Yes, please. I think we're going to stick around here a bit longer, just so someone is here close to Paul, in case something happens, in case he wakes up. We'll be over towards the end of the afternoon."

"OK, we'll see you later. I'm glad you're staying with him." Quickly, I snuck back into Paul's room. I kissed his forehead and whispered in his ear *'you better wake up'*. I swear I saw his finger twitch out of the corner of my eye. We blew Margreet and Bert kisses in the waiting room on our way out and headed home.

Cons (for moving to America): I'd miss the *gevulde koek*.

Chapter 16

I couldn't simply brush my teeth, wash my face, and tell myself that things would all be better in the morning. Lucy decided she wanted to sleep in her own bed tonight, which was fine by me. As much as I liked having her close, I needed my space. Plus, I had trouble sleeping and didn't want to keep her up. Images of Paul, all bandaged up with tubes in his mouth haunted me — I tossed and turned. My feet were cold, so I put on a pair of thick wool socks. Lying on my stomach, I realized how much I needed to pee and mustered strength to go. The screws on the bathroom doorknob needed to be tightened as the fitting hung loose. The door gave a loud squeak as it had for a couple of months. My insides felt like Playdoh when I realized these are all things that I would normally have Paul fix. *He wasn't here to fix these things. Will he ever be here again to fix them?*

I walked back towards the bedroom and glanced over my shoulder into the kitchen that was filled with moonlight. The house was so quiet, it felt so lonely. Shivers went down my spine as I crawled back into bed. My wedding and engagement rings laid on my nightstand — I usually took them off when I went to sleep as I lathered up my hands in cream, fighting the signs of aging. Staring at my rings, I thought back to our wedding day in Gettysburg, August of 1999, just before moving to Amsterdam. It was so hot, upper nineties, which the Dutch weren't used to. I remember Paul's dad Hans with beads of sweat on his forehead. The cold Mumm bubbles waiting for us across the street at my grandmother's front lawn came as a relief, probably just before anyone had a heat stroke. So many beautiful memories, of our honeymoon out west, camping by Jenny Lake, grilling up steaks and corn on the cob at our campsite, bathing in the cold lake, running out of gas in the desert and luckily finding an old ranch along the road that helped us out. Trips within Europe as newlyweds - eating pizza in Italy by moonlight, drinking prosecco by the Mediterranean sea. What a dream! But slowly, as years went by, as our careers advanced, as we tried to get pregnant time after time, then successfully, as Lucy got older and demanded more of our attention leaving less time for each other, those romantic moments became less and less.

It wasn't pizza by moonlight, more like Wednesday night is pizza night, Friday is snack bar night, everything became routine. Paul had his chores - mowing the grass, cooking. I had mine - laundry, cleaning up the kitchen. We walked the same routes around the house each day, going through the same motions, but lately I have felt uneasy, as if something was missing even before the accident. I was so wrapped up in chores and routines to notice that something was missing, and now with this new quiet I recognized my angst of moving to America. Maybe it was that deep subconscious idea that our agreed upon twenty years were almost up. Just as the Netherlands provided me with an escape in my early twenties, was America providing Paul with an escape in his forties - but from what? Something felt off and I couldn't quite put my finger on it. Why couldn't I be happy, be satisfied with the way things were? We had a nice set-up. We went to work, we came home, ate our meals together, and talked about our days. We watched movies during the weekend, went on long walks, went out to dinner (occasionally), and had friends over. Would this really be so different in the US? What else could there be? These small things should be enough. Back in the college chapel on our wedding day, that hot summer day, we promised to live honestly, to always be kind to each other, to be partners in life, 50/50. So why did the balance feel off? Why has it felt off for a while? It's as if each half was operating parallel to the other one but not in conjunction. Why can't we ever be synced? Synchronized? And with that as my last thought, I fell asleep.

****

Tuesday morning, again I woke up to an empty bed. There was a dent in the mattress where Paul's body normally laid, reminding me of our recent discussion that we needed to get a new mattress. We could get one in America, a fresh start and a fresh mattress. His sweet honey smell lingered on his pillow case. I buried my nose into it before getting out of bed. This Tuesday felt different from every other Tuesday morning. Instead of rushing to get showered and dressed, I put things off. It's as if all my actions were in slow motion. As I sipped my coffee, waiting for Lucy to come down for breakfast I called the hospital to see how Paul did overnight. The nurses informed me that his condition stayed the same, stable. My jaw clenched. I took a seat at one of the bar chairs by the island in the kitchen. Margreet and Bert were still sleeping in the guest room. The nurse went on to tell me that if all went well, they would try to bring him out of the medically induced coma later this week. Taking notes on a scrap piece of paper, I was sure to scribble down every word they said so that I could tell Paul's office. They're going to want an update. After hanging up, I dug into the canvas bag of Paul's belongings, pulled out his phone and waited for the screen's password prompt. It's too early to call them and I'd rather avoid speaking to anyone anyway, pressing the mail icon in the lower left, his work and private email accounts appeared. Squinting against the harsh screen light my pupils adjusted to the text in front of me. While scrolling I saw a message Sofie Leegwater sent to his Gmail account. Is that *the* Sofie?

Sent: Sunday, June 23, 2019
10:04 a.m.

Paul,
Shall we meet for that photography workshop after work tomorrow? I just bought a Nikon F and could use your help in learning how to wind the film onto the spool and how to adjust its lens. Sound like a plan? I had to think the other day, thank God I had a *spiraaltje*—IUD that night we were together in Amsterdam years ago. Otherwise things would have been so much different. I'm so glad our paths crossed again, and that we can fit in this workshop before your big move.
Tot morgen! Sofie

What I felt next was like every jealous rage I've felt before only ten times bigger and therefore unfamiliar — my pulse, and my heart and some deep wild fury came together in a rhythm that gained force and momentum. I dropped Paul's phone onto the granite floor, shattering the screen. The house never felt so silent — the only thing I could hear was my heart beating in my ears as if a true thunderstorm was about to hit. Running my hand across the counter top I felt my stomach rise in the back of my throat and cupped my hand over my mouth, trying not to vomit. The next thing I knew, is the closest I've ever come to experiencing an out of body experience. The walls closed in on me as I gasped for air. *Spiraaltje* and betrayal — these two words flashed in my head like alternating neon light signs. I ran into our bedroom and started ripping out every piece of clothing I could find in Paul's closet, throwing it into a heap on the bed. Like a bulldozer, I scooped up the pile, walked out the front door, straight across the street, slammed open the gate to the *overtuin*, walked out to our dock and started throwing Paul's clothes into the Vecht. Letting out every curse word imaginable — I'm sure the fish underwater could hear the soundwaves. I'm sure I woke up all our neighbors who were tucked under their linen sheets, in their expensive Dutch Auping beds. Crying and gasping for air, I saw Geert across the river, coming out onto his balcony, looking over at me astonished, but I could give a flying fuck.

"Yeah Geert — what do you think of this?! I've got news for you Geert — men suck!!" Like a mouse going back to his hole, he popped back into his house. Like getting every last drop of *vla* — custard out of those Dutch cartons, the screaming left my lungs - leaving me empty and flat. I stood on the dock looking at Paul's polo shirts, khaki's and boxer

181

shorts floating in the water and felt an enormous sense of regret. How did I let myself snap like this? Paul's in a coma. As angry and as hurt as I was, those clothes floating there — who knows if he'll ever be able to wear them again? I decided to jump in after them, with my nightgown on. The initial cold of the water made me gasp for air. I started swimming towards his clothing, now heavy with water and gathered what I could in my arms, around my neck. I waded through the water as it was too deep to feel the bottom. Sobbing and shaking I did my best to keep my head above water, then climbed up the ladder, back up onto the dock. Our boat was there tied up. I could still see blood stains on the teak wood floor. I walked back to the house, deflated, defeated, exhausted. Paul's clothes were soaking wet. I threw them under the carport. Luckily no one heard me inside. I promised myself at that moment to pull myself together, sealed my lips, and stayed strong. If anything for Lucy, and for Margreet. I heard Lucy coming down the steps, hair tossed every which way having just rolled out of bed.

"Good morning mama!" Her eyes were small with sleep. Seeing her made me want to pull it together, for her. "Why are you all wet?"

Think of something, anything. "Oh, I was out checking on the boat and slipped off the dock and fell into the Vecht."

"Ouch! Are you OK?"

"Yes, thanks. I'm OK. Visiting hours start at 8 a.m. Do you want to come with me to see your dad? You can also go with Oma Margreet and Bert later if you want. They might like that."

"I'll go with them. I need to wake up a bit more." Lucy let out a big yawn. "Can I pick up fresh croissants for breakfast at the Jumbo?" Her eyes are not as bright as they normally are.

She had her tough girl face on, there's not enough concealer in the world to cover that up.

"Of course. Good idea. There's some cash in the kitchen drawer. If you need to come home early or want me to come get you, just let me know. I'm going to visit your dad this morning, and then again later this afternoon during visitor hours."

"Good, I want to be with him as much as possible. I'll go with you this afternoon." She gave me a big warm hug, her head which came just above mine smelled sweet like cherry blossoms. Holding her I thought about how much our world has turned upside down so quickly, in just a matter of one day - she only knew half of it. I wondered if I should tell her what her father has done. Would she hate me for not doing so later in life? As I hugged her I imagined us running off to the US to my parents' house — just the two of us. We could hop in a taxi to Schiphol right now, all we needed was a carry-on and our passports. We could get on flight KLM651 to Washington Dulles International, which usually left just after lunchtime, putting us there at 3:30 p.m. East coast time. I had enough money in my savings for our tickets - I was always sure to have just enough for emergency plane tickets. I'm sure we could live with my parents until we got our feet on the ground. I could find a job there with NPR, or at Gettysburg College doing admin or something. But then I thought about how everything that I've built these past twenty years would be for nothing. All those years spent learning the language, searching for the perfect house, the perfect job, making all those friends, navigating the entire school system — all for NOTHING! At one point I must have been holding Lucy too tight for too long, she pulled away. "OK mom, you better get showered and get going."

She kissed my cheek.

"OK, be careful. And Lucy…"

"Yes mom?"

"I love you."

"Love you too."

Chapter 17

Twenty minutes later I was in the Jeep Cherokee, heading towards the hospital. As tempting as it is to tell Lucy about what her father has done, about his betrayal, there's something so inherently strong keeping me from telling her. It was really none of her business and until I have the full story, why burden her with this? Her dad is in a coma for Christ's sake, she had enough on her mind, to go and turn things even more upside down. Besides, what would I even say?

Your father is a lying son of a bitch?

I thought I married a man I could trust?

Oh, by the way - you could have had a half sibling Lucy.

Yeah, how about them apples?!

Paul looked different to me today. Yesterday he looked like a sleeping angel, my poor wounded husband. There was a soft glow surrounding him. Today he looked like a lump. A lying dull gray lump. My heart sank to my feet when I saw him. A sour smell of urine hung in the air. The morning light shined through the dirty window, casting a square of sunlight across his white sheets. Pulling up a chair to the side of his bed, I looked around to make sure no one was within sight, and that no one could hear me. The nurses were busy at their station, drinking their first cup of coffee, shuffling through forms, typing away. Leaning over towards Paul's ear, I let the words come out softly, but clearly. I know deep down he can hear me. He had to hear me,

"Remember Paul, we promised we'd always be kind to each other, respect each other? Well, what happened to that promise?! How could you?! Sofie?! Why would you throw everything away like that?! I know about you two." Studying his face to see if I could detect any twitch, any movement, I went on, "Is that why you were with her in the boat? To discuss that night you both slept together?! Paul?! Why are you hurting me like this? I would *never* do this to you. Never." I could have sworn that his heart rate skipped a beat right then and there, on the monitor. But I couldn't be sure as just at that moment Dr. Boomsma walked in.

"*Goedemorgen* Jill." Dr. Boomsma looked like she could conquer the world. Her hair was tied back in a tight ponytail, her skin was glowing. Startled, I jumped.

"Good morning Dr. Boomsma." My voice cracked as I swallowed the remnants of phlegm from screaming earlier that morning. My throat felt raw, scarred.

"I have good news for you Jill. We ran some tests on Paul. His vital signs are looking good, the results are promising. We did a CT scan yesterday and the swelling has receded. This means we can lighten up the coma to see if Paul can come back and then assess what his level of function is." She folded her hands together, obviously pleased with the results.

"Oh my gosh! That is good news! When would you

lighten his coma?" *I'm actually not sure what to think of the news at this moment. Part of me wants to strangle him right here and now.* "We'd like to do that today, this afternoon. We have standard procedures to lighten, then check his vital signs and how he responds to stimuli. Will you be here this afternoon?"

"Yes, I was actually planning on coming in around 3 p.m. with Lucy."

"OK, I'll see if I can get two nurses on duty to assist at that time. It will probably be good to test his response to familiar family voices."

"Thank you Dr. Boomsma. Truly, you've been so wonderful."

"My pleasure. You know, Paul was very lucky. This could have all gone very differently had we not gotten him in here so quickly or if he landed the water. The gods are really looking out for him." And with that she disappeared behind the curtain, like a magician. *Hmmm, which gods might those be I wonder.*

* * * * *

Back at the house, I took out my laptop with all intentions of catching up on moving to do's, but I just couldn't focus. The Vecht was my pacifier — the only thing I could think to do was go for a swim. After downing a glass of water and a cracker with cheese, not wanting to scroll through what felt like a thousand unread WhatsApp messages on my phone, I figured I'd take a half-hour swim to the blue sign and back. Paul's smashed phone was still lying on the ground — I guess Margreet overlooked it. After all, it was a black phone on a black floor. Grateful Lucy must not have seen it, I placed it back in the canvas bag, using every ounce of willpower not to re-read Sofie's email to Paul through the cracked screen. But that willpower only lasted ten seconds. I broke out Paul's phone again and read further through their email chain, line for line. Their first correspondence began with an email from Sofie asking which camera he thought she should get. A bit flirtatious, stroking his ego *after all, you are the professional photographer ;)*. He responded with a link to a camera and then offered to take her out in the boat for a lesson before we moved. There were about four messages back and forth of them making plans to get together after Paul's work. Now it made sense why Paul asked, "How late will you be home?" He used to never care how late I'd be home. He was calculating, wanting to know exactly what time I'd be home. I thought he was just being considerate! There was a bitter taste in my mouth as I read through their flirtatious written banter. My hands started shaking, and sweating. I felt nauseous. In full punishing detail — I could visualize their little romantic photo safari escapade by boat. I couldn't get the images out of my head — Paul being all captain-like, commanding the steering wheel. Sofie sprawled out with her bare legs perched on the back bench, wearing her short flowing skirt, smiling with her big white teeth. After reading the most recent message one more time, word for word, the one where she referred to her *spiraaltje*, I turned off the phone completely and threw it in the bag. I felt betrayed, like every ounce of trust and respect was out the door. Paul signed off each message with *x* — he's never signed off a message to me with *x*. He has used *love* or *liefs* but never *x*. It seemed like something a teenager would say, not a forty-five year old man! The fact that Paul was not even here for me to take my anger out on him was probably a good thing. I felt so left in the dust by him, on so many levels.

Making it out past the blue sign *Loenen aan de Vecht* — the village boundary marker, I turned around to swim back. The water felt smooth against my skin. The sunlight reflected off the leaves of the trees along the banks, highlighting the lush green against the stark blue sky. Swimming past Sofie's house I saw that her curtains were open a crack on the ground floor. She could be peering out at me. Why doesn't she just open them all the way like all Dutch people do? It used to bother me that back home, in Gettysburg, everyone always had their blinds shut, even during the day. The Dutch usually had them open, night and day. Stemming from their Calvinist background. You only closed your curtains if you had something to hide! *Bitch. Slut. Fake.* My heart started pounding again, breath became short, rage started pumping through my veins. I climbed out of the Vecht and made my way to the shower. After rinsing off and getting dressed I made a fresh pot of coffee and looked out the window towards the Vecht. *Water doesn't lie nor keep secrets.* I whispered towards the water, *"This all doesn't fit into my plan. Now what?"*

Cons for staying in the Netherlands: words like *spiraaltje* and *krentenbaard* make me want to puke.

Chapter 18

There were three missed calls from Marlies on my phone. Only then did I realize that I never told her about Paul's accident! Like a clam in a shell, I've closed myself off these past couple of days, even when I knew talking to people like Marlies was exactly what I needed. She was my lifeline. When I called her back she picked up after one ring.

"Jill! Where have you been?! I've been so worried about you! I haven't seen you since Monday - what's going on?!" Her voice sounded urgent and concerned.

"I'm so sorry Marlies. I meant to call you sooner, it's just been a nightmare. Paul was in an accident Monday night."

"What?! Is he OK?" Her voice went up an octave.

"I don't know. I hope so. He's in a medically induced coma at the Amsterdam UMC. They're going to try to slowly bring him out of it this afternoon."

"What happened?"

"He didn't duck on time when going under a bridge in our boat and he smashed his head. Sofie was with him when it happened. Marlies...." starting to choke up, I swallowed the lump in my throat.

"Jill? What's wrong?"

"I found an email. I think Paul's having an affair with Sofie."

"Oh Jill. Are you sure? What makes you think that?"

"Believe me — I know what a *spiraaltje* is."

"That son of a bitch. Oh Jill, I'm so sorry. Can I come over? Is there anything I can do to help?" I paused, letting her question sink in. Was there anything she could do to help? These past two days felt like a strange twilight zone between the past and the future. Time stood still while I was left suspended, hanging, not knowing where I'm going, or even who I was.

"No. I can't think of anything. Just talking to you helps. I was so sure he was incapable of cheating on me, ever. He's such a devoted father and up until last night, I thought a devoted husband. Sure we had our rough patch with IVF - but I thought that only made us stronger as a couple." It helped getting the words out — otherwise I would have probably crawled up into a ball and rocked back and forth. Tears welled up in my eyes.

"I feel so betrayed not only by Paul, but by people here in Loenen."

"What do you mean?"

"I feel like everyone knew something was up, everyone but me. Rumors spread fast. People know they were together during the accident."

"Jill, don't worry. I honestly don't think anyone is thinking that at all. They're probably thinking that it's just a coincidence. What's important now is that Paul wakes up. That you get your husband back, and Lucy her father."

"Yeah, except now I feel like a fool. God, I wish we would

have just stayed in Amsterdam, where we were anonymous."

"Jill, stuff like this happens all the time, trust me. What's important now is that you hold your shit together. You're a smart woman with a great career. Stand your ground." I wasn't aware of this quasi-casual attitude towards marital affairs and have to admit I'm a bit shocked. Marlies's pep talk did help though, like a big slap in the face. "This gives you a free pass to do whatever the hell you want. You want to go off and screw the cute bartender? Go screw the cute bartender. You want to move to Timbuktu? Move to Timbuktu."

"If only it were that simple Marlies. Paul's in a freakin' coma. And then there's Lucy." My eyes teared up again.

"Do you want me to come over, Jill? I'm happy to help in any way I can."

"No, thanks. I'll be fine. I just want to be alone right now if that's OK."

"Of course. How's Lucy handling all this?"

"Surprisingly well, but she doesn't know half of what's going on. She's scared of course, hiding it with her tough girl face."

"Awh poor thing. That sounds like Lucy."

"I gotta go, Marlies." Looking at the clock I saw that it was already noon. I should eat something, Abby needed to go out, the house was a pigsty, laundry and dishes kept piling up. Margreet and Bert were visiting Paul but they'd be back soon. The mental to-do list on a regular day seemed endless, let alone this chaotic time.

"Yes, of course. Keep me posted Jill, and please let me know if you need anything. One step at a time, OK?" Her voice was calming, like one of those meditation apps.

"Thank you."

"And Jill, for what it's worth, Stijn thought Sofie smelled liked mothballs and wasn't that pretty."

"Thanks, I needed to hear that."

*****

Up until this week, I spent all my time and energy curating the perfect Dutch life. As a child, of course I never knew I'd end up being married to a foreigner, living in a different country. The pieces of the puzzle just fit together and gradually over time, with some calculated planning, I had the life I've always dreamed of. But even before finding out about Paul's one night stand, before the boat accident, was I really happy? Or was I too busy to notice? Too restless to actually sit down and check in with myself? I felt as if every meaning of home I had, was now erased. I moved over to the Netherlands, planned on having lots of babies that would come home for Christmas when they were older, that I'd have to pull out extra chairs to accommodate everyone at the table, only to be told that IVF was my only option and that there would only be one child in my future. Then the icing on the cake — my devoted husband goes off and sleeps with another woman, one year after we were married! If I didn't have such good friends like Marlies and Roos, and needed to have it pulled together for Lucy, I'd probably do something damaging, dangerous even — putting me in that all women prison in Nieuwersluis, along the Vecht.

*****

Paul wasn't in his bed when Lucy and I arrived later that afternoon. We asked at the nurses' station and they informed us that he had been moved to the medium care unit, just down the hall. *A step in the right direction I hope? Medium care sounds a lot better than intensive care.* She pointed us down the hall, on the same floor, the 7th floor. Seven was always Paul's favorite number. He really did believe it was lucky. Seven was our first apartment in Amsterdam and now our house number in Loenen — it kept following us. We passed a large mural of wild flowers — *at least they made an effort to brighten up the place*. The same cream colored linoleum floor and fluorescent lights led us down a different hallway. Walking down this hallway reminded me of when I was in the hospital giving birth to Lucy. The same lighting, the same smells. At the end of the hall there was a small waiting room with cheerful faux leather grass green chairs, and a whitewashed coffee table, surrounded by six rooms. Paul was in a double room with a divider curtain. The other bed was empty, all made up and waiting for its next patient. There was a built-in couch just below a large window. I looked out and could see we were facing southwest, towards Loenen. The sun was still high in the sky and I thought of all those people out there, like little ants on the planet, going about their day while people were stuck in here, children who were sick, patients in comas, and those ants kept marching.

Only two people were allowed at a time during visiting hours in the ICU and medium care units. I promised Margreet and Bert that Lucy and I would switch with them at 4 p.m. so they could have enough time to visit. It felt good to take turns, knowing there was always someone at Paul's bedside during visiting hours in case he woke up on his own. We each had a good hour and half in the morning and in the afternoon to be with him.

It was 3:15 p.m. when Dr. Boomsma walked in with a team of two nurses.

"Hi Jill, hi Lucy. Glad you are both here this afternoon." Lucy and I nodded our heads and I reminded myself to let her do all the talking, instead of my usual interrogation style. "Now, what's going to happen is we're going to slowly lower Paul's painkiller and sleeping aid dosage. We're going to monitor how his body responds to stimuli, as well as monitor his atrial pressure. We have to keep him on the ventilator until he fully comes out of this coma. If all goes well, and he shows signs of consciousness, and his blood pressure is OK, we'll continue weaning him off..."

"And, if not?!" I couldn't help but interrupt, the words left my mouth before I had time to consider how Lucy might react and how rude it was to interrupt.

"If not, then we keep him on the same dosage, in the medically induced coma for another day. Then we'll try again in a day, or two. Monitoring his blood pressure will allow us to make sure there's no more bleeding in his brain."

"OK. We'll get out of your way and let you do what you have to do." Clearing my throat I moved back to make way for the two accompanying nurses, grabbing Lucy's hand, pulling her back with me. We sat in the chairs on the far side of the room and watched.

One nurse, must have been her late twenties. She was tall and had auburn hair piled on top of her head in a messy sort of way. She gave me a friendly smile as she made her way to the computer beside Paul's bed that had a flashing bright blue screen and she began typing away. The other nurse, my age, stepped over in her Dr. Scholl's type clogs to one of several tubes hooked up to Paul and started fidgeting with it. Dr. Boomsma called out some number to her along with the name of what sounded like a medicine. I assumed it was regarding the dosage. Lucy and I looked at each other, raising our eyebrows at the same time as we sat amongst the beeping, the typing, the checking, the monitoring, the dripping, the waiting. At one point Dr. Boomsma said loud and clear,

"Paul, squeeze my hand if you can hear me." Silence. Paul's hand didn't move, not even the slightest bit. "Paul, I want you to squeeze my hand if you can hear me." Dr. Boomsma held Paul's hand waiting. "Jill, why don't you say something to him? Ask him to open his eyes."

I swallowed and took a step towards his bed. He looked peaceful, his face was soft. "Paul, it's Jill. Can you open your eyes for me?" For a split second I could swear I see his eyes flutter, but at that very second, one of many beeps, medium tone, becomes more prominent, more frequent. Both nurses and Dr. Boomsma looked at the blood pressure monitor.

"His blood pressure is increasing. Femke, I need you to administer 50 milligrams of Propofol." Dr. Boomsma's orders were curt.

"What's happening?" Lucy asked, alarmed. She stood, leaning towards Paul's bed to have a better look, stabilizing herself by placing her hands firm on her upper thighs.

"Your father's blood pressure shot up, which means he's not ready yet to come out of the coma. We don't want to risk any bleeding in the brain. He had some and this is the way for the body to tell us that he needs more time to heal. We can try again tomorrow."

The moment Dr. Boomsma said this, I felt scared. What if he doesn't wake up? What am I going to do without him? Did he only make it to forty-five, enough time to see a child born and a high school graduation? What about the rest?

He has to see the rest! There was so much I wanted to talk to him about. So much we still needed to figure out. We were on the verge of starting a whole new adventure in the US. We needed to have a real conversation, and who knew when he'd be in a state to do that? I needed to figure out if I wanted this NPR job. We needed to figure out whether we were moving to America, as we had originally planned to do. Whether we're going to accept the offer on the house. I didn't want to make these decisions alone. Like a captain of a ship facing a storm, all my calculations and plans were thrown off course. Was this the universe's cruel way of giving me more time to figure things out, for myself?

*****

Lucy and I walked out to the waiting room, her arm was wrapped around my waist and her head rested on my shoulder. I could sense her disappointment. We must have been casting off our despondency with the look on our faces, because Margreet and Bert stood up and Margreet started crying. She then cupped her hand around her mouth and walked towards us to embrace. Her soapy perfume smell was overpowering.

"It's OK Margreet, they're going to try again tomorrow. They're just being super careful about waking him up. His body's not ready yet." I discreetly dislodged myself from her bear hug.

"I know, you're right — I was just so sure he'd wake up today."

"Margreet, before you go in there, could I speak to you in private? There's something I want to talk to you about." Her eyes showed concern. "Lucy, can you wait with Bert here for a of couple minutes?"

"OK. But mom, I told Julie I was going to hang out with her after this. She's expecting me at 5 p.m." Lucy pulled out a pack of UNO cards and sat down next to Bert.

"OK. We'll only be a couple of minutes." Margreet followed me halfway down the hallway and around the corner. No one else was around, so I figured I might as well blurt it out right there.

"Margreet — remember I used to call you when Paul and I were first together, every time we had an argument? You were like an emergency hotline for me. I figured — no one knows Paul as well as you and you're the only one who would understand when he acted like a jerk, or helped me know what to do next." Margreet let out a laugh and gave me a warm smile.

"Yes, I never minded you calling me. I know Paul can be a royal pain in the ass. He's hard on me too sometimes as his mother. But Jill, you make each other better people. You two have something special. You belong together." The more words that came out of her mouth, the more tears formed in my eyes until I couldn't hold them back anymore.

"I'm not so sure, Margreet."

"What do you mean, Jill?"

"Paul slept with another woman. The same woman that was with him in the boat, the day of the accident."

"Oh, Jill. How do you know?" Facing me, she grabbed both of my arms and looked me straight on, giving me full attention.

I wiped my tears with the back of my hand, "Because I found an email from Sofie to Paul referring to a time they slept together." I wanted to throw up after regurgitating the words.

"Oh Jill, come here. I'm so sorry." She pulled me in and I cried on her shoulder, shaking, broken. Did she already know? Does she have some sort of sixth sense? She took a deep breath. "Listen, I left Hans, but that was just because I fell *in love* with Bert. It was the seventies — things were different then. Had Bert not been in my life, I'd probably still be with Hans. But in Paul's case, he messed up. Once. How long have you been married? Twenty years? How long have you been together? Twenty-two? Jill, men, they need attention, need to be praised and appreciated. When they're not, they go look for a new *baasje*—owner. But don't worry, one thing I know for sure is that Paul loves *you*. That I'm certain of. Whatever he had with that other woman, it was nothing. I think every man, and woman for that matter, should be allowed one glitch in their marriage. Don't you?"

"I wouldn't call this a glitch, Margreet. They had sex! Your son, my husband, the father of Lucy had sex with another woman!!" The thought alone was so painful.

"Now Jill, *wees een grote meid*—be a big girl and get over it. When Paul wakes up, have a good conversation with him. Tell him you know, confront him. I know he'll regret it, he'll come clean. You need to forgive him and move on. Forgive and forget. Go get some marriage counseling if need be. But don't let this one mistake, that he made years ago, ruin what you two have."

I hated when she said *wees een grote meid* or called me *klein meisje*—little girl. It was so patronizing. Paul always said she meant this in an endearing way. But I always felt like her pep talks made me out to be a little mouse with tiny fists. I am a big girl. I'm forty-four years old! I have a career! I have a daughter! I've been living in a foreign country for twenty years now! I can handle this! But I guess when you're seventy-four years old, that thirty year age difference, in Margreet's mind, justifies calling me a *klein meisje*. But I still hated it.

"Forgive and forget?!" Easier said than done. All of a sudden I felt very alone. I was frustrated by Margreet's lackadaisical attitude — that in her mind, her son could do no harm.

"Marriage is *hard werken*—hard work. Come, Lucy's waiting." We walked back to where Lucy and Bert were in the middle of their UNO card game.

"OK, time to go Lucy."

"Everything all right?" Bert looked up at us both.

"Yes, for now. You should go see Paul. Visiting hours are over in an hour."

"OK. We'll see you back at the house. Let me cook for you and Lucy tonight." Margreet knew how much I hate cooking.

"Thank you. That would be really nice." Lucy and I started walking down the hall. Glancing over my shoulder through the crack in Paul's door I saw his bare foot peeping out from under the sheets. I used to massage his feet when we first met, while we watched TV. But over the years, as his feet got older, more calloused, I simply stopped. I stopped touching him all together and I don't know why. I just did. I used to run my fingers along the back of his neck when he drove. I thought about doing it now, but there's something deep inside me that kept me from doing it. Paul was always the one to come give me a kiss before leaving for work, or to give me a hug out of the blue. I came to rely on *his* initiative, hoping he wouldn't give up on me, that he'd keep providing the kisses, the hugs, the touching. If I would have continued massaging his feet, giving him more physical attention would he still have gone off with Sofie? Marlies said she schedules sex with Stijn for every Sunday night. She didn't always look forward to it, but at least they had regular sex, and she knew when it was coming. She said that she learned that was the best way to keep a man from going off with other women in a marriage seminar. Maybe I should have tried that. Now, I'm too late.

*****

Lucy and I hopped in the Jeep and merged onto the A2.

"Mom, how old do you have to be to get your driver's license in the US?" She asked while staring at herself in the side view mirror.

"Sixteen. You take Driver's Ed classes as part of your school curriculum. In Gettysburg, all we had to do for the practical exam was drive around the block, and parallel park between two cones." Just thinking back to Mr. Miller's Driver's Ed class brought a smile to my face. It was the first time I had smiled in a week.

"Sixteen! So I can start driving soon after we move to America?!"

"That's right. You'll have to take a couple lessons and pass the test at the DMV. But there are a lot of accidents, you know. We used to have parties out at my friend Jared's farm - lots of windy roads to get out there. Kids would drink of course, then it was tricky how you got home. Usually our parents would have to come get us. Promise me you'll never get behind the wheel after drinking, and never get in the car with someone who has been drinking!"

"I know. I promise. You've said this all before."

"I can't say it enough. That's why I like how, over here,

you can get your driver's license when you're seventeen and drink at eighteen. It just makes more sense. Whereas in America, you can drive early, but you can't legally drink until 21 which means there are more kids sneaking around and drinking more than they can handle. Most American kids were never allowed to drink on occasion with their parents, learning slowly but surely how to handle it. Of course Dutch kids sneak around too, but I'd venture to say less." As I said this we passed two boys who looked about eighteen sipping glasses of rosé out on the terrace by the Hans and Frietje cafe. "See! Look over there. You just don't see that kind of thing in America, two boys drinking rosé out on a terrace, there's proof right there!" Lucy stretched her neck past me in the driver's seat so she could see and smiled. "You know — alcoholism runs in our family. Your uncle Ben has been sober for six years." I felt Lucy's eyes turn towards me in surprise.

"Really?!"

"He couldn't handle alcohol. And I remember him telling me something he learned in his AA meetings — 'alcoholism ends in three ways - death, jail, or sobriety' and unfortunately, I fear he's right."

When we got home, Lucy changed her outfit to cut-off jean shorts and a crop top, then gave me a hug, and headed out the door to Julie's.

Con for America: They have their drinking and driving ages backwards. Teach those kids how to drink before putting them behind the wheel.

Chapter 19

As I approached the front door, I found a beautiful bouquet of pink and white peonies - my favorite flower. There was a card that read:

Thinking of you Jill. This is a good time to remind you of the story you once told me, how you'd lay out your outfits ready the night before in high school along with a pep-talk sticky note with the abbreviation: D.W.B.H., which you said stood for 'don't worry, be happy'. To quote Bob Marley twice in the same message, "Everything's gonna be alright". Liefs, Marlies

God I love that woman, such a good friend. I always thought you had to have a long shared history in order to be close friends, but the older I got, the more I found that it's not the shared history that matters - it's being on the same level, understanding each other. Knowing where the other one is coming from and meeting them there. It's about being able to laugh, cry, scream, vent, and listen.

Roos and Marlies made me feel stronger, like I belonged, was appreciated, and less alone in this world. I used to wonder if my being American made me a more interesting friend for them. But I've come to realize that, if anything, I was a nice reminder for them about how great they have it here in the low countries, because I'm always pointing that out. Like last King's Day when the Dutch broke out their orange finery, hung up their Dutch flags, and ate their *oranje tompoes*—Dutch custard dessert. Marlies asked me what I liked better, the 4th of July or King's Day. I said King's Day because it's more *feestelijk*—festive, plus all ages come together, and there's an entrepreneurial undertone. Kids selling their old toys flea market style, painting nails or faces, playing their violin or singing for money. I once earned enough money for Paul and me to go out to a fancy dinner by turning our ground floor Amsterdam apartment into a public women only restroom, one euro a pop. I removed the bathroom mirror so they wouldn't take up too much time checking their hair and make-up. Then there's all the people out on their boats dancing to DJ's or brass bands playing out in front of nursing homes while the *oudjes* sip their coffee. Sure I love a little Bruce Springsteen, fireworks on the Mall in Washington, and the fireman's carnival - but there's something about King's Day that attracts tourists for a reason. I don't recall ever hearing anyone say, "I booked a flight to America so I can be there on the 4th of July." But as much as I loved King's Day - there were festivities when I felt very out of place. All anyone had to do was play André Hazes or another Dutch folk singer and I wanted to crawl in a hole and disappear. That music has always been alienating for me. I would never be Dutch enough for that.

I had one hour alone in the house before Margreet and

Bert came home. One hour to put my investigative journalism skills to use. Loenen was a small village. Everyone knew each other's business. How did I not pick up on Sofie and Paul's vibe? How could I be so blind? Back when Ruud and Roos split — it was the talk of the town, for months. News of Ruud's affair with the golf trainer spread like rapid fire. People were, and still are, bad mouthing him. "Every time they do the custody switch of Julie — he gets on Roos's case for hanging out with *his* friends in *his* town. If only Ruud was more amicable towards her, they could coexist at parties and at least then Julie wouldn't be the *dupe van alles*—have to suffer." If people are always speculating on Ruud and Roos's divorce, I'm sure they're speculating about Paul and the hot new *dentist* Sofie! Where to start...Facebook!

Whipping out my laptop, I brought up my Facebook page and did a search under Sofie Leegwater. Bullseye, there she was, blond hair, white teeth and all. In her profile photo she was wearing a pink ribbed top, pulling her shades halfway down and looking into the camera with puckered lips. Gross. Scrolling through her photos I saw some amateur attempts at artistic photography, mostly nature shots and landscapes. There was one photo in particular that caught my eye. I recognized the World War Two bunker, between Loenen and Nieuwersluis, in the background along the Vecht. Double clicking to bring the photo up full screen I saw two shadows stretched out across the water, making that all too used muscle flexing posing, the shadow next to hers was much taller. I studied the contours of the shoulders, the head, and the posture. It was Paul. I was sure of it. The photo must have been taken just before the accident. So inappropriate of Sofie to post this on Facebook. My stomach turned. Seven likes, one heart — none of them Paul of course. He's not even on Facebook. Scrolling through the four comments I saw one from Femke! Femke, *the* Queen of Loenen who just had us over for dinner three weeks ago! Here I was so thrilled to be invited, and the whole time she's friends with Sofie on Facebook?! Does Femke know that they slept together?

Surfing the web - I pulled up the local news article from last Monday's accident *'Man (45) raakt ernstig gewond aan zijn hoofd bij bootongeluk langs de Vecht*—Man (45) serious head injury after boat accident along the Vecht'. Studying the photo again, looking more closely — I had only seen it briefly the day after the accident — I saw Sofie talking to two police officers, holding her arms up in the air. It's difficult to see Paul who was lying on the bridge with a white sheet held around him, surrounded by the two ambulance personnel in neon yellow and green uniforms, two emergency nurses, two police officers. I saw a trauma helicopter back in the field next to the all-female prison, which was just across from the bridge. I saw police officers on our boat, inspecting the scene under the bridge with their flashlights. The whole scene looked scary, horrendous even. It reminded me of something you normally see on CSI, on TV, not along the Vecht River!

Letting the images sink in, I took a deep breath and contemplated what to do with the remaining half hour to myself. Abby still needed to go out. I could walk over to Femke, confront her, ask her whether she knew anything more. What have I got to lose? My husband, who up until now I've always trusted, cheated on me and is now in a coma! What's talking to Femke going to do? What's it going to change? Nothing. But, I felt like I needed to find out how much of a fool I'd been. Did the entire village know except for me?

Have I been so blind? How could I, a journalist who always gets the full story, be living with only half the story all this time!? Just then the doorbell rang.

*****

I peered through the peephole and spotted blond hair, but couldn't quite make out who it was. I opened the door. "*Wat doe jij hier?*—What are you doing here?" I was flabbergasted and felt a sudden sense of panic take over, as I saw Sofie in front of me. Fumes of her *le temps perdu* perfume flew past me. I was sneaky enough that day after my dental appointment to call Scents in Amsterdam and ask them to look up her first name with the Loenen postcode in their system. I said she was a friend and I wanted to get her a bottle for her birthday. I lied. I'm not proud of it, but I had to know. That stuff costs 190 euro for a 50 milliliter bottle! She was holding a so-called *Oud Zuid* bouquet of flowers. I knew this because I liked to buy these lovely mixed Dutch bouquets at the market in Breukelen on Friday's. *Of all people, what the F?*

"Jill, can we talk?"

"About what? This isn't really a good time. I'm expecting my mother-in-law back any minute."

"Please, just ten minutes of your time." Her eyes were pleading. She looked sincerely upset.

"OK, come in." I led her to the table in the dining room. I didn't offer her anything to drink which went against my nature.

"How's Paul doing?"

What else was she going to say? My heart started pounding fast, my breath became shorter. I could feel the rage bubbling.

"Well, maybe you can better tell me, seeing you slept with him." The words shot out of my mouth like a loaded pistol. Sofie's steel blue eyes widened and she struggled to swallow as if there was a big lump in her throat. "I found an email on Paul's phone, alluding to how you guys slept together, saying thank God you had a *spiraaltje*—IUD at the time." It felt like I was watching myself from above. Normally, I hate confrontation, avoided it at all costs, but not now, not with this.

"Jill, please..." She gasped. I didn't give her a chance to speak.

"Paul's my husband! We're married! We have a daughter. You can't just prance in there and ..."

"Jill, that was years ago! What, like nineteen years or something. It meant nothing. You were gone for your work. Paul came over for a drink after a party, one thing led to another. It was just a fling." She blurted out midway through my sentence.

"What?! Just a fling?! We were trying to start a family. He was, and still is married. Why are you taking photography lessons from him? Just stay away!" Tears welled up in my eyes and I felt warm drops run down my cheek.

"Look, at the time I didn't know Paul was married. Otherwise, I would have never slept with him."

"What about your recent email bringing up that night again, how thank God you weren't pregnant in the end?"

"I meant that as a joke, more like, look at us now taking photos of nature as friends and how glad I was that our one night stand didn't result in a pregnancy."

"But you were with him during the accident. You two were off taking photos, or making out, or whatever it is you guys do in our boat." Her mouth hung open, offended by my accusation.

"I was with him, Jill, because that was going to be our last of two photography sessions. He was going to show me how to use my wide-angle lens and how to use water as a mirror! He said you were all moving to the US. It was purely professional. He was steering the boat. He turned around to take a picture of me. I yelled 'duck!' but it was too late. Believe me, I felt horrible when I realized you two were together, after sleeping with him all those years ago. I honestly had no idea. You kept your maiden name, so nothing rang a bell when you both came in for a check-up. I had only just moved to Loenen a couple months prior, I didn't know that many people in this town. And ever since your goodbye party, it felt like everyone in town has been talking behind my back."

As she talked, I studied her, every word that came out of her mouth I weighed carefully.

"Why did you even take photography lessons from him given your past, with the one-night stand, and the gossip?"

"We got to talking at your goodbye party about photography, and he offered. I didn't think anything of it, truly. I was just grateful that he was going to teach me some new techniques. He loves you Jill, and Lucy, that's all he talks about! Please don't let that fling that happened years ago mess things up."

"Mess it up? But, it already has!" A sadness washed over me. It sounded like she was being truthful, but that didn't take away from the fact that Paul cheated on me years ago, then lied about giving her photography lessons, behind my back. Snot started dripping. Sofie grabbed a tissue from her purse. "They tried bringing him out of his coma, but he's not ready yet. We're hopeful though."

"That's great news! Look, Jill. What Paul and I had was just a fling. It didn't mean anything."

I squeezed the wet tissue into a ball and hid it in my fist. "And just a fling?! What if you had ended up pregnant?"

"Yeah, but I wasn't, and thank God, because just as much as you don't want Lucy to have a half-sibling, do you think I want to share my child with another family for the rest of my life?! I don't want any strings attached, just as much as you." Her voice was not angry, it was kind. My head hurt from doing all the math, all the calculations and probabilities, all the 'what if's'.

"As soon as I found out Paul was married, I kept my distance. We had no contact after that night, I swear. Not until last April when he came in and sat in the dentist's chair. When you invited me to your party, I saw it as a way to normalize things. After all, it had been nineteen years. I thought by showing up, maybe it would send a signal that nothing was going on, because you invited me."

I looked at her, she looked at me. My tongue was tied. I wanted to believe her, I really did. But I still felt like my heart had been ripped out of my chest. That the man I thought was a devoted husband and father turned out to be a fraud, and that pained me to no end. The silence was interrupted by my phone ringing. It was my mom, saved by the bell, "I'm sorry Sofie, I have to take this." She nodded and stood up to walk to the door. I followed her out.

"Well, I think we're done here anyway."

"OK, but Jill, one more thing. Please know, I feel terrible. I'm so sorry to have put you through all of this. Please know that it was in no way my intention to break up your marriage. There was never anything between us. It's a small town. Can we just put this all behind us? Please?" She went to grab my hands, but I pulled them away, still holding the wet balled up tissue in my fist.

"Sorry, this is all just too much to process. Please just stay away from Paul, from me, and Lucy. It's embarrassing enough as it is. I feel like a pawn in Loenen's own soap opera chess game."

"I understand. Jill, just please know that I'm truly sorry." I opened the door. I had already clicked my mom away. I can call her right back.

"Goodbye Sofie." My eyes started twitching uncontrollably. I felt my blood pressure rising, my breath shortening.

I closed the door behind her. I felt empty—*Leeg*.

Chapter 20

Screw Loenen, screw the Netherlands. Even though our plans to move back to the US were now in total hiatus — I couldn't help but wonder what it would be like to live there again. We've been there plenty of times over the course of the past twenty years, going once, sometimes even twice a year. Visiting the US regularly was important to me so that Lucy could hear English spoken from others, besides me and the television. I also wanted Lucy to see, and know where I grew up. To know what honeysuckle smelled like and what it's like to roll down a hill because there are a lot of hills just calling out for a good roll. In the Netherlands, this doesn't exist, unless it's manmade, or if you're down in the Limburg province a two and a half hour drive away. That doesn't mean that visits to the US were easy-going and relaxing. They were often more challenging than not. There was the pressure to have a good time, and to get along with all the family members that came out of the woodwork to see us. And it's because those visits were so intense, between catching up with my three brothers, their partners, and kids

— that part of me actually looked forward to moving back and creating my own physical home instead of always having to rely on my old home, staying at my parents. I could stop by and have an Arnold Palmer (half lemonade, half ice tea) on the back deck with my parents. The fresh lemonade doesn't compare to the syrups they add water to here. I'd simply drop by, similar to what my current neighbors have with their daughters — just pop by for a quick visit.

I called my mom back as soon as I saw Sofie leave the driveway. I wasn't in the mood to talk to her, but it was always so hard with the time difference. I owed her an update, but I was scared at what she'd say if I told her about Paul's infidelity, afraid that would ruin their bond. She's always liked Paul, but she's also one to hold a grudge. The more she pried into our marriage, "Are you and Paul getting along? I never hear you talk about him," — the more I pushed the subject of our marriage away. She just misinterpreted things, drew her own conclusions. Which is what happens when your only source of information is over the phone, no hand signals, no facial expressions. I didn't want to permanently damage Paul's relationship with his own mother-in-law. I would need to tread carefully, choose my words carefully.

"Hi mom."

"Hi, Jill. Did you click me away before?"

"Yes, sorry. I just had an unexpected visitor, that's all."

"Oh OK, I just wanted to check in to see how Paul's doing, how you're doing?"

"Paul's still in a coma. They tried bringing him out today but it didn't work — his blood pressure shot up. They're going to try again tomorrow."

"Oh jeez Jill, I'm so sorry. Your voice sounds different.

Are you OK?" There's something about mothers, how they detect when something else is going on.

"I have a lot on my plate at the moment."

"You know, Jill, no matter what happens, you can always come back here and stay with us."

"I know. Thank you. I appreciate you saying that."

"No, but really, I mean it. When you left us, back in what was it — 1999, gosh that was a long time ago, I never told you this, but you left a big hole Jill. Sometimes I wonder what things would have been like if you had settled in Gettysburg. Would you have ever gone off to Europe with Paul? I could have had you guys over here for these past twenty years! I'm not sure if any mother knows what they're doing, they just act on instinct most of the time — I wanted you to follow your heart. But I'll admit, it was hard. I mean, you are my only girl." She sniffed in between her words. "I just hope by us letting you go that you didn't feel like you weren't wanted or welcome to stay. You are and will always be our daughter. I'm so proud of you and everything you've become. I know I don't tell you that enough, but I am."

"Thanks, mom. This isn't your fault, none of it is. I don't hold anything against you or dad. Every move in life up to this point has been my decision. So if anything, I think it was brave of you and dad to let go. I'm not sure I'll be able to do the same so easily with Lucy." Taking a deep breath, I leaned back on my chair. "How did it feel — to say goodbye and not know if or when I'd ever come back?" There was a long moment of silence, then I heard my mom's breath as she opened her mouth to speak.

"It hurt, Jill, in all honesty. But that's part of being a parent, letting go. It's not easy, that's for sure. Love and let go."

"But how?"

"Well — it's like the Dalai Lama once said, 'Give the ones you love wings to fly, roots to come back and reasons to stay.' I guess you didn't have enough reasons to stay."

"Mom, that's not true."

"I know, I'm messing with you."

"I like that quote though. I'll have to remember that one. I'm realizing that more and more too — that we all just do our best, and as they say in Dutch, *meer kan je niet doen*—you can't do anything more than that. Margreet and Bert just pulled up to the house. Margreet is cooking us all dinner."

"OK Jill. Hang in there, promise? We love you."

"I love you too." As close as she sounded during our conversation, that's how far away physically she felt when I hung up. An ocean in between.

* * * * * *

Huisje, boompje, beestje—house, tree, pet — a popular Dutch saying basically to explain when one is perfectly settled. The best comparison I could think of in English was the white picket fence that surrounds the traditional American home, a detached house with a lawn, a swing, rose bushes, and lace curtains. As I stared at our sturdy brick house with a lawn, a fence, a swing – I was reminded of the white picket fence scene that we so badly wanted to escape in DC back when we first met. We've actually created that same scene for ourselves here in Loenen! And then I realized, this "American" dream we were trying to escape, isn't American at all. It can exist anywhere. The Dutch strive for it too. And once you have it, it's not all that bad. It's actually nice.

When we bought this house five years ago — I went

through each room with sage and a feather, to rid the bad vibes. My mom sent me a Native American ritual book that came with the sage, feather, and three pages of instructions on how to cleanse your home of evil spirits. Diligently, I went through each empty room before moving in all our stuff. Paul and Lucy rolled on the floor laughing at me. "Laugh all you want. Fact of the matter is, we bought this place from a divorced couple. I'm sure there were loads of arguments taking place behind these walls — I want a fresh start!" And I truly believed that's what we had. Our own little America in the Netherlands, complete with a driveway, lawn, swing, and front porch. And I absolutely loved it.

These ideas of what made the perfect house, the perfect marriage, the perfect life — were instilled in me at an earlier age. In 1991, I saw *Return to the Blue Lagoon*. Lilly, played by Milla Jovovich, and Richard, played by Brian Krause, were stuck on a South Pacific island, alone together as teenagers. I was fascinated by the idea that they could survive on this island together. They were living in paradise, catching their own fish and developing a natural love for each other, one that allowed them to survive. At one point they have a rescue opportunity to leave the island but they turn it down — choosing to stay in the home they created together. I wanted a relationship like that, one that developed naturally, over time, one where you're working alongside each other so closely as friends in order to survive your surroundings but then BAM one day you realize you're in love with that person. Just like Lilly and Richard, I wanted someone that I could build a life with, build a home, create a bubble, a safe haven in which to live together. Someone with whom I could share my deepest fears and thoughts. I wanted someone who was my companion, my equal.

While I believed in fate, it turned out "what is meant to be" doesn't necessarily knock you off your feet like it does in the movies — at least not at first. I had been on a hunt all throughout college. I was obsessed with looking for a life partner who matched the movies I saw in the early nineties. I wanted that raw and pure love, the love you can't live without.

Despite my pious-like plea for some sort of otherworldly divination, I had a list of flings, or shall I say, noteworthy love education specimens. They were all studies in the various types of relationships one could have, me the student, trying to determine who could be my equal. Now I realized this may have seemed contradictory — on the one hand I was looking for fate to bring me and my future husband together but on the other hand, like a scientist, I was trialing various relationships to see which one was right. But in my mind these two things could co-exist (like scientists who believe in God)!

During my senior year of high school, I dated a professional golfer whose breath smelled like sour milk, a handsome Mormon who tried to convert me during a hike halfway through our first date, and a sweet Mennonite who took me to prom and shook my hand goodnight. During my freshman year of college I dated a jeep-driving smoker obsessed with Bob Dylan. During my sophomore year of college I dated a strict Catholic in ROTC training for the army who wanted to marry a virgin (eliminating any possibility of a future together). During my senior year of college I dated two native Gettysburgians - one a patchouli-laced hippie who owned a coffeeshop in town and liked to walk around barefoot. The other was the son of die-hard Republicans who owned apple orchards. Every time I saw his parents in the grocery store, I had to re-introduced myself. They were so aloof and uninterested in either me or who their son was dating. This was another requirement, in addition to him being my equal, smart, and driven — I had to like his parents because I couldn't imagine a life where I didn't get along with my in-laws. My parents got along well with theirs.

Within those love experiments, there was always something off though, about the aforementioned specimens. Sometimes it would take me a while to figure it out because for everything that was off about them there was an element that attracted me to them in the first place, making me want to date them. The patchouli-laced hippie introduced me to poetry, the son of the Republicans introduced me to Johnny Cash music and we had a blast riding through his orchards on a four-wheeler. I didn't sleep with all these men or even date them for that long. I didn't even find all of them sexually attractive. I was simply dating around, gathering, collecting, studying, waiting for the love to grow, see if it would stay, see if we would one day look at each other and say BAM! You're the one!

When I was in college, around 21, my mother asked me while we were eating our usual Thomas's English Muffin with Musselman Apple Butter breakfast, why I was dating two men at once (the hippie, and the son of apple orchard owners). "How am I going to know who's the right one if I don't get to know them all? Men date around all the time, why can't women?" She laughed. My parents were fairly liberal and they never really questioned me about the guys I dated, nor pressured me to get married right away and have kids. If anything, my mom and I talked fairly openly about each date. We even came up with a list at one point of all the guys I dated, giving them funny monikers like Milk Breath and Jeep Man.

Looking back, I saw my obsession with finding "the one" was rooted in wanting a home I could call my own. I knew I wanted to leave the warm and comfortable cocoon of my parent's house but I never imagined living alone. I'd always imagined building a life with someone, from the beginning of my life, from the ground up ala Lilly and Richard. But there I was, just graduated from college, with an internship at NPR in Washington but on the finding a life partner front, I was, well, lost. That obsession gave me control and made me feel if I could just make that part right, the rest would fall into place. Then along came Paul. He was my equal. I respected him. He made me laugh, knew how to get me all fired up. He brought out the best in me and sometimes the worst, but that was OK. I placed all my chips on Paul in creating this home I could call my own. Now he's in a coma and he betrayed me. My plan backfired, my hunt for Mr. Right backfired. I should have listened to my 8th grade teacher who saw how boy obsessed I was when she said, "Jill, a man is never going to make you happy. *You* have to make yourself happy." Damn it Miss May!

******

Lucy rolled in from Julie's house around the same time as Margreet and Paul. Margreet got to work on dinner. The smell of garlic and onion filled the kitchen. Margreet stood over the counter next to the stove making meatballs with her weathered short fingers. Her hands looked like they served many years of child rearing, cleaning, cooking, caring. Bert sat across from her reading the newspaper, drinking a beer out of a glass. Lucy was next to Bert scrolling through her Insta feed.

"Wow, that smells so good!"

Margreet threw the meatballs into the pan, making a sizzling sound.

"Any news on Paul? Did anything happen during your visit with him?" Just thinking of him there in the hospital brought so much unease.

"No news. I held his hand, read him a couple of articles out loud from today's paper. I feel like that might help stimulate his brain somehow." Margreet turned down the heat on the burner.

"Maybe you're right. We'll know more tomorrow, I suppose. Lucy, did you have fun at Julie's?"

"Yeah, we just hung out and watched YouTube make-up tutorials." Lucy didn't lift her eyes from her phone as she talked to me.

"Lucy, remember what I said? Please look at people when they talk to you."

"Oh right, sorry mom." She looked up, placed her phone down on the table.

"Dinner is ready in five minutes!" Margreet checked on the potatoes and vegetables roasting in the oven. "Jill, grab yourself a glass of wine. I opened up a bottle of red over there."

At one point during dinner I thought back to my conversation in the hospital with Margreet. The Dutch always had such a sober way of looking at things. Never dramatic. As refreshing as that was, sometimes I missed the drama. I liked making a big deal of my sore throat or a marital affair. But the combination of soberness and directness was growing on me. Maybe the way we communicated was so deeply culturally embedded it couldn't change? I'm not sure I could ever become as direct as the Dutch. It just wasn't in my nature, but there have been times when I wish it was. Like when the hairdresser charged me the adult price for Lucy's haircut when she was under twelve. Or when Henk down the street talked my ear off when I was in a rush to get to work.

The shrill scratch of Lucy's scraping fork against her plate brought me back to real time. "Lucy, can you please stop pushing food around on your plate?" Lucy, whose mood swings have become a daily thing, had been especially quiet. I was worried about her. Maybe I was too hard on her before. I should let things like table manners go. This has got to be tough for her especially. I made a mental note to check in with her more often, to encourage her to voice what she was feeling. Margreet has always been able to get more out of her than I was — the *Oma*-effect I called it. Those two could talk on the phone for hours, whereas I was lucky if I got two sentences out of her.

"I'm not very hungry."

"But, you love Oma's meatballs!"

"Oh that's OK, let her be Jill," Margreet waved her hand through the air. "Lucy, what did you think when you saw your dad today at the hospital? I'll bet it was hard for you." Margreet wiped her lips with her napkin and took a sip of her wine.

"I don't know. Scary, I guess." Tears welled up in her eyes as she continued to look down at her plate, food shoved off to the edges.

"It is scary. He's going to be OK though, we have to stay positive. Tomorrow they're going to try to wake him up again." Margreet reassured her.

"I know, I'm just scared of losing him." She cried, and I walked up behind her, grabbed her in my arms, and nestled my face in her neck. Margreet reached across the table and grabbed her hand.

"You're not going to lose him. Don't you worry." Margreet rubbed her thumb over the back of Lucy's hand. Bert listened quietly, sympathetically, sipping his beer. We finished our dinner, except for Lucy, and all helped clean up. Bert played a bit on our piano. He has never really read music as he preferred to make the music up as he went along, which resulted in the most beautiful melodies. Warm notes filled the room. Lucy sat in a chair next to him listening — she already had on her pajamas. He didn't play for long though — he said his arthritis was getting to him, that he couldn't move his hands like he used to. Margreet and Bert retired early to bed. Perhaps they wanted to give Lucy and me as much privacy as possible.

The NPR job kept popping into my head — I didn't want to jeopardize this opportunity, but I was running out of time. I had to be careful how I played my cards. I told them I'd let them know by the end of the month, that's in three days! I shot Catharine a carefully curated but short message, saying there was a family emergency. I told her that Paul is in a medically induced coma due to a boat accident and asked her for more time, and that I was still very interested, I just need to see how things go. If that wasn't a good excuse, I don't know what was. We'll see what she says. After signing off and closing my laptop, I headed to bed, again, alone, somewhere between numb and anxious.

That night I had a dream. A nightmare rather, in which I was swimming towards Paul in the Vecht, but the current against me was so strong, I couldn't reach him. He called my name, waving his arms, but no matter how hard I swam to reach him, slowly I drifted further and further away until he was out of sight.

Chapter 21

Thursday, 8:30 a.m., exactly one week since Catharine called me with the NPR European Correspondent job opportunity. I checked my email first thing to see if there's a response from Catharine. There's just a one-liner asking me to call her as soon as I could. I couldn't call her now, it was 2:30 a.m. Washington time.

Lucy, Margreet, and Bert were already dressed and ready to go visit Paul. They had on their coats and were loading the last coffee cups in the dishwasher.

"You smell nice, what is that?" Margreet sniffed with her nose in the air.

"Ah-ha, thank you for noticing. That's my newest fragrance, *le temps perdu.*" I waved my wrist around closer to her face.

"Well, it smells very nice. Ready to go? Are we all going in one car?"

"Yes, let's. We'll take the Jeep. I can't imagine Dr. Boomsma won't let all of us in at the same time, and otherwise we'll take turns in the waiting room." Grabbing my keys, I took a deep breath. This was it — D-Day.

Dr. Boomsma was waiting for us when we entered Paul's room. The same two nurses as yesterday were with him.

"Good morning."

"Good morning Dr. Boomsma. Is it OK if we're all here when you try to wake him up?" Paul looked peaceful lying there. The symphony of beeps from the machinery was playing softly in the background. He was in desperate need of a shave and his lips were cracked and dried.

"Yes, that's fine, so long as we have enough room here. I suggest at least three of you sit over there on that couch by the window."

One nurse stood by the blood pressure monitor, the other by his bedside with the intravenous drip. Dr. Boomsma stood at the other side of his bed calling out commands to the nurses while holding one hand on Paul's shoulder.

"OK, we're going to decrease his amount of pain and sleep medications now, see how his body responds. We need to monitor his arterial pressure. Jill, why don't you come over here, sit and hold his hand." Dr. Boomsma motioned to a chair by Paul's bedside.

A good fifteen minutes passed. We sat there making small talk, about how bad the coffee was on this floor and that you were better off getting coffee in the cafeteria downstairs. We talked about the weather, how pretty much the entire month of June it hasn't rained. Then, Dr. Boomsma looked at the computer next to Paul's bed and said, "Jill, why don't you ask him to squeeze your hand."

I swallowed the lump in my throat and licked my lips, "Paul...it's me, Jill. If you can hear me, squeeze my hand." Two seconds later, I felt a light squeeze! "He squeezed! He squeezed!" Lucy jumped up from her seat and leapt towards me. Margreet and Bert stood up straight, almost on their toes, but stayed put. Margreet cupped her hands over her mouth in happy disbelief. Tears rolled down their cheeks.

"Papa!!" Lucy sat on my lap and put her hand on top of mine — we both held Paul's hand. "Papa, it's me Lucy. We're here next to you. We love you." She was so choked up she could hardly get her words out. "You're going to be OK."

Dr. Boomsma nodded her head in reassurance. "He'll come around, gradually. We need to make sure he can breathe steady and strong on his own after removing the ventilator. Now, I'll warn you that he may be agitated or confused at first. The last thing he remembers is being on the boat. He doesn't realize that he was in a coma this whole time. So keep that in mind, OK?"

"Thank you Dr. Boomsma. What's his recovery time looking like, do you think?"

"Well, we did an x-ray of his ribs yesterday and they're healing up well. If his body continues to respond well to the decrease of the painkillers and sleep medicine, then I'd say about five more days in the hospital, just to be sure. But his recovery time at home is uncertain. We just have to see how he does. Everybody's recovery is different."

"Five days isn't too bad, is it? I was expecting much longer." Margreet chimed in from the couch.

"No, that's not too bad, all things considered." I ran the back of my hand against the grain of the stubble on his cheek. "When do you think he'll open his eyes?"

"Well, it wouldn't surprise me if he did here in a couple of minutes. I'll give you some time alone with him. If he starts yanking at his breathing tube just buzz me. It'll feel like he's breathing out of a straw at first and he might try to rip out the tube. Don't take too long though. When people come out of a coma, they're very tired. They need their rest. I'd say spend about fifteen more minutes with him, then give him a couple hours of rest. Come back at 3 p.m. — I think that will be best for him now at this stage. If you have any questions, feel free to ask at the nurses station, or you can save them for this afternoon. I have to finish my rounds." Dr. Boomsma grabbed her chart, put her pen in the front pocket of her white coat and made a slight bow before leaving the room.

"Dr. Boomsma." I called out after her just before she exited the door.

"Yes, Jill?" She peered over her metal framed glasses.

"Thank you for taking such good care of him." I looked over at the two nurses as well. "You've all been so wonderful throughout this entire process. I can't thank you enough."

"You're welcome Jill. Just doing my job, but you're welcome." And with that she left the room, as did the nurses.

We sat for a good twenty minutes gawking at each other, talking to Paul, still in slight disbelief that Paul was responding so well. Lucy updated him on school and hockey. Margreet told him about her garden, about how their neighbor was nice enough to come trim their willow trees and mow their lawn. I had plenty to say to him, but preferred to do that in private, when he's off all the monitors and machines. I could tell he was getting very tired. Even us talking was too much too soon, so we decided to give him some rest.

*****

Monday morning, four whole days since Paul was brought out of his coma. If he continued to do as well as he's been doing, he could come home tomorrow afternoon. His eyes were

230

open, he was talking, he looked much better. The bruises had disappeared, bandages removed, less tubes, less machinery. He couldn't remember much about the accident itself, which Dr. Boomsma said was totally normal, but his long term memory had kicked in. Intentionally, I decided not to discuss anything about Sofie yet. I didn't want that to influence his recovery. It seemed too soon. I'd rather wait until he was home to ask him things like "What the hell did you do?", and "Are you in love with her?", and "Why did you do it?".

All this time, I was thinking about how Sofie at one point could have had Paul's baby growing inside her. She and Paul's baby! Lucy's half-sibling! I had nightmares about Sofie shoving the baby in my arms at the front door so she and Paul could go off to Tahiti while I changed diapers and made bottles, their baby whaling in my ear. Thinking in my dream — *but this isn't what I signed up for!*

Chapter 22

A morning mist hung over the vast flat farmland between the Amsterdam UMC hospital and Loenen. The iconic black and white Holstein cows were grazing in the green grass. It was chilly in the car. I always had the temperature set to 69 degrees and Paul always changed it to 72 degrees. Today was no different.

"Jill, it is June you know." Paul sat beside me as I drove, looking out his window over at the farmland off the A2, as if it was his first time on this planet.

"Actually, Paul, it's July. You've been out for a couple of days."

"Oh, right. Boy am I glad to be out of there! I'm so looking forward to my own bed, fresh coffee, you and Lucy, just being home." He reached over and placed his hand on my right thigh. It was the large hand of a middle-aged man; a beautiful hand with strong fingers and neatly trimmed fingernails; as familiar as my own hand was to me. I mustered up a smile and continued to watch the road in front of me. Today was a milestone, the day we've all been waiting for, the day Paul could come home — but for some reason I couldn't help but feel a splintering of pain and worry spread through me. I had so many questions for him, but was afraid of knowing the answers. Plus, I didn't know when to bring it up — was there ever a good time to confront someone about anything after they almost died?

We pulled up to the house. Lucy made a welcome home sign and blew up a couple balloons and hung them out by the front porch. Dr. Boomsma recommended that Paul walk with a cane for a few days until he regained some strength. I ran over to the passenger side and helped him get out of the car, stabilizing my legs as I pulled him up. He gasped and leaned on me like a child as we walked 10 feet to the front door. Lucy's hair was still wet from the shower, making a dark spot on the shoulders of her red t-shirt. Margreet and Bert were standing just inside in the living room. Bert held Abby down by the collar so she wouldn't go berserk when she saw Paul. God forbid she jumped up on him and knocked him over! Paul hadn't set foot in this house in nine days, but it felt like an eternity.

Paul closed his eyes once he was inside the house and took a deep breath, "Ahh, the smell of home. I love that smell — laundry mixed with dog and remnants of cooking. You become so immune to it when you're here every day, but when you're gone for a while, you really appreciate it again." Margreet, Paul, and Lucy walked closer to him and gave him a big hug. Everyone started laughing and crying at the same time, myself included.

"Are you hungry Paul? I made a quiche." Margreet pointed to the kitchen.

"Yes, you know me, I'm always hungry. But if it's OK with you, I'm just going to plop down here in this chair."

Paul sat in the closest chair he could find.

"Of course, I'll bring everything out here. Lucy, can you give me a hand?" Lucy followed Margreet into the kitchen and they came out with a pile of plates and the quiche. Out of the corner of my eye I noticed Margreet and Bert's suitcase was already packed by the door.

"Margreet, you're already packed? Leaving so soon?" I nodded towards her suitcase as I distributed forks around the table.

"We should be getting back to Groningen, plus we want to give you all some space. We've been here for well over a week." She has always respected our privacy and was intuitive enough to know when it was time to leave — another quality I loved about her. We all sat down to enjoy Margreet's food and retold our own versions of the last nine days. Paul didn't remember much of the accident itself and sought clarification on a couple of details, "So a helicopter brought me to the hospital?", and "Was I really totally out, in a coma for that long? What did that look like?", and "I remember having nightmares, very vivid, like I was hallucinating."

"Yes, Dr. Boomsma said nightmares were typical for coma patients." I reassured him. As the conversation continued, I could see him getting tired. His eyes became less focused, he became more quiet and slightly withdrawn. "Paul, maybe you need to go rest now." I started piling up the plates.

"Jill's right. We're going to head back to Groningen now so you can all get settled again, have your house back. Jill, thank you so much for allowing us to stay here."

"Allow? Are you kidding? What would I have done without you here for all this?! Thank *you*!" Standing up to give Margreet a hug, my face fell into her salt and pepper hair as she embraced me tight in her soft cushiony body, like a big pillow. Bert squeezed my hand, just like he did when I first met him, and pulled me in for a peck on the lips, his beard too soft to actually scratch. Paul stayed put and Lucy and I walked out to help them with their suitcase. Bert beeped his horn and they waved through their rolled down windows until they rounded the corner, making a right at the windmill, out of sight. A sense of quiet washed over me as I walked back into the house with Lucy. We put our arms around each other.

"I'm so glad papa is home. Aren't you mama?"

"Yes, of course. I'm glad he's home too."

*****

It felt strange to have Paul beside me again in our bed, having slept alone for the past nine nights, except for the occasional night with Lucy. It was muggy for July in the Netherlands. Dutch weatherman Marco Verhoef predicted a heatwave with tropical temperatures reaching 84 degrees this week. No matter what the weather report, he always presented it as a glass half empty. Summers in the Netherlands have gotten warmer over the years due to global warming, but I can't complain as it reminded me of summers in Pennsylvania, nice and sticky, no jackets needed, less wind. Our bedroom window was open. Despite having screens installed on most windows, mosquitos still found their way in — I could hear one buzzing past my ear.

"Jill, can we turn off the lights now?"

"No, sorry, we can't, not until I find that little bugger and zap him with my mosquito racket. You know I can't sleep until I find him."

"Argh, OK. Well, I guess that was the one good thing about sleeping in the hospital — no mosquitos."

"Glad you're able to look on the bright side. Ah! Found him, here on the curtain!" The small mosquito secretes a slight burning smell as I walked to the bathroom trash can, tapping the racket so it fell in. "Now we can turn off the lights!" I jumped back into bed and pulled up the linen duvet.

"*Welterusten*—Good night." I switched off the lights. There was still some daylight shining in from behind the blinds. The clock showed 22:22. I made a wish. I once heard that you're supposed to make a wish when the clock shows all the same numbers, but so far my wishes haven't been granted this way.

Except for the occasional hum of an airplane flying overhead towards Schiphol, it was silent. I could hear Paul breathing softly beside me and felt the rise and fall of the duvet cover. We both laid there, unable to sleep, like newly acquainted strangers who have known each other for the longest time, but didn't know how to act, as if we were on our first date. My mind jumped in all directions - the NPR job, *I have to call Catharine!* Lucy's college forms. *I sent those off right?* I forgot to show Paul the pile of Get Well Soon cards that have poured in from Loenen friends. Then I thought back to my conversation with Sofie. *Is what she said true? It all meant nothing? Is Paul still the man I fell in love with years ago in DC?* I felt so alone, too foreign for home, too foreign for here, never enough for both. If I'm lucky, I'll have another forty years ahead of me. Is this what midlife feels like? Where do I want to spend those years? Back in the US, a place I don't really recognize anymore? Or here, a place I've come to get to know so well but since finding out about Paul's fling, feel betrayed by?

I watched an interview with our Dutch Queen Maxima a couple of weeks ago. The Dutch presenter Matthijs van Nieuwekerk asked her what King Willem-Alexander meant to her and she replied, "He's my anchor. He pushes me to be the best I can be, but he also knows when to hold me back." I remembered thinking — *that's Paul!* Paul's my anchor! He's always encouraged me to be the best version of me, but always there to play devil's advocate. He's always telling me how proud he is of my radio segments and brags about them to his friends. If a colleague annoyed me at work or I didn't get the promotion I wanted he'd say "screw 'em, they don't deserve you." Before doing a social media post that would make me look like a fool, or committing to a project not worth my time he'd catch me just on time, "Are you sure you want to post that? I think people might take it the wrong way", or "Think back to when you worked with them before, you hated it remember?" Not only was he my anchor, but he was my compass. But now he's gone and messed it all up! How can I live with a man who cheated on me, who broke my trust? Is trust something you can regain? Thoughts like these ricocheted in my mind along with an incredible urge to confront Paul. Why not just ask him? Let him know that I know what happened all those years ago — well over a decade! Why keep something bottled up? It's time to get things out in the open. After all, isn't that the Dutch way?

"Paul? Are you awake?"

"Yes. I can't sleep, it's too warm."

"There's something I want, I actually *need* to get off my chest."

"Sure. What is it?" He laid there waiting, nothing in his voice that indicated he had any clue what I was about to say.

"I know Sofie was with you during the accident. I also know that you two slept together." I felt a fury build inside me. Holding my breath, I stared straight above towards the ceiling. My tinnitus was back with a vengeance — it felt like my head was going to explode from the roaring swooshing sound. I tasted salt and didn't know whether it was rivulets of sweat or tears. "I found an email exchange between you two when you were in a coma. What the hell, Paul? After just one year of marriage? When we were trying to start a family? Keeping it a secret all these years? And then lying about meeting up with her for photography lessons? How am I supposed to trust someone who goes behind my back like that?"

After what seemed like an eternity of silence, "You're right, Jill. I haven't been honest with you." Paul swallowed a lump in his throat and turned towards me, placing his hand on mine as I laid like a stiff plank. It was definitely a tear I tasted, I felt a second droplet slide down my face, over my ear, onto my pillow. "I messed up, ages ago, and had a one night stand with Sofie. But it was just once, it meant nothing. I'm *so* sorry Jill." I've never seen Paul cry before, until now. The bed started trembling as Paul grabbed my hand tight, sniffing and crying like a little lost boy. "I swear – it was my biggest regret. I didn't see the point in telling you. When I saw her at the party, I was shocked. That was the only time I saw Sofie outside of getting my teeth cleaned since, I swear. She asked me to give her a couple photography lessons, nothing more, nothing less. And I never told you about the photography lessons, well, because we were leaving for America anyway. What was the point? There were just two lessons. I guess I didn't want you to be suspicious. I honestly didn't think there was anything wrong with it. Plus, you were busy as it was. I felt we've been out of touch lately with this whole move to America. I mean, I honestly thought that I could just leave this all behind me. I'd never see her again. You, me, Lucy, we'd move to Pennsylvania — this was just a stupid fling that happened years ago. It's long buried." I laid there silent, in a state of bereft. I saw this coming, and I didn't see this coming. Hearing this all from him, the source, the truth landed — dead center in my heart, bullseye.

I flung his hand off mine — there was a moment of silence.

"Of all men in the world, I never imagined you'd ever cheat on me! Ruud, sure. All those other jackasses out there, sure, but you?! And with that blond bimbo that cleans teeth?! How she manages to keep her teeth so white when she smokes like a chimney is beyond me! Now I get why you smelled like cigarettes that one night you stormed out of here, and her perfume! You lied to my face Paul." Punching my pillow I sat up. My heart rate was sky high, I could feel the anger boiling inside of me.

"I know, I'm sorry. I messed up. It's that simple."

"I can't sleep beside you tonight — and no, it's not that simple. Look, I know I'm not the most effusive person in the world, never have been, but I'm affectionate...at times. But does that mean you have to go off and look for that with another woman?" I grabbed my slippers and pillow to sleep somewhere else. Anywhere but next to Paul.

"Jill, please, I'm trying to have a conversation with you. It was a difficult time for us, back when we went through that IVF process. I felt like a factory, a machine that had to perform on the clock. I know IVF is usually about the woman trying to get pregnant, but we were both vulnerable. I don't want to lie anymore." Paul was too weak to chase after me. I became worried all of a sudden, if I let this go too far it could set back his health. He could have a stroke or heart attack, fresh out of a coma. No idea. Hesitating at the door, I turned around to look at him lying in the bed. There was just enough light coming in behind the blinds casting soft light on his face. He looked sincerely devastated, sitting up in bed, chin down, his face cradled in both hands.

"Do you love her?"

"No! Sofie means nothing to me!"

"So, you don't have any feelings for her?"

"No, absolutely not. It was ages ago!"

"I found an email you know, from her to you, on your phone. Alluding to your one-night stand…" I felt the tide rising and there was no way of stopping it. "She could have been pregnant back then for cryin' out loud Paul! Do you have any idea what that could have meant?! Do you have any idea how much that would ruin everything we've built together? Our family, Lucy, how, and where we live? We would've had to stick around here for the rest of our lives so you could play dad to some other child. Lucy would have a half-sibling! Hell, maybe Lucy would have never existed. I don't want Sofie in our lives, let alone your child with her! This is all so ludicrous! How can I forgive something like this? You always gave me crap for wanting to get a Dutch passport, but thank God I did, because at least that way I can take that NPR job and stay here, regardless of our marriage. I don't *need* you, you know!" And with that I slammed the door behind me and walked upstairs. On my way to the guest room, I opened Lucy's door a crack to make sure she's still sleeping, which thank God she was. Before closing her door I whispered softly *sorry*, hoping she'd hear that in her dreams. The sheets were stripped from the guest bed since Margreet and Bert's stay. Wiping a hair that was stuck to my neck from sweat I laid down, exhausted on every level.

Minutes turned to hours on the clock as I tossed and turned in bed, rehashing everything in my head, weighing Paul's honest confession with the rest of the equation. But no matter how hard I tried, I couldn't come to terms with a final outcome, I was stuck, more stuck than I've ever been before. Could it be that this land that I thought I knew so well and it's people was all one big faux experience? How could I have been so blind? Had I just stayed with the patchouli laced hippy in Gettysburg would everything have been fine? The only thing I could think of to help me sleep right now was music — reverting to the old trick I had as a teenager, I went downstairs and quietly grabbed my phone and headphones. I found a Billie Holiday album on Spotify, laid back down on the mattress protector and hit play. Tomorrow is another day. The last words I remember hearing from Billie's deep husky voice in her song *The End of a Love Affair*, *'So I go at a maddening pace, And I pretend that it's taking his place, But what else can you do, At the end of a love affair. Do they know, do they care, That it's only, That I'm lonely, And low as can be, And the smile on my face, Isn't really a smile at all.'*

Chapter 23

Lucy's knock at the door woke me up. It was 8 a.m.

"Mom?! What are you doing laying here? And why do you have your headphones in your ears while sleeping?" Lucy had her hair tied up in a bun and her soft bathrobe on, arms crossed.

Groggy and aching, I rolled over to face her, pulling out my earbuds, "Oh jeez, good morning to you too Lucy. Sorry, your father was snoring so loud and I figured we'd both get a better night's sleep if I came up here." *A total lie, not sure if she bought it.* Her teenage 'uh-huh' with a slight eye roll said probably not, but she didn't pry further. "Come, help pull me up, I'm getting old."

"No you're not mom, you just need to start doing yoga again." Lucy pulled me off the bed with both hands.

"You're probably right." We walked downstairs, petting Abby on our way to the kitchen.

"Happy 4th of July by the way!"

"Oh my gosh — I totally forgot!" Normally, in order to hold on to my American roots I hung up the American flag, lit some sparklers, and played Bruce Springsteen music at a loud volume while firing up the grill for some burgers. "We'll have to see how your father is feeling today. If he has enough energy, we could go out on the boat maybe for dinner, bring some food along with us? That is, if the boat's not too traumatizing for him. I can get some good old coleslaw, make a potato salad, grill up some burgers."

"Yes! Lucy licked her lips and rubbed her hands together. If she could eat a cheeseburger every day for the rest of her life she would.

"Mom, aren't you going to check on dad?"

"Why don't you do that sweetie, I'll make some coffee." Not ready to face him yet, I dutifully set a pot. I don't hold grudges as long as my mom, but I doubted I could get over last night's confession anytime soon. Peering in the fridge I saw we were out of milk. Maybe it would be nice to get some fresh croissants for his first morning back. I figured I could kill two birds with one stone— get a couple groceries since Lucy is here for Paul and walk to the store, letting Abby out. I could use some fresh air. Lucy came back to the kitchen.

"He's still sleeping."

"Doesn't surprise me — he's still in recovery. Let's let him sleep. Can you stay here with him? I'm going to go to the Jumbo and get some fresh croissants and a couple things for dinner tonight."

"Sure. Can you get some Nutella too?"

"OK, but you know that stuff will give you pimples right?" I grabbed her jokingly, pulling her in tight. Seems like just yesterday I took her to her first K3 concert, the Belgian trio band that little girls loved so much. Now she's making her own provocative TikTok dances! Grabbing a leash and my sunglasses to block the morning glare, I headed out with

Abby for the ten minute walk to the Jumbo. I took the scenic detour, straight through the Dorpstraat, which felt like it was straight out of a Charles Dickens book, so picturesque with immaculate gardens and perfectly painted shutters lining the brick laid streets.

The smell of fresh croissants wafted past me by the Jumbo's front entrance. After securing Abby's leash to a bike stand, I grabbed a cart and walked in. I scanned the room to see if I recognized anyone, which thankfully I didn't. I wasn't in the mood to speak to anyone. I started making my rounds through the store that's become so familiar. I could walk through each section with my eyes closed — I grabbed some milk, ready-made coleslaw and potato salad, lettuce, tomato, and burgers. Rounding the corner of the meat section, I walked over to the bread section which bordered the checkout line and started filling a plastic bag with croissants, still warm from the oven. I could never maneuver those grabbing tongs. It took me 30 seconds to grab one croissant, so I ended up using my hands. I headed off to the express check out aisle. An old Dutch woman with her walker butted in front of me. *I hate when they do that. Why is butting in line and unsolicited advice common practice for Dutch people over sixty?* A young guy with pasty white skin and wire frame glasses scanned my groceries.

"Do you have a Jumbo pass *mevrouw?*"

"No."

"*Spaar je zegels?*—Do you save stamps?"

"No."

"Do you want to start?"

"No, thank you."

"But you can save for the Schott Zwiesel glassware set."

"No, thanks. You see, I'm moving."

"But there might be a Jumbo where you're moving to."

"Look buddy, I'm moving to the US. We don't have Jumbo's over there OK?"

"*Bonnetje?*—Do you want your receipt?

"Ahhh, no! Too many questions, sorry."

Chapter 24

Back at the house, I replayed my conversation with Sofie over and over in my head while placing the groceries in the fridge. *It was just a one-night stand years ago. Should I care? Does it even matter at this point?* Lucy came up behind me after eating her croissant and gave me a peck on the cheek before biking off to hang out with friends. As I made Paul his favorite breakfast of *filet americain* on a *pistolet*, cured meat as red as Rudolf's nose on a white hard bun, Marlies called me. I haven't seen her since before Paul's accident.

"Jill, *hoe gaat het met je?*—How are you?" Her warm voice was comforting and familiar, as if she was sitting across from me at the office.

"Oh Marlies, it's been one hell of a week."

"You mean two weeks."

"Oh my gosh, yes, two weeks. Has it been that long since I last saw you? The days are flying by. Paul's back at home, I think I texted you that already, so that's good news. But Marlies, I've uncovered the most upsetting news and I'm trying to wrap my head around it."

"What's that Jill?" Marlies says, concern oozing through the phone.

"I found out Paul slept with that dentist, Sofie! The blond that we had Stijn go up and spy on at our goodbye party!"

Her gasp is so loud I had to hold the phone away from my ear. She switched into journalist mode, firing off questions, "What?! When?! How?! OMG Jill!"

"It was a long time ago, but still, it has thrown me for a bit and I really can't handle any more surprises right now. I mean first the NPR job offer, then Paul's accident, then to find out about their one-night stand, it's just all too much Marlies!"

"I'm so sorry Jill. That's some heavy stuff you're dealing with." She let out a big sigh into the phone, sounding as overwhelmed as I was.

Sniffing and wiping tears with the back of my hand I shifted gears, "And then this whole NPR job offer, something I've wanted my entire life on a plate in front of me. This has all just turned into one complicated meal."

"Did you decide about the NPR job? Do you want to talk about it? Maybe over wine at Mout?" Marlies always had a way of drawing me back in, making me feel welcome, wanted.

"That's sweet of you. Believe me, if I'm not thinking about Paul's recovery, and his fling, I'm thinking about that job and what to do next. Catharine wants me to call her, but with the time difference and all that's happened I haven't had the chance."

"OK, well if you want that job, you better call her soon. Jill — you'd be crazy to turn this opportunity down! You've always wanted to move up the ranks with NPR!"

"I know. I want to have one last conversation with Paul before calling her. I plan on having that conversation today. Did I tell you that NPR would give me a Sennheiser shotgun mic with a furry ferret that I could use in those Dutch gale force winds? That would be so much better than the omnidirectional mics we've been using at Radio 1."

"You better let me borrow that mic." While laughing Marlies took a sip of a beverage.

"Ha-ha, of course."

"NPR is in the big leagues. I mean, think of the population you'd reach! A lot more than our two million, that's for sure. They'll pay for a studio space for you right?"

"Yes, and an assistant, plus editorial team back at headquarters. Plus, all seventeen foreign correspondents get a Comrex machine. If I want to go live, I just plug into NPR's headquarters, putting me on the audio board with the host. It's the size of a hardcover book! You could be in the middle of the desert in a warzone and still connect to NPR headquarters!"

"Oh Jill, just listen to how excited you are talking about it. You better take that job! What an amazing opportunity. I'll take it if you don't." Marlies's smile came out in her voice. A sudden sense of guilt washed over me, as if I'd be leaving her behind at Radio 1. We made such a good team and I owed it to her how far I've come in the radio sector. She's the one who taught me all the editing tricks in the beginning, how to write a good script, how to remain calm in stressful situations, think on my feet, be more curious. She taught me little language nuances, like how it was more polite to say *zou je*—could you instead of *kan je*—can you in correspondence.

When reporting from the field for Radio 1, there was

always something unexpected that happened. Like when an actual customer came knocking on the prostitute's door who I was interviewing, making for an even better story. Or the earthquake that took place while I was interviewing the CEO of the *Gasunie*—gas union up in Groningen, who despite local cries to stop digging deep for gas production, kept digging. And the time when the police found 220 kilograms of cocaine in a container of bananas while I was interviewing one of the Rotterdam harbor managers. The unexpected is good in radio — that's part of the story, that's my cue to follow the unexpected, because that could be *the* story. Maybe I should apply that way of operating to my own private life, see the unexpected as good and roll with it. I don't need to have everything figured out, whether that be a move to America, or a summer holiday, or what we're having for dinner, or whether an expensive wine glass breaks, or what I wear to a party, or whether I get my 10,000 steps in. Who cares?!

"What about the time difference?" Marlies's question brought me back to real time.

"Well, because of the time difference, recordings are usually live. *Morning Edition* goes live starting at 5 a.m., so 11 a.m, for us. Usually live stuff will be between 11 a.m. to 1 p.m."

"That's perfect, so really during regular office hours."

"Yeah, more or less, but my days would be busier than with Radio 1. I'd have to travel outside the Netherlands to do feature stories."

"Well, as long as you bring me along for some of those trips, I'll allow it." Marlies' deep warm laugh filled the phone line. "OK, I gotta go. Keep me posted, OK Jill?"

"Thanks Marlies, I will. I promise."

* * * * *

When Lucy pulled up on her bike it was 3:30 p.m. and she was not alone. Roos and Julie were with her. Roos was carrying a large baking pan covered in tin foil. Catching sight of them opening the gate through the window, I walked across the gravel to greet them.

"To what do I owe this pleasure?"

"Well, once we heard from Lucy that Paul was back home and seeing it's the 4th of July, we made you Rice Krispie Treats!" Roos slid her large stylish sunglasses to the top of her head and handed me the baking pan.

"Rice Krispie Treats?! I haven't had those in years!" Peeking under the tin foil I took a whiff and was thrown back to childhood birthday parties and barbeques.

"I know, I remember eating them once years ago when Ruud and I went to visit his sister who lived in Connecticut. I loved the sweetness of the marshmallows. I had to make something for you guys. I was planning to bring soup yesterday, but got caught up with work stuff."

"Well, this was very sweet of you just the same, thank you!"

"How's Paul doing?"

"He's much better. And thanks again, Roos. I mean, I don't know what I would have done had you not been with me that night. I was a mess."

"Of course! I'm glad I was there too. Julie and I have been thinking of you guys each and every day. It must have been so scary for you when Paul was in that coma." The girls had already ran into the house for something to drink. Roos and I stayed out on the driveway talking. Twisting the toe of my shoe in the gravel, looking down, I hesitated. I want to bring up the whole Paul issue, that I was having trouble forgiving Paul, but felt sorry for him in there, recovering from his accident. What Roos went through with Ruud was different. He didn't just have a fling, he had an affair. But was the difference really so big? How can one forgive and forget? Is a one-night stand more forgivable? I mean, we all make mistakes at some point in our lives. I guess that's the difference? A one-off mistake or a repeated mistake? It all boiled down to whether two people loved each other. But the whole trust thing. How can you trust someone again, even if it was a one-off mistake? Who says they won't do it again? All these questions I wanted to ask Roos, they were at the tip of my tongue. Sometimes, I felt like divorce was a contained disease. I always saw the same divorcees together, going off to the Dutch island of Vlieland with each other for a long weekend. Are faults in a marriage magnified by hanging around divorcees?

"Roos? Can I ask you a personal question?"

"*Tuurlijk*—of course! Ask away."

"I come from a household where we don't talk that openly about things — I guess I'm just overly cautious."

"Well, go ahead, shoot. You know you can ask me anything. If I don't want to answer, I won't."

"OK, fair enough...When you found out about Ruud's affair, how did you get over it in the end? I mean, what led you to decide on a divorce?" My armpits started to sweat and I could feel a drop of sweat roll down my back.

"Ah, I see where you're going with this. I guess I don't talk about it much, do I? It was all pretty traumatic at the time, it took me months to get over it, years even." Roos huffed. "As much fun as Ruud is, I knew I couldn't live with him after he repeatedly went behind my back with that golf trainer. My trust in him was broken, and trust is a very hard thing to win back." The glare of the sun on Roos's face forced her to put her sunglasses back on.

"Do you think if it had been a one-night stand it would have been different?"

"Of course! That is, if there was regret involved. We all make mistakes. But the fact Ruud was seen with her multiple times, making me the laughing stock of Loenen, that was the breaking point for me. It wasn't fair to me, nor to Julie. Plain disrespect."

"I don't think you were the laughing stock of Loenen, but I get it." Just then Lucy and Julie came outside making the sweet puppy dog face they always make when they wanted something.

"Mom, can I have dinner at Julie's tonight? Please?"

"Well, I thought you wanted to do a July 4th barbecue with cheeseburgers on the boat? You can all stay here for dinner if you want?"

"No, that's OK Jill, but thank you. Paul just got home. I think you need rest, not to be entertaining us. It's really no problem if the girls want to eat at my place tonight. Maybe that will be nice for you and Paul to have some time together in the boat."

"Well, if you're sure it's no trouble. I'm fine with it."

"Great, I'll make sure she's home by 9 p.m., OK? Give Paul a hug from me! And take those treats along with you for dessert!"

"Thanks Roos, I will." I waved as they biked away. Roos called over her shoulder, "Happy 4th! Don't forget to put up your flag!" She pointed to my empty flagpole in the front yard.

She was right, it was the least I could do to celebrate

my roots. Walking over to the shed, I dug through camping gear and power tools until I found our American flag tossed on the back of a shelf. The military would frown upon our wrinkled crumpled up flag, that we didn't fold in a perfect triangle, like I was taught in girl scouts. Paul put handy clips on it last year so that I could attach it to the flagpole's string. Hoisting it up I sang, half-jokingly to myself, *Ore the land of the free, and the home of the brave. Play ball!*

"Jill, what are you doing?" Paul walked out onto the porch with his cane.

"Are you ready to say the *Pledge of Allegiance?*"

"What's that?" Paul looked at me as if I had two heads.

"That was something we had to recite every single day in school growing up. You place your right hand over your heart, then recite an entire pledge of allegiance to the flag."

"Whoa, you guys actually did that?! I've seen it in films, but didn't realize that was actually a thing. Isn't that like communism?"

"Eh, you get used to it." Paul came up next to me and placed his arm around my waist after securing the flag. "Come, time for a boat ride, I can help you step in."

* * * * *

There wasn't a trace of blood left on the teak wood floor. I played Bruce Springsteen's *County Fair* on the boat's built-in speakers. I took the steering wheel this time and let Paul relax on the back bench. We made our way through the Mijndense Sluis, the lock separating the Vecht River from the Loosdrechtse Lake. Five other boats were crammed into the lock with us as the lock keeper came around to collect our money and hand us a ticket. The water's force pulled the boat towards the gate of the lock as water was being sucked out. This being my fifth summer by all this open water, I've learned how important it was to hold onto the side of the lock with all your might. We've seen way too many boats tie themselves to the side, only to have to cut their ropes because otherwise their boat would hang from the wall.

"You did a good job back there Jill. Your first time doing all that steering and maneuvering on your own!" Paul pulled out a beer from the cooler and snapped open the can.

"Thanks for the pat on the back, but it still stresses me out. I like it better when you steer and I can just sit back and relax with a glass of wine. I'm so afraid I'm going to crash this thing."

"The only way to learn is by doing. Besides, that's why we got an old secondhand boat, it doesn't matter if it gets dinged up."

We made our way out towards the lake. Ducks passed by and lily pads floated along the side of the bank. The breeze was soft and the smell of sunscreen mixed with dank water filled the air. We waved to other boats passing by with their dogs and kids sprawled out across the bow. Some had bodyboards attached to the stern with kids on top, laughing and screaming.

"Is this too much for you Paul? I mean, you did just get out of the hospital."

"No, not at all, this is perfect, just what I needed, fresh air. I've missed this! And to think I was so close to losing this."

"I know, don't even say it — it gives me chills just thinking about it. You know I'm prone to that sort of thinking anyway, worst case scenarios." I moved to the back of the boat and sat next to him. There's an extra wooden steering handle by the back bench, allowing me to keep my eyes focused up front so I didn't run into anything or anyone, but could still steer. "Paul, can we use this time to have a good talk? There's so much weighing on my mind and...well, with the whole boat accident and all, I feel like there's never a good time to talk about it."

"OK, sure, what do you want to talk about?" He repositioned himself to face more towards me.

"Well, I'm still bothered by this whole Sofie thing, even if it was years ago. We were married, and that was when we were trying to build a family. I can't stop thinking about all the what if's." Paul took a sip of his beer and placed his left hand gently on my thigh.

"I'm sorry Jill. I was young, stupid, selfish. It was an asshole move. But I mean, here you were learning Dutch, getting your master's, planning out our life step by step. I don't know. I guess I felt ignored."

"But isn't that what you wanted? Weren't you happy that I was making an effort to adjust to a country that wasn't my own? As much as I wanted to come over for a cheaper masters and to start a life here with you, I was taking a huge risk and leaving my family behind, my hometown."

"Yes, of course, but you have to understand it was strange for me to be back in the Netherlands too. I almost felt like I failed in a way. I was proud of my internship in DC. I actually liked the prospect of staying longer. I get that your master's program was cheaper in Amsterdam. I get that there are more vacation days over here. But I actually liked living in America. And I was looking forward to going back now with you and Lucy."

"But I just don't get how that all led to you sleeping with another woman, after one year of us being married? And then to offer her photography lessons, it just doesn't make sense, or seem right. It's hurtful." My throat tightened.

"Jill, it meant nothing. I was stupid. You were off with one of your friends from your master's program. The neighbors had a party, Sofie was there. We were all pretty drunk. I mean, I was what, twenty-five? She invited me over and one thing led to the next. I regretted it as soon as I was cognizant of what I'd done. That's why I never brought it up. I didn't feel it was necessary. We were never in touch after that, until she coincidently moved to Loenen and I saw her when I got my teeth cleaned."

"But why would you go off and give her photography lessons?!"

"Because she asked me, and photography is my hobby."

"Well, you could have said no."

"The fact I didn't think twice about giving her photography lessons should be enough to prove I have no feelings for her. I simply saw it as a teaching opportunity. *Ik zweer het*—I swear. Can't we just move on?" A seagull flew overhead. The sound of the tractor engine in our boat was so loud and distracting. It was vibrating so much that it rattled our water glasses that were touching. I moved them apart and suggested we put down our anchor so we could turn off the engine and have a bite to eat before heading back. After fixing us both up a plate, including the expensive pickles I bought from the American store on Leidsestraat specifically for the 4th of July because Dutch pickles are sweet and don't have that crunchy dill taste, I sat back down next to him, protecting my butt with a towel from getting scorched on the dark blue leather seat cushion.

"Mmmm, this is so good. Thank you for putting this together. Happy 4th!" Paul raised his can of beer, "*Proost!*"

I raised my insulated Tervis tumbler my mom got me last Christmas, keeping my wine nice and cold. "*Proost.*" Paul finished his burger in four big bites while I slowly munched on mine, mulling over our conversation.

"Look Paul, I know I was operating like a factory when we went through that whole IVF process. The thing is, I've only ever known how to tackle goals, in this case having a baby, by being systematic about it." I wiped a wad of ketchup from the corner of my mouth. "But I was scared. Here I was, in a new country, learning a new language, figuring everything out. We just got married, and then only to find out that we're unable to have all the children I always dreamed of having." Paul put his plate down and repositioned himself to face me even more. Looking up at him after having my eyes fixated on the floor of the boat, I saw that his face was soft, his eyes were warm. "I realize that wasn't the best point in our relationship. I was so consumed with becoming pregnant — it took all the fun out of our marriage. I'm sure I came across as a drill sergeant, making sex a timed chore, always taking my temperature, all those hospital visits. But that's the only way I know how to handle stressful situations and the unknown is by turning it into one big chart." Paul wrapped his arm around my shoulders and pulled me in closer. "I was resentful. In a way, I felt tricked. My body tricked me, and I felt vulnerable — I felt like I was swimming in the deep end. As if, even though we made the decision together to come over here, I was somehow trapped in *your* country, all bets were on *you*. And well, I was scared. In that sense, it's probably good I found out about Sofie now and not then. I'm not sure what I would have done, so early in our marriage, before having Lucy."

"I know, and I'm so sorry I hurt you Jill. I'm sorry you

had to find out about all this while I was in a coma, that I wasn't there to explain from the get go, leaving you wondering." Paul kissed my forehead and then placed his forehead against mine. "You were vulnerable, and I can relate to that, because that's exactly how I felt in America. I'll never forget how your mom bought all that stuff for my first apartment. We still have that broom." Just the thought made me laugh. The sun was getting lower. I looked at my watch and saw that it was already 7 p.m. Lucy would be home in an hour, and it would take an hour to get back, through the locks, to the Vecht. I promised her sparklers tonight.

"We should head back. I can pull up the anchor, if you can give me a hand to put it over there in that bin?" A bunch of green gunk came up along with the anchor. We quickly lifted it into the plastic container we stored under the bench. I revved up the engine and we headed back toward the reed-lined waterways leading to the lock. We devoured Roos's sticky Rice Krispy treats while we waited, licking marshmallow from our fingers. Once we made it through to the Vecht River, I could see the old Loenen church tower up ahead, a visual reminder each time of how beautiful Loenen really was and how lucky we were to live here. So little has changed physically, except for the Cronenburg castle that once stood in the field off to the left, built in the 12th century! And I thought the Jenny Wade House in Gettysburg, where the only civilian killed in the Battle of Gettysburg in 1863 was old. So much history, and now a different generation of Loenenaars are boating through the Vecht, and walking the same brick streets. I leaned forward over the edge of the boat — I watched the ripples rhythmically sliding along the side of the boat, soft white wispy clouds overhead, sky as blue as Paul's LA Dodgers baseball cap.

"Paul, I really want this NPR job. It's my dream job and I don't feel like I can pass up this opportunity." There was a long moment of silence. Paul placed his hat backwards and I bit the inside of my cheek. "I know you were looking forward to working in the US. I realize this past decade has always been about Radio 1, and that you've had to step in on many occasions to be accommodating. I haven't given you enough credit over the years. You know I'm not from a household that voices how we feel. But I'm telling you now, thank you." Taking a deep breath I glanced over at him. Paul said nothing at first, he straightened his back. "And the thing is, I know I complain about the Dutch complaining, about the cold rainy weather, about old Dutch people butting in line. But the fact of the matter is that we've built a life here, together. I don't want to lose that. So many memories — of Lucy with her lantern singing door to door on *Sint-Maarten*, biking around Amsterdam with her in the *bakfiets*, setting her shoe by the fireplace for *Sinterklaas*, chocolate letters, *pepernoten*. Then later in Loenen with ice skating in the winter, Lucy meeting up with friends out on the lake, our late evening conversations out by the water over a glass of wine, morning swims as the sun came up. I mean this place, this river, has become such a huge source of comfort in my life. And then this job comes, giving me the best of both worlds — as it would allow me to stay here in Loenen, but also report back to my roots, America — a place that felt like it's drifting further and further away, but this job is like a rope that keeps it attached to me. A channel I can tune into each day. I don't want to leave the Vecht, the *borrels*, the three kisses, the open curtains. I try to picture what that'd be like and I can't. Lucy can defer, do a gap year. Or she can go and we'll visit, she'll be fine. Why would we move? Besides, Gettysburg is not the Gettysburg I grew up in. When we go back to my parents' house to visit, it is overrun by my brothers' kids, their wives, and dogs — it's not the house I grew up in. I have an amazing career opportunity ahead of me, I'd be crazy to pass it up. Now that I know you're OK, I feel I can go for it. I'm afraid if I don't go for this opportunity, I'll never forgive myself." I felt a huge sense of relief, like a deflated balloon, an empty tube of toothpaste that had every last drop squeezed out of it. There - I got it all out.

Paul stood up, turned and looked out over the water, and I expected the worst, that he'd say that he was angry, that it has always been about me and my career. That he'd come up with a million more reasons why we should go. But instead, he turned back towards me, reached out his hand for me to grab and said, "Let's just see what happens. Let's see where the summer takes us, one day at a time. No more planning."

Chapter 25

Seven weeks later

Like a mirage, heat waves evaporated off the tarmac in front of a huge American flag waving proudly over Dulles airport. *Welcome to America.* I've seen this scene from my window seat many times before, but this time was different. We were not visitors anymore, we were residents. As we exited the plane, we immediately boarded the Passenger Transport Vehicle (PTV), also known as the mobile lounge, or moon buggy due to its strange otherworldly appearance. The white 54-by-16 foot carriage mounted on a scissor truck has been used to transport international arrivals to the main terminal for as long as I can remember. Paul, Lucy, and I rushed to get in the first one that left so we could avoid the ever-increasing line at customs.

"Thank God I'm allowed to go through this line for US citizens instead of visitors," Paul said as he looked over to the right, where the line was twice as long with only two customs officers working.

"I know, me too. I feel bad for all non-US citizens. It's

not the most warm welcome, making them wait that long in the line." I grabbed his hand as we walked through the line together, Lucy in front of us. Paul and I have had three marriage counseling sessions so far since I found out about him and Sofie. The first sessions were on Zoom seeing we wanted a therapist in the US to continue working with — Dr. Monahan was a short drive for us in Pennsylvania. So far, so good. Marriage is hard work and especially when there was trust to be regained. Lucy knew about us going to marriage counseling, but she thought it was because we're soon to have an empty nest and because of the big move, career changes — big transitions all at once. Which was also true. She was quiet for a good portion of the trip, her nose in a book or watching one movie after the next.

"How are you doing Lucy, are you doing OK?"

"Yeah, I'm fine. Just getting a little nervous for college, that's all. Bummed we couldn't fit in a week at the beach." She opened the front pocket of her backpack to took out her passport for the upcoming check.

"Oh sweetie, I can only imagine. It's been a crazy summer and so much is happening in such a short amount of time. At least we have one week to get settled and adjusted to the new time zone. We'll do the beach next year. Promise." I tucked a pluck of her light brown hair behind her ear.

"I can't wait to see Oma and Opa Amerika! They are picking us up, right?"

"Yes! That much we did plan — dinner at their house, spend the first night with them, then head to our rental place in the morning to unload everything." The 3 acre lot of land we bought four years ago was scheduled for the perk test next week, which would determine when we could actually start building. The townhouse we rented four blocks from my parents, two blocks from Lucy's college campus, had a one-year lease, so enough time for the build and to get settled.

I wasn't going to stress about it. One day at a time. I've learned there's no use getting all worked up about the future. Turned out, the very next day after my July 4th boat ride with Paul, Catharine sent me an email telling me that NPR had already given the European Correspondent job to someone else. Their foreign correspondent in China was sick of the surveillance. In Shanghai, where he was based, the Chinese were tapping his phone, his computer was hacked into, people he interviewed were being interrogated. He actually put in a request a year ago to be placed on the European desk. He'd had enough, so NPR transferred him over to Paris to cover all of Europe. Catharine said it was out of her hands, that she was sorry, and that she would try to pull some strings in the Washington office to see if she could set me up there. Time will tell. I didn't want to get my hopes up too much, not after that. I was trying to take a step back, not to rush things, not plan. Family, health, marriage, that's what was most important. Career could go on the back-burner for now.

"I hope Abby's OK. I hated seeing them load the animals into the cargo section. I watched the animals one-by-one move up the conveyor belt from my seat on the plane." Lucy tried peering behind the glass separating us from the baggage claim.

"I'm sure she's fine. As soon as we get our luggage we'll head over to odd sized baggage and pick her up."

We made it through customs smoothly and picked up our luggage and Abby. The rest was being shipped over. As the electric doors opened to the arrival hall, I immediately spotted my parents standing with big smiles on their faces, my mom's arms reaching out like a snow plow. Her dark brown hair that she's never had to dye looked longer and she lost a bit of weight. My dad looked older, but his blue eyes lit up when he saw us. Lucy ran up to them first and gave them a big hug. Paul and I made our way over, taking turns for a big embrace. I caught a whiff of my mom's Awapuhi Paul Mitchell shampoo. My dad seemed to have shrunk a bit, as my shoulders came just above his as we hugged.

"Welcome back, Jill! We're so happy to finally have you guys on this side of the pond." She grabbed one of our rollers and we started walking out to the parking lot. A wall of heavy heat hit us as soon as we exited the airport. "I've always hoped this day would come."

Hearing my mom say this felt like a dart hitting the bullseye of defeat. *Are we here because I couldn't make the Netherlands work? Or because this was always the plan anyway?* A sense of panic took over as thoughts like *What have I done? And everything I built up is now gone. And Did I make a mistake?* We made our way up the 270 North which ran into the 15 North towards Gettysburg. I was struck by the green traffic signs. I was so used to the blue signs in the Netherlands. I wasn't sure which I liked better. I saw the Catoctin Mountains ahead and I took a deep breath — a sense of calm took over.

"1,2,3 - we're free!" I sang as we crossed over the Mason Dixon Line where Maryland meets Pennsylvania.

"Mom, you always say that. Don't you think that's getting a little old?" Lucy rolled her eyes, smiling at the same time.

"I'm simply reminding you of the importance of the Mason Dixon Line." I grabbed her hand in the back seat. My mom looked at us through the rearview mirror and smiled. "Ah, I love this view. This has got to be one of the most picturesque parts of Pennsylvania with the rolling hills, orchards, fruit stands with fresh sweet corn on the cob. I did miss this."

"Camp David is just over there on that ridge." My mom pointed off to the left. "Although, Trump is spending more time at Mar-e-Lago in Florida than here."

We took the first exit for Gettysburg which brought us along the Battlefield. There was a red barn up ahead with a backdrop of blue sky and wispy clouds. The wooden snake fence lined the road as we made our way into the tourist section of town. I saw people out on Ghost Tours, walking behind their guide decked out in Civil War garb. There was a line that went the whole way around the block at Mr. G's Ice Cream Parlor. The hotel where Paul and I had our wedding reception years ago towered over the surrounding buildings on the square. The town was well kept, with flower baskets of geraniums hanging from lampposts, freshly painted facades, and neatly arranged storefronts. Although, as I looked up at the power lines above ground, I was reminded of how fragile the infrastructure is compared to the Netherlands. Any storm could knock out the power in this town and often did. My mom saved her stinky thirty year old Yankee Candles for that reason. As we pulled up to the parking lot next to my childhood home I heard my parents' dogs barking. A strange mixture of familiarity, hope, and uncertainty churned in my stomach as we made our way into the house.

"Your father made you chili with cornbread, your favorite." My mom helped us with a few bags. Abby took off in the backyard with my mom's two dogs. As we walked into the kitchen, smells of chili powder and cilantro floated through the air.

"Mmmm, thanks dad. It smells so good." My dad fixed himself a vodka with lots of ice from the noisy built-in ice-maker in the fridge and sat down on one of the bar chairs. His iPad was propped up on a stand with his latest crossword puzzle. My mom noticed me looking.

"Ah yes, that's all your father ever does anymore — crossword puzzles. He even follows a crossword puzzle blog. They sit here all night chatting online about crossword puzzles. Can you believe it?"

"You're kidding! Dad? Really? Well, at least you're enjoying retirement to its fullest. It's a good thing we're here now — you'll have something else to do from time to time besides crossword puzzles." My dad let out a laughing snort and handed us all a bowl for the chili.

"Would you like a glass of wine Paul? Jill? Lucy, what would you like something to drink, half and half?" Every summer when we come over that has been her go-to drink, half lemonade half iced tea with lots of ice in a Tervis Tumbler.

"Yes! Half and half please, Oma."

"Wine would be great Sally, thanks." Paul took a seat on a bar chair across from my dad.

"Me too, thanks mom."

"Paul, would you mind going over there to that curio cabinet and bringing me three wine glasses?" My mom pointed to the far corner of the dining room which was next to a large bookshelf. I saw Paul hesitating to browse the bookshelves as he often does when he's in other peoples' homes and he pulled out a large book from the top shelf.

"Hey — is this one of those all-American high school yearbooks?" Paul looked over at me as he opened the yearbook, as astonished as a boy in a candy shop. "I didn't realize you had a copy."

"Of course I have a copy. GHS — Gettysburg High School baby." Seeing how preoccupied he was I went to grab three wine glasses for my mom as he flipped through the pages.

"Well, well, well - look here. *Jill Stone - most likely to succeed.*" He looked up at me with his eyebrows raised, his pointer finger holding the page.

"Yeah, and now look at me. Unemployed and back in my hometown."

"Jill, come on, you know you'll find something soon enough. Just enjoy your time off. Maybe something else will open at NPR in DC or you can work for the local station." My mom poured me a big glass of red wine and handed it to me. "Cheers — to your safe arrival and re-patronization!"

* * * * *

Jetlag had us exhausted by 9 p.m. so the three of us headed to bed early, Lucy in my childhood room, Paul and I in what was now the guest room across the hall. When I went in to kiss Lucy goodnight, I saw the remnants of the tape that used to hold up my Cure poster on the ceiling. The chest that used to hold my precious belongings now held toys for my nephew for when my mom babysat. My handheld Smurfette mirror was still on the dresser. I guess there were just some things my mom couldn't throw away. I crawled back into our bed that had as many layers as the *Princess and the Pea* and was reminded how the Americans liked their comfort and 'things'. I stubbed my toe twice already on all the furniture. I had become so accustomed to the *strak* minimalist Dutch interiors, open concepts, white, gray, black. The summer sounds of crickets made their way through the window I had opened a crack. The air conditioning that blasted 24/7 was too cold, so I closed our door and opened the windows, letting in the hot humid air that I preferred.

Even though my body was exhausted, my mind was still awake. I grabbed my phone and earbuds, hoping that if I listened to Morrissey I might doze off. The first song on the playlist was *Home is a Question Mark*. I propped up my pillow and listened to the lyrics that I had never really paid much attention to before, *Home is it just a word? Or is it something that you carry within you?*

Before I fell asleep, I scribbled the lyrics down on a piece of paper next to my bed on the nightstand, writing in the dark. The next morning I jumped as Paul removed my ear buds. I must have fallen asleep with them in my ears. Paul gazed down towards the nightstand and glanced at my notes.

"Morrissey huh? Nice."

"You know these lyrics? This song?"

"Of course, who doesn't?"

"Oh, I didn't realize it was that popular."

"Well, maybe it isn't, but it's a good song. Good message too. Good morning honey." He sat on the bed beside me and leaned in to kiss me. There was a sparkle in his brown eyes and dimples showed on both sides of his mouth when he smiled. "I like to think of home as a ball of light I carry with me, you know, visualize it, that makes it easier. It's all in here." He pounded his fist lightly to his chest.

"How philosophical of you, Paul. Is that meant as a joke? That's a nice thought though. Never thought of it that way." I jumped out of bed and opened the curtains. Soft pink cotton candy clouds surrounded the rising sun. There was a team of construction workers who were switching between Spanish and English as they unloaded materials to replace the neighbor's roof across the street. I saw the Lutheran Church's steeple one block away, the church I attended as a child before moving to a country mostly composed of atheists. I saw the train tracks 30 feet away, and was reminded how annoyed I was as a teenager when the cargo train came through town in the middle of the night, blasting his horn, thinking *how is that even allowed, why doesn't the government just put up one of those railroad crossing gates?* I saw remnants of the payphone I used to prank call from my bedroom window. It was as if I was seeing my hometown through a new pair of glasses — everything seemed more vivid, magical even.

Later that day, Paul, Lucy, and I took a bike ride on Culp's Hill — part of the National Military Park. Lucy, who has biked her entire life, but only on Dutch flat ground, could not get used to the hills. She was huffing, puffing, and complaining the entire time.

"You have to stand up and peddle Lucy when you go up the hills! Come on, the last hill is ahead and then we can take a break at Spangler's Spring — there's a creek there, we can cool off our feet."

Beads of sweat ran down my back. It was only 9 a.m. but the temperature had already climbed to 91 degrees. When we arrived at Spangler's Spring, we took a seat on some rocks and grabbed our water bottles. The rock was too hot to sit at first, but I eased into it, then took off my socks. The burbling sound of the creek's water was soothing. My thoughts were immediately thrown to the Vecht River. I missed it. Even though the creek in front of me was much smaller than the Vecht, it's dark water and dank smell was similar. Dipping my toe into the rushing water, I watched how the water managed to make its way around the obstacle I inserted, just like the rocks peeping out and the tree branch. I remembered coming out to this creek with my friend Anne when I was twelve, throwing a frisbee. I remembered being terrified when biking down the hill behind us with my brother and Uncle. My brother John didn't know how the breaks worked and flew through the air, landing just behind a rock. I recalled the sense of relief I had when he stood up behind the rock laughing. I remember making out with my boyfriend in junior high over in the wheat fields in front of us. All these memories played out before my eyes like short movies. It felt surreal to be sitting here now in my forties with my family — two worlds colliding, American and Dutch, past and present.

We continued biking the rest of the route. Towards the end we stopped at a large monument of General Lee on top of a grassy hill. Laid out in front of us like a tapestry was a beautiful panoramic view of Gettysburg, nestled in the valley, the blue ridge mountains just behind.

"Wow — what a view! I'm always amazed at how beautiful the town looks from up here." I moved my head from left to right taking it all in.

"It is beautiful. Look — you can even see the college campus and Pennsylvania Hall from up here." Lucy pointed off to the left. Her college orientation started in just a few days.

"And down there is my favorite tree, standing alone in the middle of the cow pasture. I've been passing that same tree my entire life, ever since my mom and Uncle took me out here on walks as a baby. That tree probably even withstood the American Civil War!" I snapped a picture with my iPhone of the tree, then one of Lucy and Paul leaning against the fence with the valley below. I took a similar picture that always hung in our stairwell — when Lucy was three years old, pretty much as this exact spot. Now look at her!

Suddenly it hit me — this is what home looked like, this was it. That inner beat, that's been pushing me forward, plowing through life's path — the way the boats plowed their way through the glistening water of the Vecht River, the way the plane moved forward bringing us from the Netherlands to America, the place I need to be — not because it was necessarily planned that way, controlled, meant to be, but because it just is, home. A home I carried with me.

And that's just it. Home *isn't* just a word. Home *is* something you carry with you. Is it really that simple? But why is that concept so hard to practice? I guess because you can't carry something with you until you know who the hell you are. I didn't have to categorize myself as Dutch or American, I was both. Just like we had friends for different phases of our lives, we had places for different phases of our lives. I grew up in America, I had an American childhood and it was a good childhood. America has changed in so many ways, but it's still America. Spending my young adulthood in Washington and Amsterdam, like many young people do, was a privilege — I saw that now and felt nothing but gratitude. Life's roadmap starts taking shape early on and the decisions I've made have had a direct influence on places I've ended up. Standing on Culp's Hill, I realized I was back full circle, and I wouldn't want to have it any other way! I looked forward to seeing where Lucy would end up. Where Paul and I would end up.

A couple of months ago, before finding out about the fling, before the boat accident, when we were planning our summer holiday and discussing staying at my parents' place, the house where I grew up, as usual, I got stressed. Paul said to me, "Jill, Gettysburg is never going to be the Gettysburg you grew up in. Your parent's house is there, but the dynamics of how people use it has changed. You have to get used to Gettysburg 2.0. It's not home like you remember home being." He was right. But not only my parents' house and Gettysburg, but maybe I have to get used to Jill 2.0. People change. Places change. How we see people and places changes. And until we're comfortable in our own skin can we accept those changes with an open mind and heart.

All this time I tried so hard to control everything around me, situations, flights, vacations, people, my place in the family, family itself, my career, education. In doing so, I became a restless control freak who always thought the grass was greener on the other side. But it doesn't work like that. Margreet was right — *loslaten*. Let go. So simple, yet so hard to do. I needed to let go of that control, just be happy with what's in front of me. I needed to find peace in the simple things. Moments aren't just moments, memories aren't just memories, they're gifts. Because lord knows, there will always be curve balls thrown my way — Paul's one-night stand, Paul almost dying, and a dream job offer. I needed to let those curve balls come, I needed to welcome those curveballs, but I could only do that if I carried home in my heart, that concept of home. I couldn't bat those curveballs until that realization landed — until I found my place in the world.

Once back at my parents' house, I took out the pros and cons list I still had tucked away in my Moleskine agenda and ripped it in half, and tossed it into the trash can. Paul looked over at me, and grabbed the *Gettysburg Times* from the coffee table, raising his eyebrows, "Are you OK?"

"Yeah, I'm OK. Just shredding some old documents that are no longer needed." I smiled and he went back to reading the local newspaper.

And so I made the decision to change. Right there on day one of our new life in our new place Gettysburg, with Paul and Lucy by my side and Morrisey lyrics scribbled on a notepad beside my bed. It might seem that change was impossible, given my character, but I understood exactly what there was to lose. The point wasn't whether or not I liked it. The point was it had to be done. I had no idea whether a job would work out for me in the US. I had no idea whether Lucy would like a small liberal arts college, or whether Paul would like his new job at Leaf. I had no idea where we would be in five years from now, or even five months from now. All I knew was that I didn't want to lose Paul, or Lucy, and that each and every day slipped out of my fingers way too fast. I had better make the most of this place. After all, if a boat can have two home ports, so can I.

Acknowledgements

Having spent half my life in my hometown and the other half in the Netherlands — an ocean in between me and my roots, I've learned that calling two places home is in theory simple, but in reality it's complex and filled with emotion. I often felt like I operated in some sort of a middle zone — a constant balancing act. But, over the years, I've realized what an enriching process it can be, the process of finding your place in the world and making peace with that place, at that particular time. How much of where we end up set-tling has to do with fate, or circumstance? When is a place home? Although this is fiction, I hope this story conveys the truths those living abroad experience as well as something they can relate to and therefore be comforted by as they find their own place in the world.

Even though my name is the only name on the cover of this book (a dream come true), many people helped me along the way, and this book wouldn't exist without them.

Thank you to my developmental editor Andie Huber (no relation) who I met in Amsterdam, leading not only to a great editor, but also great friend. The emails and coffee dates between us are too many to count! Thank you to my proofreader at Exactly Editing, Rebecca Blunden — LinkedIn and mutual connections really do lead to great things.

Thank you to Natasja Bijl and David Chislett for giving me the courage to self-publish.

Thank you to all the Lisa's in my life — Lisa Doctor who cheered me on from California, Lisa Friedman who led the writing feedback group that I was part of, allowing me to share my early writing in a safe environment as well as learn more about the craft, and Lisa Hall who did her layout magic.

Thank you to my beta-readers who read through early drafts and provided their feedback - Sophia Harris, Liesbeth Ton, Jill Maclaren, Miriam Fournet, Patricia Diaz, Lisa Failes. And for the second round with Saskia Hazelhoff, Julia Bailey, Saron van Diemen, and Colleen Geske.

Thank you to illustrator Eveline Wijdeveld and graphic designer Cigdem Guven for their artistic skills in making the perfect cover for this book.

Maartje Terra for sharing her medical expertise, Rob Schmitz at NPR for sharing his journalism background, and Sophie Langkemper for helping with PR.

A shout out to my Gettysburg girlfriends Heidi Sumser, Mary Bigham, Lauren Schultz, Leslie Magraw, Marijke Muller, Ashly Springsted, and Adrienne Williams-Kief and my Amsterdam girlfriends Joke Aerts, Saron Hanson van Diemen, Julia Bailey, Imola Berczi, Colleen Geske for being my biggest cheerleaders and keeping me grounded and sane through this crazy ride, especially during the pandemic.

Thank you to my Dutch in-laws; Janna, Saskia, Marieke, Egbert, Gert, Nynke, Aad, Rudolf, and Jan Willem for always showing interest and welcoming me into your family with open arms. Thank you to all my lovely neighbors, dear friends, and book club in Loenen who let me talk their ears off about this book. An ode to the Vecht River and the beauty she shows each and every day.

A huge thank you to my readers. I wrote this for you and hope that this book entertained you as well as perhaps provided some comfort, especially for those finding their place in the world.

Thank you pandemic for providing the space, quietness, and time to tackle the creative process of writing, bringing a story to print, something that's been on my bucket list since I can remember. At least there was a silver lining to the pandemic.

And finally, the last and biggest thanks to my family, especially my parents, Chad and Val Huber, who always let me fly my wings, no matter what and my Uncle Ross who inspired me to write. My husband, Joost, who gave me the space and love needed during this writing journey, knowing full well it was something I had to do. And to my children, Noor, Mary, and Tom for lighting up each day. I can't wait to see where your dreams take you.